To Jan

Who always returns from the hairdressers both invigorated
and bursting with new ideas…

Anodorhynchus hyacinthinus

Many regard the hyacinth as the most beautiful of all macaws. Those who have had the fortune to see this magnificent bird in person are always astonished by its dazzling deep blue plumage. Coverage is complete but for bright yellow flashes beside the bill and thin sunshine spectacle rings around the eyes. The largest species of macaw, hyacinths are now heavily protected. Very few remain in the wild and those still existing in Paraguay and Brazil have seen their habitats decimated by increased human activity. Hyacinths are not deep forest birds but prefer open areas of savannah where they live in small social groups. They benefit from extended lifespans and are normally placid. Unlike African grey parrots, who demonstrate remarkable linguistic skills, hyacinths are not particularly noted for having unusual cognitive abilities.

But there are always exceptions…

CHAPTER ONE

There is a smell, of all the smells in the world, which has delighted generations, heightening anticipation and creating wonderful feelings of delicious expectation. This seductive smell makes people close their eyes, raise their chins and inhale deeply with a dreamy smile on their faces. Of course, the world is full of such smells and some are excellent indeed, such as welcome rain sizzling on a sunbaked pavement, bread fresh from the oven, or a newly mown English lawn, green and striped. Many other odours are perhaps less evocative but remain, nonetheless, immediately recognisable: WD40, oranges, ozone, molten tar, Burton-on-Trent.

We live on a surprisingly whiffy planet and as a consequence have been generously gifted by nature with the means by which to detect these odours. (Incidentally, the positioning of our noses, so conveniently sited as they are between our eyes, has also greatly assisted in the design of spectacles.) So, on the whole and taking all things into account, there is a positive cornucopia of great smells and it's one of these more agreeable aromas with which we are concerned at this particular time.

It is the wonderful smell of coffee brewing.

Doreen Coddle stood listlessly, twirling a lock of hair around her finger with that characteristic abstract nonchalance unique to women, waiting for the coffee to percolate. She was on the phone, her sleek black mobile pressed to one ear, a sour expression on her normally placid face. This particular conversation required privacy and so she'd excused herself from company and slipped away into the small kitchenette, but now the woman on the other end of the line was being plain tiresome and Doreen had no time for that, thank you very much. She had just suggested a particular course of action and, as a consequence, the woman was protesting as only a haughty Latin American aristocrat can protest. Doreen let the heavily accented contralto blather on for the length of time it took the old-fashioned percolator to burp thrice then stopped the woman in mid-word with a sibilant hiss. Maria desisted immediately, showing uncharacteristic restraint as she lapsed into a fuming silence. It took a special kind of authority to stopper up the nimble tongue of the mistress of the President of Paraguay – and Doreen had that authority.

Oh, yes, she had it in spades!

Now in her late forties, Doreen Coddle did not appear in any way remarkable for one endowed with so much power – and indeed one certainly needed to be a remarkable personage to be on nodding terms with the mistress of the President of Paraguay. She was of a more generous silhouette than she would have liked, the result of a sedentary life, a hopeless addiction to chocolate and the production of two sturdy children, and it sometimes depressed her that almost every effort she made to trim down her weight seemed to trigger an adverse reaction. She suspected there was an as yet undiscovered law of physics describing how, when dieting, the compulsion to graze between meals was directly proportional to weight lost. Now, there's something really useful physicists could turn their minds to instead of wasting time on black holes and – er, time. In reality, Doreen had long ago acknowledged that raiding her private sweetie store to satisfy an attack of between-meal munchies probably had something to do with those lying scales registering a steady upward nudge of the needle with each passing year.

However, although not a great beauty by any standard, neither was Doreen cursed with any distressing ugliness –

but it sometimes rankled that, in a crowd, she would inevitably be one of the last to stand out, unless, of course, the selection process was determined by hair colour alone.

No, it could not be denied, Doreen was neither a Plain Jane nor a stunning beauty but instead found herself comfortably located within that convivial middle ground occupied by vast swathes of the human race, being neither tall nor short, stick-thin nor truly dumpy and neither elegant nor clumsy. She was an average mother of average height and somewhat above average weight, with an average complexion just on the right side of pale, and she had resigned herself to spending the rest of her life slowly becoming more and more comfortable around the middle. Nonetheless, there remained a waist in there somewhere and a careful choice of clothing could still raise a smile of satisfaction in the dressing mirror and more than just an affectionate squeeze from Bernard.

However, when it came to the really essential life skills, the things that truly mattered to women across the globe, she excelled in three vital areas; she'd married a good man, brought up two wonderful children – and most crucially of all, she had an impeccable taste in shoes.

But, sadly, none of those fine attributes were helping at the moment.

Doreen sighed inwardly and ran an exploratory hand over her hip as she let Maria stew in simmering silence. Yes, there was no doubt about it – despite a strict diet dripping with carbohydrate, sugar and fat, her body was finally answering the siren call of gravity. Mercifully, her features remained essentially unchanged. She had pale, greenish-grey eyes, fine brows, clear skin and a thin-lipped mouth. Her hair, her pride and joy, was always cut in a very nice bob, but those luxuriant waves had recently found themselves host to a very, very unwelcome guest – and this was a guest who had no plans to move on, no plans at all.

She'd first become aware of this interloper two days

ago and the sight had almost reduced her to tears. Two days! How could so short a time have had such a devastating effect? How could it have changed her life so much? The guest was still there and very soon one of its cousins would be coming to stay as well. Then another would join them both, and another. Doreen sighed. Her first grey hair was going nowhere. It was making itself entirely at home, settling in for the duration, a distressing, unwanted, insignificant but ultimately deadly ashen thread emerging like an infection at her temple.

This catastrophe merely reminded her she now lay firmly in the grasp of middle age. Her youth had long departed, and like just about everyone else, she hadn't even noticed! This, above all, was the source of her current bout of unease and dissatisfaction, and spurred on by that single grey hair putting its feet up beside her ear, she'd taken out her frustration with Moaning Maria. Doreen had to admit it was grossly unfair – but it did help. A lot.

For a long time every facet of Doreen's existence had been remarkable for actually being unremarkable – and that, in a nutshell, more or less describes the lives of almost everyone on the planet.

Then *she* came.

Until that moment there had been no real extremes in Doreen's life, neither peaks nor troughs to liven things up a little, and she had somehow found that fact to be increasingly sad. She'd been essentially content with Bernie and the kids, with her career, but there had always been that quiet nagging voice inside, the one whispering that surely there was more to life than this. She was in no doubt other women heard the same whisper, including many of her friends. This is life, it murmured over tea and a plateful of buttered scones, do something with it before it's too late! Bernie would have been surprised to discover Doreen had felt that way. He was a good husband and gave his all to provide for the family, but again, that had been before *she* came. That woman! That remarkable, warm-hearted, astonishing, passionate, charismatic woman.

She changed everything.

Suddenly, Doreen's life had more ups and downs than a Merthyr Tydfil bus route. Who would have believed it!

Oh, and by the way, be careful what you wish for. Be very careful indeed.

Her thoughts again turned to that awful grey hair while she continued to let Maria fume. She knew it was pointless plucking it out. That would merely initiate an avalanche of eager replacements, all keen to avenge their cruelly uprooted colleague. Damn, why did it have to happen now, just as she was getting acclimatised to her disappearing waist? She checked the mirror again, just to see if she'd been mistaken, but it was still there contaminating her lovely colour. The sight of this solitary interloper had made her sharper than usual with Maria.

Patience. Always. Especially when dealing with prickly characters like the volatile, sharp-tongued and extremely excitable Maria Consuela Bernicia Rosalinda Melgarejo: concubine, mistress, pneumatic ex-call girl and savvy bed partner to one of South America's most egocentric and bombastic presidents. He liked to think his beloved people still called him El Toro – The Bull – but although El Presidente was snorting, belligerent and muscular in his public life, he was not quite so bestially potent between the sheets. El Toro's horn tended to be short, blunt and downward-turning these days, much to Maria's chagrin.

Now there was something Doreen had no complaints about, even after twenty-seven years of marriage. Bernie had been her childhood sweetheart and she still found him as enticing as the day she went on the pill as a sixteenth birthday present to him, some time way back in the foggy dimness of the eighties. To tell the truth, Doreen actually had to come off the pill just before their wedding and in one of those strange coincidences which often pepper our lives, her mother, that very evening, had sat her down and advised that now she was about to marry she should strongly consider oral contraception to prevent any untoward accidents. Poor Mum; she never knew the truth to her dying day.

Bernard Coddle had approached the young and fresh-faced Doreen Williams in their school bike sheds one lunchtime in March. She was fifteen, he a year older. No awkward shuffling of the feet and sheepish mumbling for Bernie. No, indeed. He had simply walked up to her as she was padlocking her bike and said, 'Doreen, you're the prettiest girl in school and I want to go out with you.' Overwhelmed by the subtlety of his approach, Doreen simply had nodded and when Bernie marched off, head held high, she'd walked to her history lesson in a bit of a daze. The lively consequences of the Enclosure Acts had held no interest for her on that particular afternoon!

They married young and the kids came quickly after that, doubtless something to do with coming off the pill. She and Bernie had done a lot of squeezing in those days. Martin came first, a bouncing bundle endowed with three superlative skills: smiling, puking and farting. A year later he was joined by Joanne. Doreen's hopes for a less messy baby were sadly shattered. Jo was everything her brother was, with the added bonus of an ability to fill her nappy with truly astonishing frequency. Doreen had thought there was something very wrong with them both until her mother informed her they were merely continuing a fine family tradition.

Doreen found motherhood daunting and by far and away the most difficult task a woman could ever attempt. Catastrophic injuries were avoided on an almost hourly basis and the house needed steam cleaning at least twice a day – but when things went well it was just the best feeling ever. Their summer holidays in Weymouth were legendary, but then they really splashed out and went abroad for the first time. To Saundersfoot. She'd made cardboard passports for the kids which they waved at the tollbooth woman on the Severn Bridge. When they finally arrived, a passing truck had clipped the town sign, reducing it by one letter to Saundersfoo. That holiday had passed into family history, never to be beaten.

Time galloped by, uncaring and swift, so when Doreen reached her thirties she had two boisterous youngsters to control in addition to keeping down a full-time job. Bernie had his plumbing business to keep him busy, *It's A Doddle For Coddle* proudly emblazoning the sides of his van. Stresses and strains tore at her family in much the same way as they did for just about every other family she knew. Some went under, others survived. Hers fell into the latter category. Just! Now Jo and Marty were both postgraduates and had proper passports of their own, the type where the photo actually looked lifelike and an embedded chip allowed you to roam the world. Saundersfoo had been replaced by Faliraki, Weymouth by Ibiza. The kids were gone, living their own lives and only returning when the laundry needed doing. Doreen wouldn't have had it any other way.

Maria had never experienced such difficulties, bless her flashing almond eyes. She had no children and planned none for the future. Her ovaries were locked up tight and strictly off-limits to any passing sperm. She was a woman with an eye on the main chance and no snivelling, figure-ruining, nipple-chewing infant was going to stop her achieving what she desired most. Status. Money. Power. El Toro provided them all with traditional South American presidential flamboyance.

Doreen could almost feel Maria's Latin incandescence radiating from the phone pressed to her ear. She'd now been forced into this wholly unnatural silence for nearly a minute, yet Doreen knew she could keep her waiting for as long as she liked. Power indeed. The woman was literally panting with frustration. No doubt her bosom was doing that wobbly thing which made El Toro go weak at the knees, but Doreen didn't care too much about Maria's trembling hooters.

'We all have to make sacrifices, Maria,' she said finally, taking pity on the poor woman before she started ripping out her own hair. The conversation required a patience she didn't really feel, necessitating the use of that calm voice she knew exasperated Maria so much. 'You are part of a larger picture. Your needs must sometimes be put to one side. No sex. That's an order.'

'But –'

'No, Maria. I will not hear any more. I admit it is unfortunate for you to be involved with such a petulant, self-centred, arrogant bully-boy, but it is your duty. I tell you again, it is vital to deflect El Toro. He's just irritating the Bolivians now but they are a grim and determined lot when they get going. Use your most powerful weapon. Deny him your connubial services. Coupled with the rumour I have just decided you are going to spread that not all is well in the presidential trousers, this should be enough to achieve our aims. In my experience with men such as El Toro, the merest suggestion of soft cock syndrome would prove too humiliating. You only need to point out, in your inimical way, just how embarrassing it would be if his chuckling populace discovered the extent of his sexual inadequacy. How much it would demoralise his military. You only need to deflect him minimally while I work on the Bolivians, then, once conflict has been averted, you can restore his vigour with some of those imaginative techniques for which you are so renowned. I'm confident you'll find some way to correct his distressing lack of rigidity.'

'Yes, Mother,' replied Maria in a suitably deflated tone.

'Good. Now then, my dear, you will keep me informed, won't you.'

'Certainly, Mother.' Poor Maria sounded most despondent. Doreen decided to offer a little reward.

'And when the dust has settled, I'll arrange for a presidential trip to London and we can go shopping for shoes.'

'Oh, thank you, Mother,' squealed Maria with genuine delight. Now, that had cheered her up. Considerably.

'I love you, Maria. Do not ever forget that.' Doreen finished the call and took a deep breath to calm herself. Goodness, she'd almost lost her temper. South American dictators and their lively concubines could be so tricky to handle. She mulled over the situation while the coffee machine continued to belch spasmodically, and wondered why this burden had settled on her shoulders. The answer came immediately, as it always did in these moments of reflection, accompanied with the fond memory of that day in February over fifteen years ago, the day her life changed for ever.

The day *she* came.

She wore a beautiful cashmere camel coat, very classy, and a dusky blue silk scarf over her head. Doreen had never forgotten the sunglasses. Why did she wear dark glasses indoors? In February? She was very tall and austere and, once they were on their own, took off her glasses and fixed Doreen with a steady stare.

'Doreen Coddle,' she said in a husky Yankee twang, 'Ah'm Katherine Hepburn and ah want to talk to you about saving the world!'

To say Doreen was stunned would have just about been the biggest understatement of her life. Kate laughed merrily at Doreen's goggle-eyed expression. 'Do you know, dahling, that's the exact same look I had on my face when Clemmie Churchill drove up to my front door in her lovely Rolls-Royce and told me it was my turn to save the world. I think it's a natural reaction, but hear me out.'

'I – I –' stuttered Doreen impressively.

'That's my girl,' chuckled Kate, patting Doreen's inert hand. 'Ah'm going to tell you a story, sweetheart. It's a very long story, one which spans centuries, but take it from me you'll not get bored. You'll discover why your hair is the colour it is and why you, of all women on earth, are destined for this task. Don't worry, dahling, surely ruling the world can't be as difficult as bringing up two children, and you've made a very fine job of that.'

'I – uh!'

'Still monosyllabic? Only to be expected. Sit yourself down. Ah'll brew up, as you British like to say, and then we'll begin.'

And so it was that Doreen Coddle inherited the title from Kate and became Gaia, Supreme Goddess of the Sisterhood of Helen, Defender of Knowledge and Mother of Blessed Lycia, descended by clear and unbroken bloodline from Helen of Troy herself, committed by solemn oath to nurture, preserve and protect the Earth for the sakes of her own children and those of every mother on the planet.

What a day!

Doreen poured the coffee, picked up the tray of steaming mugs and chocolate digestive biscuits, and nudged her way out of the kitchenette through a pair of battered swinging doors and into the salon beyond.

'Here we go, girls, and I've found some naughty bum-fatteners to dunk!'

Doreen Coddle ran the world.

She was a hairdresser from Chipping Sodbury.

CHAPTER TWO

The lush green fields of the Severn Vale wheeled sedately, turning slowly as the bird circled high above, his senses alert to the faint thermal rising from the chequerboard of sun-heated pastures far below. He soared effortlessly as the rising updraught caught him, lifting him on wings spread wide. He rarely flew this high, preferring to flit among the trees, but the day was so grand he just had to give in to instinct. The feeling of freedom was profoundly pleasurable, as it was to all birds who could be bothered to heave their sorry feathered butts into the air. This particular bird had little sympathy for his cousins who merely strutted and fluttered on the ground. They were invariably nervous, always looking over their shoulders for predators. He avoided nervous birds if he could. Their conversation tended to be stressful, to say the least. Another swirl of warm air caught him at an awkward angle and he adjusted his body without even thinking, such was his consummate mastery of flying. He prided himself on his skills and could be as nimble of wing as a hawk, no mean feat for such a big bird. Yes, it was a lovely afternoon and he basked in the bright sunshine, his back and head warmed pleasantly by that friendly yellow ball in the sky.

Presently, peering to the side, he spied the Lady River Buzzard a little way off. She swung in closer, riding the airs effortlessly, and joined him on the other side of the thermal, the two swinging around in a lazy, unhurried circle, nonchalantly spiralling ever upwards with leisurely elegance. Slowly, she caught him up until the two were flying almost wing tip to wing tip. She was acquainted with him and called out politely. He replied with a brief squawk of his own. With the courtesies nicely handled, the buzzard dipped her wings fractionally in respect, then rolled away and dived, peeling off to patrol her favourite hunting grounds along the banks of the Severn. Any vole or rabbit foolhardy enough not to keep its eyes peeled wouldn't survive long with such an accomplished hunter stalking from above.

He watched her glide away until she was just a tiny dot, then looked to his own affairs. Below, he recognised the intricate jigsaw pattern of tree-dotted hedges, of roofs and roads, streams and ponds, and took great comfort from their familiarity. Down there, amongst the scattered dark green copses and golden squares of rape, lay the tiny village of Prior's Norton and home.

Home! The bird was entirely familiar with the human concept of home: a place of belonging, somewhere comfortable and safe, where good food and interesting conversation could be enjoyed, and where love could be shared. The bird knew all about love. He loved as a child loves, unreservedly, uncomplicated, as deep as the soul; and he knew his love was returned with the same simple intensity. This was the cornerstone of his life. Most people just couldn't understand, just did not comprehend how a creature, a mere bird, could enjoy and reciprocate such an intensely human emotion, but the bird did not care about them. All he cared about was his mummy and daddy.

He took one final look around. The landscape was breathtaking: the rollercoaster humpbacked Malverns to the north; the bare-breasted convexity of May Hill crowned by its nipple of fir trees to the west; the dark rolling woodlands of the Forest of Dean spreading south, the shining silver band of the river snaking through its fertile grasslands; and dominating the east, the long solid ridge of the Cotswold escarpment. Yes, it really was very nice indeed – but not quite as nice as Brazil!

Tucking in his wings, Bertie angled down into a delightful shallow dive, his feathers ruffling pleasantly. Wind hissed softly as his speed increased, but he did things with his long tail to scrub off some of the excess velocity, keeping things nicely dignified. After all, he was a hyacinth macaw and knew all about dignity.

Below, he saw Celeste sitting at a table set on the lawn beside a shady tree. She was engrossed in her book and so he trilled a happy call. She looked up, waved and patted the chair next to her. 'Here, Bertie. Mummy loves you.' The sound of her voice filled him with a deep joy and he spiralled down in a tight corkscrew, banking to display his full wingspan, before executing a perfect landing on the back of the chair. It swayed and creaked under his weight. He sidled over for petting and nibbles. Celeste obliged both generously, putting her book to one side and concentrating on her beloved Bertie. He lapped up the attention and, as he always did nowadays, broke into a paean of contented purring.

Presently, she rummaged in a bowl and handed a fat walnut to him. He crushed the tough shell with ease and extracted the oily nut inside with delicate dexterity. 'Thank you, Mummy,' he said, as polite as always. He'd been brought up well.

'My pleasure. Do you want some more?'

'Yes, I do,' came the immediate reply. He knew the answer to that question and was rewarded with another nut as an extra treat. Celeste stroked along his back and down the length of his majestic tail feathers. Now thirty-seven years old, Bertie was well into his prime, a stocky, heavily-bodied macaw with a head bigger than her fist, forty inches in length and with a five-foot wingspan. His thick plumage was immaculate, a deep violet-blue, dazzling in the warm sunshine. His entire body was covered in glorious azure except for glowing yellow patches bordering his bill and matching panda rings around his alert brown eyes.

Not a feather was out of place. He groomed every day without fail and was as fastidious in his personal habits as any fashion-conscious teenager. Celeste tickled under his viciously curved black bill and the purring waxed. He closed his brown eyes and lapped up the attention. Now that Sebastian was gone, he had no rival. The Persian found country living just too messy. He was simply too hirsute; a town cat, he needed to be near a grooming salon. A few months at the cottage had reduced his effeminate fur to a muddy tangle of matted knots interspersed with the occasional captured twig. The final straw came when several robins checked him out as a possible nesting site. He now lived in pampered luxury with Patti Duke-Warrender at her London home where, apparently, he'd taken to pissing on her prized peonies. Bertie was not surprised at the cat's total lack of respect and thought his departure no loss to the household, but was saddened when his great friend Barnstable scuttled off to hamster heaven at the advanced age of four. Bertie really liked the little chap, often feeding him nut after nut just to see how big his bulging cheeks could actually get, and stood with Celeste when James buried him under the oak at the top of the garden.

So now the household just comprised Bertie with his mum and dad, and all three couldn't be happier.

It had been two years since Vivian Bell won the election, an election precipitated by Bertie, whose innocent and entirely unexpected outing of James Timbrill had been the last straw for the old Government. Now sulking in opposition, they and James had parted company with little love lost on either side. Incredibly, James was still the MP for Gloucester North, even though he'd tried really hard to retire. Unfortunately, he'd not taken into account the strength of feeling and stubborn loyalty of his constituents, who had cajoled, badgered and bullied him into standing as an Independent, and he'd romped home at the election with all the other candidates losing their deposits – no MP had a greater majority. He had entirely misjudged their mood, expecting condemnation and vilification, but instead finding that they cared not one jot for his well-publicised proclivities. He was universally liked in the city and commanded huge local support – unlike at Westminster, where his life was made spectacularly uncomfortable by every other Member in the House.

Unsurprisingly, the political establishment was horrified at his reappearance and viewed this trend towards active local democracy as a direct threat to their cosy lifestyles and troughing ways. At first James was the only Independent MP in the House and had a tough time. Parliament was a place where original thinking had long been discouraged. Spank-happy leather fetishists they could just about tolerate, the Speaker sensibly invoking the general principle of stones and greenhouses, but a combination of both independence of mind and political persuasion were regarded with deep antipathy.

And then the inevitable happened. An unusually high number of by-elections had, astonishingly, all returned Independent MPs, cutting into Viv's majority and eroding his power steadily. Commonly referred to as the IMPS, James now found himself as unofficial leader of a loosely affiliated group of six Independents who owed no allegiance to any party and were pledged to reflect the wishes of their constituents. As was pointed out regularly in the political press, the only whip he now enjoyed was Celeste's!

Inevitably, and to much chortling amusement, as Gloucester's IMP, he was now widely and aptly referred to as the GIMP. Some of those who'd also suffered from Hugo Chaplain's malign influence re-entered Parliament as Independents and looked to James as their saviour. By some bizarre quirk of fate, all became known by their geographical location. Peterborough's independent adopted the somewhat unfortunate title of PIMP, Shrewsbury became SHRIMP, Blyth became BLIMP and

Crewe, CRIMP. Poor unfortunate Loughborough very definitely became LIMP, and finally there was the other one no one could ever remember because Exeter simply didn't alliterate. Although the subject of much ridicule in the corridors of power, and universally vilified in the House, the IMPs were held in great respect by their constituents, many of whom developed a thriving interest in politics once they knew they actually had a say in proceedings.

The other parties did not like this.

James found life suddenly very agreeable indeed. He and Celeste had been happily married for two years. Wife, lover and mistress still, she controlled him with consummate skill, providing a rock-solid home life which helped him cope with the pressures of Westminster. Sustained by her love and the unqualified support of his constituents, he had gained a reputation as an excellent Parliamentarian, either voting for, or against, the Government in accordance with the wishes of his constituents.

The other parties did not like this, either.

Being an IMP, he was no longer at the beck and call of the executive. His status as *persona non grata* meant his mobile phone remained mercifully silent. Mornings were usually spent in the constituency, dealing with local matters, conducting consultations and attending surgeries. He canvassed views utilizing an interactive website which explained the arcane mysteries of Westminster in layman's terms. This website was much visited and whenever he held meetings, James found his constituents intelligent and well aware of the implications of upcoming legislation. James debated and answered questions, then his constituents voted on whether they felt he should or should not support the Government and James trotted off to the House to oblige them accordingly.

And boy, did the other parties *really* not like this. Not one bit!

Viv's Government had enjoyed the usual hundred days' honeymoon period before slowly sliding into a morass of ill-conceived legislation and financial scandal. The trouble was, as it had been with the previous government, the calibre of his MPs. This was questionable to say the least, and the lure of fiddling their expenses, hawking their services to vested interests and awarding themselves obscene pay rises proved just too much of a temptation. The gravy train was up and running bang on schedule again, with stops at Greed Junction, Backhander Halt and Dirty Money Depot. The public had shown their disgust in the usual way, firstly with another lively egging campaign, then following this up by returning IMP after IMP at each by-election – and slowly but surely, Bell's slender majority shrank. People liked what James was doing. Only he and his little band of IMPs were effective in tackling voter apathy and general political despondency. The main party MPs were again exposed as career politicians, their absolute priority being to continue their careers, usually to the detriment of their constituents. These characters possessed second-rate brains but excellent vision – both eyes firmly fixed on the main chance.

With James and the IMPs blazing a trail of honesty through the House, these inadequacies were highlighted time and again, giving leather-loving bondage boy James ample opportunity to take the moral high ground on honesty and probity – something which always tickled the press, exasperated his former colleagues and entertained the public. Suddenly, politics was fun again.

James enjoyed bumbling around his constituency meeting people. He opened new shops, awarded prizes at village fetes and led sponsored walks for charities, and wherever he went he was invariably met with a grin and a wink. Elderly ladies, in particular, always seemed far more interested in his private life than his political effectiveness. He now expected a little teasing before matters turned political, but no longer found such good-humoured comments offensive and managed to fend off all enquiries as to the specifics with a knowing smile. What would have been a perversion too far a few years ago was now accepted as a lifestyle choice. Well, it was in Gloucester, anyway!

If James was at home, nobody bothered to call him after lunch. They knew he would be indisposed. It was well known he spent most afternoons 'meditating', as Celeste once told the press. This fooled no one, of course. The entire country knew exactly what was going on, and 'meditating' was fast becoming a popular euphemism.

'Shall we go home and meditate, dear?'

'I'm going to meditate your arse off!'

'If you think I'm going to meditate in the back of that crappy little Vauxhall Corsa, think again!'

This caused untold problems for British Buddhists.

Celeste, too, had become something of a celebrity, despite her very best efforts to avoid such a catastrophic career move. She preferred to live a quiet life at home in the country. She sometimes missed London. Well, the shows at any rate, but little else. It was definitely a young person's place, dynamic and bustling, but Gloucestershire was drop dead gorgeous and the people fantastically eccentric, which made up for its occasional cultural poverty.

Media interest remained unabated after the election and she had to fend off tiresome enquiries and turn away interview offers on an almost daily basis. Lenses poked over the hedge and took long-range snaps but no paparazzi had the courage to get any closer. Bertie's fearsome reputation was sufficient to discourage even the most determined hack, but she was thankful that these irritations had finally declined in the last year or so, leaving her to pastoral tranquillity.

It had all been far too exciting, but now the three of them had settled into domestic bliss, a hackneyed phrase but in this case actually true.

Thoroughly contented after his nutty snack and made drowsy by the warmth, Bertie was taken unawares by a short snooze, so Celeste returned to her book. She relaxed in perfect comfort, despite the unusual nature of her outfit. She wore a high-necked blouse, double-breasted with shiny silver buttons; a stiff Victorian-style corset; a calf-length pencil skirt, pleasantly tight about her hips; nylons and towering stiletto court shoes. Impractical on a lawn, certainly, but at least the turf got aerated regularly. All this sun-heated black leather exuded a deliciously earthy aroma which she found delightful. Her uniquely burnished red hair glowed like molten copper, the wavy tresses held back tightly by a simple studded strap, the ponytail flowing down over one leather-clad shoulder in a torrent of liquid ginger. This was her signature look, and despite her best efforts to avoid such a fate, she had graced the front cover of not a few magazines, from gossip rags to coffee table classics. Laboratories across the country scrambled to produce a hair dye that replicated the colour but somehow still couldn't quite get it right.

Peace settled like a balm over the garden. Constricted delightfully by her stylish costume, Celeste smiled in utter contentment. All was well, all was calm, all was under control. James was on his way home from Westminster for a well-deserved weekend of meditation and the outré costume she wore had been carefully chosen as a welcome home treat. She had something special lined up for him, a task for him to complete. He'd attempted this task a number of times before and had always been unsuccessful, inevitably because his excitement got the better of him, but she'd been training him diligently and was confident her wonderful slave and gorgeous husband would come through with flying colours this time. If not – well, there was always the whip to help him concentrate. And, of course, the whip would still be used as a reward for success.

Frankly, thinking about it, they were both in a win-win

situation whichever way it went.

Man, life was just dandy. What could possibly go wrong?

A room. A discreet space, neutral, anodyne, comfortably anonymous, a positive symphony of taupe, yet possessing an impressive panorama. Perched high in the heart of the City, famous buildings could be glimpsed through the tinted windows, both historic and modern. The dome of St Paul's nestled in the shadow of new glass and steel towers, thrusting, shiny and brash. London was fast becoming *the* global capital.

The room was thoroughly isolated, both physically and electronically. Men sat around a central table. Gloomy men. There were more furrows on their brows than in the fertile fields of Lincolnshire. They perceived their power, so effortlessly gained and compulsively clung to, was beginning to slip. They felt under attack, under pressure as never before. They were not happy with the way events were unfolding. There had been grumbling. And sighing. Lots of sighing.

In short, they were having a good old-fashioned man-sulk!

There were four in the room. There should have been five but one had inconveniently suffered a cardiac arrest the evening before and was at this moment the worried half of a man/machine entity beeping away merrily in the London Heart Hospital. Perhaps the thought of this meeting had contributed to his current indisposition. It said much for the compassion of his colleagues that not one had considered enquiring as to his state of health. None of them would dream of wasting time visiting their sickly colleague.

These five men were grandees. King-makers all. Men In Grey Suits, or MIGS. And they held on to their power like a tramp holds on to his mangy dog. The MIGS transcended such mundane concepts as politics. They were inclined neither to the left nor right nor centre. They were, in fact, inclined only to look after themselves, and formed an unofficial cabinet which controlled Britain. Each was a commercial baron, a merchant prince, a captain of industry, moguls rich beyond avarice and cunning beyond measure.

These five men had recently got heavily into debt – but not in the same way as that experienced by millions of struggling families throughout the rest of the country. They had connived with corrupt officials to force through subtle changes in legislation, thus creating an environment which encouraged unsustainable personal debt – and then their companies had moved in smoothly to service that debt, increasing their wealth exponentially through payday loans, high interest short-term loans, credit card loans, in fact loans of every kind. They had effectively become the masters of Britain by financially enslaving the population.

In addition, as if that wasn't enough for any man, these five also either directly owned or indirectly influenced nearly a quarter of Britain's assets, including all the power companies, two of the ratings agencies, a hefty chunk of the insurance and pension market, a tenth of the FTSE top one hundred companies – and every DIY shop in Basildon. James once owed unknowing loyalty to these men in a roundabout sort of way, being part of the establishment himself, although at the time he was entirely unaware of their influence on his career. James's old boss, the ex-PM, he of the broken nose and formidable perspicacity, even he had to bow his knee to these men, and now, after two years, they still burned with rage over the changes instigated by James, changes which subtly shifted power within the heart of British politics. The big parties they held in the palm of their hand, had done for decades, but these new IMPs could not be controlled in the usual way.

The four had been discussing the state of their alliance. It was neither a lively nor inspirational conversation. Far from debating their way forward and formulating plans and strategies, they were becoming mired in recriminations. Petulance. Dismayed that their influence was under attack and being slowly but steadily eroded, they had been lamenting the loss of one of their more effective organs, the Joint Services Operations, Non-Military, and its supremely competent leader, Hugo Chaplain. The loss of JSON had been a sore blow. How could anyone in power be controlled if there was no one to collect the dirt? Bell was easily malleable, as any senior politician always is, having been associated with numerous questionable actions in his frenzied desire to reach the top, but these damned IMPs were vetoing much of his legislation, legislation designed to support the MIGS and their policy of continual enrichment. Dammit, some of them were even finding their rate of accumulation was declining. They still getting richer all right, but at a much slower rate, and that was simply not acceptable. Not acceptable at all. And like all arrogant egotists, they took to whining like spoilt kids when matters did not go their way.

A mobile phone rang, silencing the conversation. The ringtone was Pink Floyd's 'Money'. The man listened without speaking, his face slowly darkening. 'You imbecile! Are you telling me I cannot rely on you to control the situation?' he ground out. 'Well you're the Prime Minister, do something about it. Now!' He slammed his mobile onto the table in disgust. 'My defence contracts are no longer secure. That's billions in jeopardy,' snapped Sir Thomas Woolley. 'Bastard PM can't even get a simple vote through Parliament nowadays.'

'I did not come here to listen to your pathetic complaints,' snapped Abraham Brasenose. He'd finally had enough, having just endured more bleating than a herd of Blackface sheep lost in a foggy Yorkshire dale. The phone call was the last straw. 'We've all suffered in one way or another so shut the hell up.' He was their leader, a man so influential and wealthy a mere nod was enough to condemn tens of thousands to unemployment or send the pound spinning downwards like a sycamore seed falling in autumn. He was the evil genius behind the Leyland cypress, benefitting from a double whammy of selling untold millions of the trees to unsuspecting gardeners nationwide, then cleaning up the hedge trimmer, chainsaw and stump grinder market. 'The real question facing us is not how much we're losing but why the economic and political landscape is changing. Money can be plentiful again but only if we counter these new changes in the country from which we have gratefully extracted so much.'

'There's the rub,' agreed a waspish-looking man, thin and angular, with the close-set eyes of an assassin. 'Abraham is right. We should have been looking closer at these new Independent MPs. There's a wind blowing through politics and we have to learn to bend or we will break.' Adam Netheridge had no sympathies for his fellows. He thought them soft. He was the youngster of the group and was sometimes treated accordingly, but wondered what their attitude towards him would be if they realised he'd poisoned their missing colleague. A subtle plan had just come to fruition and now Lord Robin Newnham was reaping the benefits of ingesting monkshood with a curry, a rare poison noted for inducing cardiac instability. Naturally forewarned of the consequences, Netheridge had ensured an astonishingly quick response by the paramedics, for which his victim was already expressing gratitude. He planned to prosper accordingly.

Netheridge was a man with a damaged moral compass.

He was in good company.

'The common man is shaking off the cloak of apathy which we have worked so hard to stifle him with over the last twenty years. I'll not see all that good work go to waste,' observed Brasenose.

'I agree,' said Woolley, still smarting. 'People are

slowly emerging from their political indifference. They're getting involved again, and this needs to be avoided at all cost. Apathy is our secret weapon; when people don't care, we can do what we like. An alert and inclusive electorate is dangerous to us, and Timbrill's politics are thoroughly inclusive and his constituents distressingly alert.'

'So what are our alternatives? What pressure can we bring to bear on the man?' asked Brasenose. 'He's undoubtedly the key. These new IMPs regard him as their unspoken leader.'

'That damned GIMP,' snapped Woolley. 'He's trouble. People are waking up. It's the small stone that starts an avalanche.'

'Colourful metaphor, but not much help.'

'Chaplain should have reined him in.'

'Well he didn't and now we're left to sort out this mess.'

Netheridge cursed James roundly, his language atrociously offensive. He was the least influential of the group, which actually meant he was the least wealthy. They were multi-billionaires all – but he was merely a billionaire a few times over.

'I'm glad to see the extent of our problem has finally focused your mind.' Brasenose's tone was as dry as a Bedouin's sandal.

'It's not bloody fair. We've worked hard to get where we are,' muttered Woolley.

'For Christ's sake, we need action, not this self-indulgent grumbling,' snapped Netheridge, still fuming. They were so bloody spineless. Perhaps he should start looking at ingenious ways of despatching them all, one by one, Agatha Christie-style. Mmm, now there's an idea, he thought.

'Timbrill is famously immune to blackmail, our usual weapon of choice,' observed Brasenose.

'Well then, let's employ pecuniary persuasion.'

This sent an almost undetectable ripple of unease

around the table. Now they would have to invest some money – and as stinking rich as they all were, none of them liked the thought of that.

'How much?' asked Brasenose, voicing their collective discomfort. 'What's the going rate for an MP nowadays?'

'Depends on the MP,' said Woolley. 'I've collected souls in exchange for a pair of opera tickets. Others are inconveniently burdened with a sickening flux of morals, and they're the most expensive to buy. I think we need the experience of someone with street knowledge to pitch the – ah – invitation at the correct level.'

'I think Mr Netheridge, having just displayed a fine turn of gutter language, is the natural choice. As you were the one to advocate a bribe then perhaps you should put up the collateral,' Brasenose suggested suavely.

Netheridge boiled with anger, but kept his expression neutral. Bastards all! Definitely time to start procuring some more monkshood.

'That's agreed, then,' said Brasenose. 'You'll initiate an operation?'

'Certainly,' agreed Netheridge. And you're next on the list, you slimy turd! 'But we have to consider a back-up plan. Timbrill may well refuse the invitation, however generous. He has a disturbing reputation for honesty. We must consider alternatives.

'There's his wife.'

'Yes?'

'Also immune to blackmail. The woman's proclivities are nationally admired. That leaves us with limited options.'

'Are you suggesting a physical threat, distasteful as it may be?'

'Sadly, she's again already proved to be annoyingly resistant to such methods. No, Chaplain's failure has made that course impossible. No doubt she will contact the police, who will throw their entire weight into the case. Since JSON's demise there are now a disturbing number of honest officers infecting the force. Another symptom of our decline.'

There were curt nods of agreement. Two years ago the MIGS had had the Met and ACPO in their pocket, but no longer, and that new Lord Chief Justice, Cruikshank, was proving to be a right slippery customer as well. A real thorn in their sides.

'The bird,' growled the man at the end of the table, contributing for the first time. He was always taciturn at these meetings, preferring instead to observe his fellows. He knew their weaknesses, could discern the fine variations of deceit between them, had even discovered Netheridge's sly poisoning, having paid one of his assets handsomely for an independent toxicology report. The man was as subtle as a blood-crazed ferret running up a trouser leg – and just as charming. He'd have to keep a close eye on young Adam, the nasty little tyke.

'Yes?' enquired Woolley. Matthew Black spoke sparingly at these meetings, but his words were pithy and always worthy of consideration.

'Use the bird. If you have the bird, you have the woman. If you have the woman, the man is yours.' Black was an industrial titan, a grizzled man, thickset and bullish. His companies operated a cartel, an intricate, hidden, oh-so-clever arrangement allowing him to manipulate the paint industry. All of it. From infant faces to the Forth Bridge, everything painted in Britain – and a goodly part of Europe as well – was painted with products he manufactured from companies he owned, and it had made him immensely, astonishingly wealthy. That's the whole point of a cartel.

'The bird?'

'That blue parrot.'

'Get your facts right. It's a macaw.'

'I don't care if it's a pink and purple parakeet from Piddlehinton, it's the key. The pressure point.'

'Avicide?'

'Pointless. You merely eliminate your lever.'

'Kidnap, then.'

'Exactly.'

'You mean we're going to have to look after it?'

'You fail to understand the principle of kidnapping,' said Black. 'The victim is taken, shown once under controlled conditions to prove it's still in good health, then disposed of quietly. The woman will for ever hold out hope that the bird will eventually be returned.'

'Pluck it!' exclaimed Netheridge enthusiastically.

'I beg your pardon.'

'Kill it, pluck it, then send feathers on a regular basis to fool her into thinking it's still alive.'

'I like your thinking,' said Woolley.

'The damned thing is still dangerous,' said Brasenose doubtfully.

'It's a bird, for God's sake. How dangerous can it be?'

'Ask Chaplain's associates. They're out of prison now. I think you'll find they consider it very dangerous indeed. Ask them about their scars.'

'Drugs and a cage, that's all it takes.' Netheridge warmed to the idea. 'Miller can handle the details.' He had a man.

'Miller. Ah yes, the thug.'

'He's a tool. We all surround ourselves with tools,' snapped Netheridge.

Out of the mouth of babes, thought Black sourly. He had better things to do than sit here arguing with these idiots. Newnham, Woolley and Brasenose had inherited their fortunes, along with some unpleasant genetic defects, whereas he and Netheridge had forged their own empires. The difference in thought processes fascinated Black. The wrinklies, as he sneeringly dubbed them, clung frightened to their fortunes, ever keen to accumulate but wary of innovation. He and Netheridge were an entirely different kettle of fish. Both were proactive, both had started with nothing. Netheridge's vast fortune was lightbulb-based.

He'd identified and then bribed key officials, arranging for EU legislation to be introduced phasing out the old-fashioned filament bulbs in favour of low energy LED lamps, lamps that were manufactured exclusively by his companies. Marketed as immeasurably more reliable, Netheridge ensured a subtle flaw had been engineered into the design, causing the lamps to fail prematurely and so necessitating constant renewal. The mark-up was eye-watering! Even Black had to acknowledge Netheridge's ingenuity on that scam.

Black was proud of his own history. He had started as a shop assistant and worked his way up to the very pinnacle of his trade. His fortune now increased at the rate of many thousands of pounds a minute. Every minute. Of every day. Each year, his personal enrichment swelled by more than the gross national product of many minor countries, yet he never forgot where he came from.

Swaffham. What a dump! He'd hated his unhappy childhood there so much he'd arranged to have the town blighted by two huge wind turbines. It's great to be rich!

Nevertheless, their alliance remained very productive, and he did need to keep a close eye on his colleagues. Particularly Netheridge. A dose of monkshood could arrive at any time. All of them were capable of such treachery if the rewards were great enough. As he was himself, of course.

It would be unfair to say their association was based on mutual trust and comradeship.

'We're agreed then. We will send an invitation and if that fails, turn our attention to the woman, and by extension, her bird. We may well discover that the macaw is the key,' said Brasenose. 'You'll get your employee on it immediately.'

Netheridge nodded. If Miller could figure a way to administer poisoned chicken curry to a notoriously fussy eater, then extending an invitation to Timbrill should be a walk in the park.

Failing that, he'd simply kidnap the parrot. After all, it wasn't as if he'd have any trouble identifying his target. Just grab the largest blue bird in sight and stuff it in a cage.

This was going to be easy.

CHAPTER THREE

James crawled forward, eager to reach his goal, knee joints cracking in protest against the floor. Celeste watched haughtily from the sofa, unmoved by his difficulties. They, of course, were self-inflicted, and she allowed herself a small smile of fondness. He was born to bear such burdens, her poor leather slave. A soft creaking attended his snubbed movements, a discreet sound accompanied by an occasional faint chink of tensioned buckle.

The Kneeling Man was at it again. Doing what he did best.

Bertie cocked his head at the familiar sound, watching idly from his perch by the lounge window. It was dark outside, the curtains drawn, the phone off the hook, the room cosy and intimate, warmed by the fire and lit by a scattering of candles. Daddy had been away for a few days, but now he was home for the weekend. They both very much anticipated his return from Westminster, but in different ways. Bertie loved the attention, the conversation, the stroking and hand-feeding of the best Brazil nuts to be found in London, whereas Celeste's welcome was of an entirely different nature. Time to play – and to set him to his task.

Time to meditate!

He was edging closer now, so close she could detect the faint aroma of warm leather emanating from his clothing, then he settled directly in front of her, taking up position between her parted legs. Sitting back on his haunches, he wriggled against his bondage, useless arms strapped around his chest in a straitjacket, peering up at her with

31

wide-eyed expectation. She idly stroked his flank with her calf and felt the silky texture of his leather body suit slide across her skin.

James floated in a haze of deeply masochistic bliss. His body may have been restrained but his mind most certainly wasn't. In fact, he frequently found himself experiencing total mental freedom, especially when Celeste left him alone in the bondage wardrobe. The trance-like state induced by these physically adverse situations helped clear his mind, stripping away the unimportant to reveal the truth. He often used these times to consider the subtleties of his job, to examine the machinations of those he worked alongside, searching for connections and motives. It was all rather inspiring, as well as providing him with a profound personal pleasure.

However, on this occasion, his attention remained focused on his Mistress. As always, her intoxicating presence bewitched him. He drank in her flame-haired loveliness. Her emerald eyes sparkled with anticipation. Goodness, he was as hard as an unripe pear. Suited, booted, hooded, gagged and bound, he was entirely occluded from the outside world. There was not much give in the restraints and all he could do was wriggle a bit – but then wasn't that the idea? He inhaled the sweet aromas of supple leather, totally reliant on Celeste to release him from this delicious predicament. He trembled at the sight of her. His Mistress. His beloved goddess, the woman who breathed life and passion and purpose into him. He was as besotted with her now as he had been from the moment he set eyes on her at that infamous party of Patti's.

Struggling a little simply stoked his passion. Straps creaked and flexed. His punishment helmet was laced as tight as a duck's fundament, the gag made his jaw ache, his fingers were going tingly, his eyes stung with sweat and his middle bits were on the point of exploding.

It was a moment of sublime emotional contentment. He moaned very softly, unable to contain his arousal.

'No noise, now,' she admonished softly, 'or you'll not get your treat.' A hollow threat and they both knew it. This was about as likely an occurrence as a motorist cruising down the M4 in a pleasant and agreeable manner suddenly deciding to make his day complete by turning off to explore the delights of Reading.

However, the ritual had to be played out, and every time it was, their relationship gained strength. Mistress and slave, lovers, husband and wife, all the same. Celeste peered into the clear goggles sewn in his helmet and saw a deep respect tinged with eager anticipation lurking there. Good, he was already experiencing the desired psychological transformation. The speedy descent from highly respected maverick MP into complete sexual subservience was the foundation of their little games. Her predatory cast, the disdainful tilt of her chin and studied aloof indifference to his predicament elicited another deep moan. Breath hissed serpent-like through the eyelets punched in the hide covering his nostrils. She liked the sound very much and, cupping his chin, gazed indolently into his feverish, staring eyes.

James felt his heart lurch. He found that heavy-lidded expression of idle contempt exquisitely arousing. Celeste's eyes were the most piercing malachite green, the vibrant colour enhanced by her extensive use of heavy eyeshadow and naturally pale complexion. She wore her fiery hair loose, great waves of copper falling over her shoulders. Delicious blood red lips pouted succulently, just parting to show a flash of white teeth. She breathed through her mouth, each slow, deep, measured exhalation fanning James's leather-covered features. He smelt her breath, inhaled it, accepting her waste air as a gift. A surging wave of bone deep adoration washed through him. God, she was so good at this!

Celeste thrust him away and he sprawled at her feet, unable to maintain balance. Beneath the straitjacket, as if that wasn't restrictive enough, his entire body was enclosed inside a form-fitting body suit of gleaming black hide, banded and strapped at six-inch intervals from waist to ankle, the taut material flowing like liquid tar to consume every square inch of his body. Except his bottom. Here, twin circular apertures exposed a pair of very red, very striped middle-aged politician's cheeks. Celeste had concentrated on warming them earlier with a springy riding crop, whacking him on the caboose with accurate strokes and undisguised enthusiasm. His bum now looked like two halves of tomato sitting on a black granite work surface.

Vermicular and helpless, with arms bound tight and legs pinioned together, he could do little more than squirm on the floor, rubbing his erection over the carpet and straining against a ribbed collar to stare up at her untouchable imperiousness. Celeste smiled voraciously. He was so helpless, so entirely reliant on her for everything: for pleasure, for pain – and for release. As a natural dominant, she would not have it any other way. Neither would James. Leather suited him. Always had done. She adored its pliant touch, its ability to cling, its strength and its elusive, subtly arousing aroma. The material had become an essential ingredient in their little games of Mistress and slave.

Unlike James, who needed no encouragement at all to dive into full leather enclosure, Celeste had decided on a minimalist approach. She no longer had to cover herself from his gaze, although she still often did because he liked to see her suitably attired as his Fetish Goddess. On this occasion, however, she had chosen something a little different, something designed to show off her curvaceous silhouette.

The corset was both a beauty and a beast! Before dressing himself, James had poured her into its constrictive grip, tugging hard to reduce her waist to an insect minimum, chuckling at her grunts each time he yanked on the laces. The black leather was stretched taut, squeezing her ribs and making her pant slightly, and covered from below her naked breasts to the top of her pubic bone. Nipples coaxed into organ-stop stiffness by arousal – and probably by restricted circulation as well – nosed out in perky expectation. The corset was complemented by a pair of full-length leather opera gloves encasing both arms almost to the shoulder.

She wore nothing else. Her nakedness excited James. Long gone were the days when she remained fully clothed, when he was strictly forbidden to explore beyond the hem of her dress. It was now access all areas, a sexual Schengen Area, and those parts which once seemed so unreachable were now frequently exposed in all their delicious glory.

As they were at this particular moment.

Shaven, naturally. Since her husband officially had connubial access to all regions, she ensured her tufty parts were shown no mercy. Celeste found it ironically amusing that having spent so much time in the country, she was now a firm advocate of the Brazilian approach to bodily hair!

She decided he'd now spent enough time trying to drill a hole through the carpet and, wrestling him back onto his haunches, leaned forward and removed the gag, pulling the huge plug out of his mouth. She settled back in the sofa and, crossing her legs, casually caressed his face with her foot. He held himself still, as was required, the movement of his head somewhat restricted by the ridiculously unforgiving collar. Slowly, her meanderings approached the mouth-hole in his helmet, toes wriggling eagerly inwards when they found the small oval entrance. With another uncontrolled groan of joy, he closed his lips around their contours and sucked gently. She had the most beautiful feet he had ever seen, shapely and smooth, arched at the top and with high curving insteps that allowed her to wear spectacular footwear in perfect comfort. Towering spike heels did not represent a challenge to Celeste, in fact her feet were so curved she now found it difficult to wear flat shoes and preferred four-inch stilettos for normal day-to-day wear. While in the privacy of their home and for bedroom play, as well as on special social occasions, she reverted to a full six inch heel, much to the admiration of the press – and her glassy-eyed husband.

James worshipped her feet in a dreamy haze of sublime euphoria, running his tongue all over and licking between her lovely toes, kissing their tips very gently. Her nails were beautifully proportioned despite being clipped short to protect the stockings she often wore. They were also unpainted so he could see each pale lunula, the delicate white half-moon visible even on the minuscule nails of her little toes. So absorbed was he with the task that it came as a shock when his head was jerked away and another plug stuffed in his mouth, but he knew this gag well and focused his eyes on the small nail brush now extending outwards a short distance from his hidden lips. Celeste held the bottle of nail varnish, presenting the open end to him.

'You know what to do,' she said. 'I'm expecting great things this time. I don't want any mistakes.'

Each previous attempt James had made to paint her nails in this manner had been doomed to failure. He'd succumbed to such trembling excitement he'd made a terrible mess, much to Celeste's annoyance, so he was determined to get it right this time. Still enclosed within the straitjacket, still collared, hooded and gagged, he bent forwards and dipped the end of the nail brush into the bottle. It was not an easy task but he was reasonably experienced now and after dabbing off the excess against the neck of the bottle, stroked the brush tip with precision to leave a smooth line of brilliant scarlet varnish deposited on the nail of her big toe. Back to the bottle again and the process was repeated. Slowly, he painted her nails one by one, concentrating intensely, gripping the gag brush tightly between his teeth. To manoeuvre its tip required considerable physical dexterity, the nature of his bondage requiring his whole body to be controlled rigorously.

Celeste liked that very much.

James almost went cross-eyed trying to focus. Her smallest toe was the most difficult. The nail was perfectly formed but tiny, needing no more than a fleeting touch of the brush. With one foot completed, Celeste recrossed her legs to present the other. Sweat now dripped down James's pinioned limbs but he never wavered in his task and presently all her toenails were painted a very shiny ruby red.

Celeste was pleased. 'James, my darling, I think you've cracked it at long last. You've done a lovely job, well done! Much better than last time, in fact that's not short of perfect.'

'Well done!' repeated Bertie idly. 'Lovely job.'

'See, even Bertie can appreciate your efforts. I think that deserves a little reward. Best leave my feet alone for a while to let the varnish dry, so I'll let you rest before we continue.' She removed the nail brush gag and cupping his hooded cheeks with both hands, kissed him very gently. Her lips were soft and warm. A mischievous tongue explored. James whimpered. He whimpered a lot in these situations. She smiled roguishly and drew his head in and downwards. Her knees fell apart. He shifted his weight and leaned against the chair. She laced her fingers together at the back of his neck to ensure he didn't pull away, not that he had any plans to do so. Now, that would be just plain rude, wouldn't it, especially to a lady.

She relaxed, holding him there for a long time, occasionally raising one leg then the other to idly examine her freshly painted toenails. James's face stayed firmly where she'd put it. He seemed to be experiencing an as yet undiscovered law of attraction, one which compelled his features to stay firmly in position even when she released her grip. Frankly, wild horses wouldn't have been able to drag him away. He snuffled for breath like an asthmatic mole, not at all unhappy with his predicament, and offered enthusiastic husbandly service with tongue and lips. At this particular point in their game, that was his only function and even though at times he was in the last stages of imminent suffocation, he gave himself utterly and totally with no concern for his own comfort.

'Enough,' she murmured eventually, 'or we'll both be coming far too soon!' She let him collapse in a slithering heap of creaking leather and began to run her feet over his squirming body, kneading, stroking and massaging with heels and toes. She arranged him with deft touches until he lay supine and still only using her feet, opened the zipper over his impressively bulging middle bits, the tab fitted with a specifically designed loop through which she could hook her big toe. The hide peeled apart to reveal James's pale body beneath. Her dextrous toes went to work again and shortly emerged with their prize, hard and ready, his exposed stiffy, flopping on to his belly like a beached walrus.

But without the tusks. Or the fishy smell. Or the whiskers. Especially the whiskers. As she was now an advocate of the Brazilian, she made damned sure he was as well.

At no stage in this procedure had she moved from the sofa nor used her hands in any way. James felt the soft touch of her nimble toes on his Bishop Rock Lighthouse. His wonderful wife was skilled on so many levels. He was already hardened by a snazzy little leather cock and ball harness, embossed with the House of Commons portcullis, but the gentle pressure of her feet left him gasping. She was just so damned good at this! Cool air wafted over his gentleman's region. She scooped up his sausage and, holding it vertically between her soles, caressed slowly. He gazed up at her and saw that familiar whetted expression, that eager smouldering in her emerald eyes. Her colour was up now, her cheeks flushed, her red lips parted in anticipation. Her arousal was as obvious as his. This was going to be great.

Without warning, she dropped his wobbling todger and withdrew her feet. 'I'm ready for the stockings now,' she said, somewhat unsteadily. Parts of her were very warm indeed, but she wasn't ready just yet. She wanted to tease him some more, to extend the evening for their mutual benefit.

The nylons were black and filmy, classically seamed and with Cuban heels. She pulled them on in easy stages, lingering unnecessarily to prolong the moment, checking to ensure the seams were arrow straight down the backs of her long legs, always working the thin material higher with languid strokes of her gloved hands. She coaxed the stockings ever upwards, stretching out all the ripples, and snapped each in place around her upper thighs. James could see the broad, black elasticated bands encircling the very tops of her legs and shivered pleasurably at the sight.

Her feet went back to work. James started violently at the first touch of sheer nylon on his John Thomas. This was due more to an unexpected jolt of static electricity than to her dreamy caress. Celeste giggled. 'Poor James, these misfortunes do plague you, don't they?' She rubbed the stockings together to induce another charge and touched him again. James squealed at the shock on his cock. 'Sorry,' she breathed in a manner that suggested she was not sorry at all, and using the sole of one foot, rolled his tingling winky back and forth over his belly as if making shortcrust pastry.

She eventually withdrew and, standing, looked down at him. He was a panting wreck, his static-induced erection now nicely hard, if a slightly alarming shade of purple from the tightly-buckled harness. 'Enough of that, I think it's now time we moved on.' While a goggle-eyed James drooled avidly, she donned a pair of black leather knee boots with six-inch heels – the maximum height she could manage without platforms under the soles. The boots slid on with the aid of an ornate silver-chased shoe horn, a gift given gratefully by the American High Heel Appreciation Society. Sturdy silk lacing ensured they were drawn very tight to the contours of her legs and feet. She teetered slowly towards him, hips swinging seductively, her height boosted by the tremendous boots, and stood with one foot on either side of his head.

She was so close he could smell the warm leather. Silver eyelets twinkled, the laces creaking with strain. Her lovely feet were spectacularly arched by the curved vamps. The boots receded up her endless legs – from his lowly perspective they seemed to go on for ever. His mouth went dry. Lying on the floor looking up, she towered over him like an erotic goddess. The imagery was powerful and intensely arousing to them both.

Celeste peered down at James's enthusiastic Mr Dinker. A flick with her toe sent him bobbing back and forth. Another whimper. She could see he was profoundly aroused. Not bad for a sedentary man in his late fifties, not bad at all. 'You look ready,' she mused and, gagging him again, straddled his waist and plumped herself down, gloved fingers guiding him home. She settled on his thighs, squatting, squirming, forcing him ever deeper.

Actually, James would have argued that 'forcing' in this context was perhaps too strong a word. There was no forcing necessary. He had to force himself to go to Westminster each week, or force himself to pay his council tax bill, but *this* could not be described in any way as forcing – and all notion of coercion evaporated the instant she began to rock back and forth.

Celeste shuddered at the sublime sensation. She'd technically been a virgin before marrying, but no longer. James was a delightful, passionate, exciting, nicely endowed but above all, immobilised lover, and neither would've had it otherwise. Having finally lost her cherry, she now embraced coitus with the same extravagant enthusiasm enjoyed by the rest of the human race. Their arousal peaked. The excitement was too much and satisfaction was achieved in a flurry of thrashing, sweat-streaked limbs and panting moans.

Or at least it did for Celeste. It was difficult to tell exactly what was happening to James, but judging by his spasmodic wriggling and ragged respiration it was probably safe to assume he was also having a splendid time.

Or maybe a stroke.

Bertie watched the climax of their mating ritual with little interest. Boredom had set in long ago. Heavens, it took these pink monkeys so damned long! Surprising their species hadn't died out waiting for something to happen. No such trouble for him. He and Milly were done and dusted with lots of noise, some moderate flapping and the occasional weather warning in ten seconds flat.

Including foreplay.

Now that's a proper man for you!

CHAPTER FOUR

Buoyed by his deliciously enjoyable weekend, James returned to London in both a happy frame of mind and laced into a pair of exceptionally tight leather punishment briefs. Angela shook her head sadly when he walked into the office, stiff-legged and grinning hugely. She knew exactly why he winced as he sat down.

'She does like to strap you in tight, doesn't she?'

'My wife is talented in that direction, yes.'

'Promise me you'll take them off if your toes go blue. Again!'

'I'm not *that* much of a masochist, despite reports in the papers to the contrary. Right, what have we got this morning? Anything I need to know about?'

Angela Hutchinson had stuck with James through thick and thin. They had first met when James worked at the MoD. How long ago that now seemed. So many things had changed, but Angela hadn't. She was still rosy-cheeked and blue-eyed, still blessed with waves of naturally blonde hair – and still formidably talented. Next to Celeste and Bertie, she was his closest friend and confidante. A blushing English rose she may have been, but those innocent, wide-eyed looks belied the sharpest of minds.

And a fearsome temper; James had never forgotten the menacing way she handled the office pencil sharpener.

James's needs were modest. Unlike most MPs, who seemed to equate the size of their staff with their perceived importance, he only needed one assistant – Angela. Frankly, most of the time his presence wasn't really required at all. She was in charge whether he was there or

43

not, and continued to run his official life with consummate, effortless efficiency. In addition to updating his constituency website, one of her prime tasks involved shielding him from the torrent of anonymous hate mail that poured in every day. The Establishment did not like James. Trolls lurked everywhere. She responded to their cowardly vitriol with crushing sarcasm and humour, pointing out spelling and grammatical errors, advising on evening classes to boost their command of English, suggesting various places to insert all manner of unlikely objects, and generally having an excellent time. Her nephew, showing a rare talent that promised a stellar future career in MI5, had bought a clever little piece of software from the darker recesses of the internet and installed it in James's computer, allowing Angela to trace and log all his incoming communications, just in case some outraged nutter threatened to go all mental over the worrying prospect of increasing democracy in the West Country.

All MPs have an office in which to house their staff. The lucky, popular and important ones are provided with offices in the Houses of Parliament themselves. Sadly, James did not qualify, failing spectacularly on all three criteria, so he'd been allocated a tiny broom cupboard in the Norman Shaw Building opposite the Palace of Westminster, where the hoi polloi of MPs were housed. He didn't mind at all. His cupboard was amply big enough to house them both and that was good enough. Loyalty personified, she'd resigned from the MoD and stuck with him through the turmoil of the last election. The two of them against the rest of Westminster. Like The Lone Ranger and Tonto.

But with more leather.

In his new role, he spent far less time at the House than any other MP, preferring to maintain the personal touch in his constituency rather than sitting on arcane committees and figuring out ways to claim even more expenses. Besides, he didn't like being away from Celeste and Bertie unless it was absolutely necessary. This minimal attendance also suited those many MPs who expressed their disapproval of him openly. Frankly, they made it abundantly clear that the less they saw of him around the place, the happier they felt, and this unkind ostracism extended to the eight restaurants and six bars and lounges dotted around the grand old building. So, after working all morning, James left Angela and her prawn salad ciabatta and went in search of some lunch off the premises.

The area around Westminster was far too crowded with milling throngs of tourists, all waving their cameras and posing in front of Big Ben, and so he strolled, hands in pockets and deep in thought, to a very nice little coffee shop in Dartmouth Street just ten minutes away. He was welcomed as an old friend, ushered to his favourite window table and enjoyed a bowl of homemade chicken broth with warm tiger rolls and a plain, ordinary, no-nonsense cup of coffee: no frills, no fancy Italian accoutrements, no barista from Walthamstow massacring a Tuscan accent. Just filtered coffee. Black. No sugar. OK?

He then texted Celeste to give her an update on the state of his constricted parts and put in a formal request for extra straps and spanking the next time he was home, knowing these were never denied. With that to look forward to, he browsed through the papers, sipping his drink, but now being a man of a certain age, the strong coffee soon made its presence felt. The briefs probably didn't help, either. He settled his bill and searched out the little boy's room. The spotless facilities at Choccy, Toffee & Coffee were located out back, separated from the lounge and, unhappily for James on this occasion, extremely private. No sooner had he pushed through the swing door, when he was grabbed from behind and bustled unceremoniously into the only cubicle by three large and very determined gentlemen. All four squeezed in and the door was slammed and locked. Normally, James was happy to spend time in an enclosed space – wardrobes figured near the top of his favourites list – but he preferred to be alone in these moments of blissful confinement. This was entirely different.

James turned indignantly and was about to protest, when he received a warning finger pressed hard against his forehead. 'Zip it, Timbrill, not a word,' hissed their leader, a shaven-headed man, hard and chiselled, with nasty little dark eyes and an aura of smouldering violence. Bertie would have hacked his face off in a moment as a matter of general principle. The man's two companions stood behind, silent, with carefully cultured, gimlet-eyed sneers on their simian faces. A solid wall of muscle and bone stood between James and freedom.

It was all rather unpleasantly claustrophobic.

The shaven-headed man moved up to stand even more uncomfortably close to James, which in actual fact simply meant swaying slightly forward in the crowded cubicle. A strange gleam of whetted anticipation hardened his black eyes. 'You need to concentrate on what I'm saying,' he said very softly. 'Here, let me help.' Without warning he grabbed James's leather-clad balls and gave them a good old-fashioned twist.

To the right.

Now, it would be fair to say James was fond of his balls. Very fond. Only three people had ever touched him in his special little place before: his mother, who'd efficiently cleaned and talced his infant marbles while coochie-coochie-cooing him outrageously; James himself, who, with enormous enthusiasm had embraced testicular self-examination twice a day from the age of fourteen; and now his wife, whose cool, leather-gloved fingers did unspeakably pleasurable things to the Timbrill family conkers. This man was the fourth – and James didn't like it very much.

'Listen very carefully, Leather Boy.' His grip tightened painfully. James squirmed, a squeak escaping gritted teeth. The briefs offered no protection. Sweat popped on his brow. 'You will be contacted from time to time with specific instructions. You will follow these instructions to the letter. Failure to comply will result in … unpleasantness. You will never question these instructions and you will never attempt to identify their source. You will not contact the police. Should you fail to comply with any of these, your wife will then be regarded as a viable target, exposing her to equal – unpleasantness. And your wife's parrot. Especially your wife's parrot.'

'He's a macaw,' gasped James. Bertie was fussy about that. 'Get your facts right.'

'Thanks for the correction, you smart-arsed toff.' Another twist, this time to the left, and James keened in agony. The man sneered. 'Thought you would've liked that, pervert! Don't forget, now. Be a good boy, do as you're told and from this moment on your life will be surprisingly rewarding. Here's a small golden handshake. Welcome to the team.' Gorilla Number One placed a bulging sports bag on the loo seat. The man with his grip on James's knackers gave one final squeeze, then polished off the interview with a sharp, straight-fingered jab to his stomach. James collapsed in a heap, winded, scrotum screaming, his disinterest in the proceedings now overwhelming. He grovelled on the floor between pan and wall as Gorilla Number Two extracted his mobile and lobbed it down the khazi. Then all three goons tried to exit the cubicle at the same time, only to get snarled up in the door frame. Wedged firmly and with arms flailing, they pushed hard. The cubicle creaked alarmingly. Baldy swore, but was caught fast in a hard-muscled sandwich. All three pushed again; the frame finally splintered and they popped free, the door swinging back with a bang on its broken hinges.

'Idiots!' he muttered with real venom, shaking his lapels and stalking out, trailing chastened gorillas in his wake.

James groaned. The floor smelt suspect, an aroma of

47

badly-aimed pee and bleach. He huddled in the recovery position for quite a while until his legs began to work again then slowly levered himself to his knees, rubbing his bruised stomach. He felt pretty crap, to tell the truth, and his mood was certainly not lifted when he unzipped the sports bag and looked inside.

A quarter of a million pounds peered back.

His shoulders slumped. 'Damn!'

James did not consider himself a man of action. Men from Gloucester rarely did. He felt excessive physical exertion only made him look undignified. For God's sake, he didn't even run to get out of the rain any longer, but he also knew he needed to exit the scene as soon as possible. If the staff – who he now realised by their notable absence must all be deaf as a post – discovered him, then the police would certainly become involved. They all knew he was an MP and the Met took attacks on MPs very seriously indeed. Instinct told him this was probably a bad move.

He needed to talk to Celeste and thus fished his phone out of the toilet sump. Unsurprisingly, the screen remained stubbornly blank despite an impressive amount of random button-stabbing, so he tidied himself as best he could, took the bag and hobbled out of the facilities as nonchalantly as his bruised broad beans allowed. A fire exit door stood ajar in the passageway beyond. James peered through and discovered an alley leading back to Dartmouth Street. Various bins clustered beside various back doors. The alley was not long and appeared mercifully deserted. He hefted the bag – two hundred and fifty large was surprisingly heavy – and rather than risk attracting attention in the coffee shop, slipped through the fire exit, making sure the door snapped shut behind him. Gathering strength and dignity, he made his way down the alley, limping painfully like a saddle-sore gaucho at the end of a hard day's herding. He paused at the corner and peered around, and was thankful that the men were nowhere in sight.

The encounter had left him shaking, nervous and very uncertain. He hesitated, unsure what to do, and leaning against the wall with eyes shut, took a few moments to compose himself. His chestnuts throbbed horribly and his belly hurt with every breath. He considered his position. There was no way he would ever accept a bribe. Take just one payment and they have you for ever. He looked back up the alley. The bag had to go. There were plenty of bins to choose from, might as well make it the nearest.

'They went that way.' The words startled James. They seemed to rise from a large bundle of rags and cloth wedged in a cosy niche just inside the alley entrance. To his amazement, a threadbare blanket draped over the bundle moved and a hand appeared, bony finger pointing. 'Three men. Nasty-looking bastards, too. They went that way.' A grubby face materialised out of a fold in many layers of hoods and scarves. Limbs moved lethargically, uncurling to reveal a frail woman. She looked much older than she probably was – pavement life was obviously harsh on the complexion. A mandatory Bag Lady red woollen bobble hat was perched precariously on top of a mess of washed-out ginger frizz streaked with ashen grey. Individual hairs sprang in all directions like a hedgehog who'd just been surprised by an electric fence. Despite his predicament, James's natural West Country courtesy was just too ingrained to ignore and he found himself unable to walk away. The pain in his plums also contributed significantly to this general reluctance to move. He peered into a face pinched by worry yet oddly serene with indifference to her less than salubrious surroundings.

James put the bag down. 'Thank you, but I don't think I'll be following them.'

'Of course not. Only a fool would do that. I don't see you as a fool. Strange sort of mugging though.'

'What do you mean?'

'I saw you go into yonder cafe full of the joys of spring. I saw them follow you in with the bag. Now everyone comes piling out the back door. They were in a hurry, you're obviously bruised and battered but now have the bag. None of my business, but even I know muggings don't work like that.'

'Can't pull the wool over your eyes, can I?'

The woman cackled like a crazed Shakespearean witch. 'Not with this hair you can't. So what's a fine-looking gentleman like you associating with dirtbags like that?'

'Not my choice, madam.'

'Mmm, well, take my advice – might be wise to avoid them at all costs. As I said, nasty looking. Dangerous. Wouldn't want to meet them again in an alley like this, would you?'

'Not really.'

'Normal people don't use fire exits out of an eating house unless they haven't paid. You don't strike me as a man who doesn't settle his bill.' She nodded back down the alley, head bobbing on a neck long enough to provide a home for several scarves, then looked at him more carefully, eyes narrowed in scrutiny. 'You hurting bad, sonny?'

James couldn't conceal the drawn look of pain on his face. Perspiration sheened his forehead. 'A bit. It's nothing.'

'Liar!' she snapped. 'That's not you. I see an honest man. You can't hide anything from me. I know it hurts.'

'It does a little,' he admitted.

'Go home,' the beggar ordered. 'I'm sorry, there's no help I can give you, but be careful. These men might come knocking on your door again. They knew where you'd be today, that means you've been targeted and followed. Understand?'

James regarded her for a few moments. There was a lively and perceptive mind hidden under all those rags. A woman that clever shouldn't be living in an alley. He withdrew all the notes from his wallet. 'Thank you, you've helped with good advice and for that I'm very grateful. I'm honoured to give help in return. It's not much, but it's everything I have. Please tell me you'll spend this on some hot food.'

His words seemed to break through the woman's gruffness. She stared up at him. James was captured by her intensity, but there was a touch of madness in her green eyes. She suddenly looked awfully familiar. He searched his mind, but could not place her.

They shared a moment in silence. James could easily bear a silence, unlike so many of his fellow MPs. They loved the sound of their own voices. None of them would have stopped since there would have been nothing to gain by the encounter. With no cameras around to capture the moment, nothing would have appeared in the media, and so no advantage gained. Instead, there was just James and the woman. He had a powerful feeling of deja vu. She detached an arm from the burrowed recesses of her blanket and squeezed his hand in thanks as she took the money. 'You are so very kind,' she said gently, the wild cast in her eyes softening. 'Hot food, I promise.'

James smiled wanly. Jeez, his knackers hurt. 'My pleasure, madam. Be safe.'

He strode away as quickly as his injuries allowed. Now, where had he seen her before? He was so consumed in thought he completely and intentionally forgot to pick up the bag.

The woman watched him go. The blanket stirred and a pigeon's head appeared. 'All right, Agnes, let's see what's in the bag Mr Timbrill was so careful to leave behind.' She opened the holdall and pulled out a great big thick wad of twenties. There was a moment's silence, then she tossed the wad back into the bag and stared thoughtfully at James's back until he limped round a corner and disappeared.

'My, my, I don't think we need worry about the price of bird seed for a while,' she murmured.

Miller sat in the usual meeting room deep in the heart of The City. A fine view, he thought idly, staring out of the window while Woolley and Brasenose bickered and argued. What the hell was wrong with them. A bunch of nervous old men with too much money and an incurable addiction to power. He curled a weary lip at Adam Netheridge who in turn rolled his eyes in exasperation.

'Gentlemen,' Miller said loudly and forcefully enough to silence the room, 'I'm happy to report first contact with Spanker Timbrill.' Yeah, he thought, my fist in contact with his belly. Mmm, that had been a pleasant moment. Miller had always been given a wide latitude by Netheridge and took full advantage of his operational freedom, but grabbing hold of another man's goolies didn't quite cut the mustard as much as a good thump in the guts.

'All went according to plan. The encounter was brief but – ah, instructive.'

'I can imagine,' rumbled Black. Miller had proved himself on numerous occasions to be direct, brutal and sadistic. 'And the invitation?'

'Delivered.'

'Good. It's always best to establish the nature of these relationships from the beginning.'

'A bag full of money is a powerful incentive,' agreed Woolley. His own avarice blinded him to any other conclusion. Naturally, he expected James to react in the same way he would himself. A pecuniary incentive backed up by the threat of violence usually obtained the required results and, of course, the moment Timbrill accepted just one payment then the man was theirs, heart and soul, to be corrupted for as long as he was useful.

Miller's mobile vibrated. He took the call while the others congratulated themselves on their cleverness, but Netheridge studied his man's face and knew all was not well. This assessment was swiftly confirmed.

'Gentlemen,' announced Miller flatly, once the call had

ended. 'I regret to announce Mr Timbrill has misplaced the invitation.'

There was a stunned silence. Miller smirked, despite his flash of anger at hearing the news. He so loved to see them all discomfited. 'I tasked one of my colleagues to observe the target post-delivery. He emerged from the venue without the invitation. My colleague entered the venue to make enquiry. My colleague has confirmed the invitation was not left in the venue. Despite an extensive search, it has not been located. Therefore, we have to assume Timbrill has not accepted the invitation and it has been lost.' His information was delivered in terse, accurate packets, one piece of information per sentence. Military style. Actually, Herefordshire style. Thanks for the SAS education, boys.

'Goddammit,' muttered Brasenose. 'What the hell's wrong with the man.'

'You mean we've lost the money!' snapped Woolley.

'Actually, I've lost the money,' Netheridge pointed out mildly. 'You've lost nothing.'

'Ah, er, quite,' blustered Woolley.

'So where is it?' asked Black.

'If it's not in the venue, nor with Timbrill, then maybe your colleague has it,' suggested Woolley. 'Thought he'd help himself to a small perk, perhaps?'

Miller did not rise to the suggestion. 'My team is hand-picked and personally trained by myself. I trust them implicitly,' he said.

'Well, if it's gone, it's gone.' Brasenose waved a hand dismissively. Miller was astonished at how blasé they could be – if the cash had been his, he'd have hunted it down to the ends of the earth and then been merciless to the thief.

'That's all very well for you to say,' objected Netheridge. 'I've just shelled out a lot of money with no tangible return on my investment.'

'Stop whining, Adam,' said Woolley. 'We'll all make a

contribution if you feel like that, although I have to say I'm surprised you're bleating over such a trifling amount.'

'I'm not. The amount is negligible. I'm just disappointed we were unable to obtain immediate results.'

Miller observed Netheridge closely. Just losing a quarter mill had to hurt, even for him. Funny, none of them would have batted an eyebrow spending extravagantly on a yacht or a couple of first-class Russian whores or even half of Hampshire, but to just lose it completely? Ouch! 'I think you've underestimated his resolve,' he said crisply. Black snickered to himself. Miller passed the buck with smooth professionalism. Had the invitation been successful, it would have been a 'we' situation.

'Or perhaps you were not persuasive enough,' probed Woolley, always keen to blame a scapegoat.

Miller was having none of that. 'Be assured, I was,' he retorted grimly. 'Would you like a demonstration? I think you'll find I had an excellent grip on the situation.'

'Enough jokes,' snapped Netheridge. Despite his nonchalance, he was quietly fuming over the loss of his cash. 'Timbrill has made a serious tactical error and needs to be punished. He does not seem to appreciate the gravity of his situation. He was warned of the consequences and has chosen to ignore that warning, although apparently in an entirely unexpected way.' Who actually *loses* that much money, especially an accountant? 'As a result, his actions have now made his wife and her bird legitimate targets. I suggest we direct our attention to them, and in particular, the bird. Agreed?'

'Agreed,' the others said in turn. Miller examined his nails, seemingly disinterested. He did it for effect, knowing this low level of insubordination really ticked off his employers, but they needed him and his unique skill set. He appeared lost in his own thoughts as a silence stretched out in the room, but in fact was counting in his head.

'At your leisure, Mr Miller,' ground out Woolley eventually. Damn, eleven seconds. Almost a record.

'Oh, sorry, I didn't know you were waiting for me,' he apologised suavely. Netheridge snickered. Miller was brilliant at annoying them. 'I was hoping, like you, that our invitation would be a sufficient incentive. Sadly, this has not proved to be the case so we must now move to the standby phase of our operation. As agreed previously, the alternative target has been under observation for some time by my team. They've been on her tail for weeks.'

'Are they any good?' asked Woolley peevishly. 'I don't want amateurs on the job.'

Miller snorted in contempt at the jibe. 'MI5 are novices in close quarter surveillance compared to my experienced team.' Miller had trained his men personally. Even those jokers from JSON were no match for him. They'd been caught. By a bird, for Christ's sake. There was no way he'd ever make such a fundamental error. Careful man, was Miller.

'I have been analysing her movements,' he continued. 'There have been no significant departures from her normal domestic routine. With regard to her home, its rural location ensures it is reasonably secluded. I have identified access and escape routes. I have also made preparations for the incarceration of the macaw at a nearby facility. There are one or two minor arrangements still to complete with my team, but essentially I am in a position to move on your instruction. If required, I can guarantee the macaw will be in our hands by the end of the week.'

The men looked at each other around the table, then nodded in unison.

Miller smiled. 'Thank you, gentlemen, it looks like I'm heading west. Time to break out the wellies and grease up the sheep.'

CHAPTER FIVE

'You must tell the police! I'll not have another man touching my husband's private parts.'

Celeste was adamant. James stood before her with his trousers and leather pants down around his ankles. She was shocked at the marbled bruising on his space hoppers. They were definitely the wrong colour. Plummy. Literally! His spuds had actually darkened like a pair of Victorias fit to fall in autumn. Add into the mix the PM's pen tattoo and James's lower half was beginning to look exceedingly artistic. A sort of Jackson Pollock-inspired post-expressionist study in blue.

Bertie bobbed on his perch, watching them both with great interest. This looked like it was shaping up as a typical evening for his mum and dad. No doubt Dad would start kneeling soon – he did look good kneeling, especially in leather – and when that happened a jolly good time would be had by all.

'Is that wise, darling? I feel I'm already taking a risk telling you. These people need to be taken seriously.'

'I think it's safe to assume we passed way beyond risk when you dropped off their cash with the old lady.'

'I'm not taking any bribe,' said James flatly. 'I needed to get rid of that bag as soon as possible. Besides, she looked like she could do with a bit of help.'

'Darling, I think what you did was absolutely wonderful. That's why I love you so much.' She peered at his injured undercarriage again. 'I think I'm going to run you a nice hot bath with extra bubbles, then we'll get some soothing lotion rubbed into those. How does that sound?'

'Will I be tied up?'

'Of course.'

'Gagged?'

'Naturally.'

'Then that sounds absolutely splendid. It's a radical treatment regime from the cutting edge of medicine, but I think it'll really help with the bruising.' He paused, suddenly unsure, then sighed unhappily. 'Frankly, I'm still in two minds as to whether I should have even mentioned what happened.'

'Like you can possibly imagine I'd not notice something was wrong,' she observed with impressive sarcasm. 'Honestly, James, we are talking about my favourite parts of you. Well, apart from your red hot bot, of course.'

'I don't want to put you in any danger. I'd never forgive myself if any harm came to you. Or Bertie.'

'It won't. My baby will protect me, won't you, sweetheart.'

'Oh, yes,' said Bertie, 'I will. What am I saying?' he added conversationally.

'I'm sure he will, but they'll know if we go to the police. These sort of people always know, and there's no way I'm risking getting you involved. Or Bertie.' James stepped out of his trousers and pants, his lower nakedness wafted by dangling shirt tails. He winced at the tenderness in his marital department. 'God, I'm getting flashbacks to those burglars in London. You don't think it's anything to do with them, do you? They're out of prison now.'

'I don't know. Maybe.' They stared at each other for a few moments. Bertie sensed they were both at a loss. It didn't happen often, especially with Celeste. She was a woman who knew her mind, who took control. Especially over her mate. It didn't look like he was going to see her in her finest plumage after all. He guessed The Kneeling Man would be equally disappointed.

'Hello, sailor,' he chipped in helpfully, feeling the

silence needed filling. He peered at Celeste, a little concerned at her pensive frown. She chewed at her lower lip, a sure sign of doubt, but Bertie had absolute faith in his mum and remained warmed and comforted by her presence. His love for her was simple and unshakable, but he was also well tuned to her moods. She was definitely unsure, as if she wanted help. The Kneeling Man usually made her smile, particularly during their complex mating rituals, but he, too, was on edge. He also seemed to be in some considerable pain, and wriggled in discomfort. Perhaps they both needed a helping hand with whatever problem concerned them, maybe a few words of encouragement. He thought hard and eventually came up with two solutions.

The first involved a really large bowl of creamy, plump Brazil nuts followed by a pear or two. Bertie dwelled on the image. Yes, that's what he'd vote for if it was up to him, but somehow he knew on this occasion it wouldn't help. No, he needed to pursue the second alternative. Mummy and daddy required assistance from another human. Mrs Badham came to mind immediately, but this problem did not seem to involve dusting the house or the immediate deployment of a vacuum cleaner. Gavin next door and his inquisitive cows, perhaps? Again, he pondered for a moment before rejecting Gav and moving on. Sadly, there was not much moving on to do. Bertie's world was now almost exclusively centred around home life; indeed, few other humans had ever impressed him enough to warrant a place in his memory.

But there was one. Oh, yes, there was one who had made quite an impression. Grey, thin and unsmiling, easily manipulated, but a good friend nonetheless, this one had helped his mum before, but, most importantly, had also introduced him to Milly. Yes, he well remembered this man.

'Wilf,' said Bertie casually, dropping his suggestion into the silence. Celeste and James both stared at him in wide-eyed shock. Goodness, he hadn't seen that look in a while! Rather missed it, if truth be told. 'Wilf,' he repeated, this time with a little more emphasis. Come on, guys, keep up!

'Wilf!' exclaimed Celeste, much to Bertie's relief. It had taken some time, but she seemed to have got the message at last. Bertie sometimes wondered just how these funny little apes had come to rule the planet.

'Wilf!' stuttered James. Thank heavens, even The Kneeling Man was catching on. He usually brought up the rear in these matters, being a man and all that. All three exchanged stares. 'Well cover me in pancake batter and spank me till Shrove Tuesday, I think that's a damned good idea,' exclaimed James at last.

'What a clever boy,' said Celeste, stroking Bertie's head. He immediately started purring with pride. Yes, it was good to be the brainy one of the family. 'He's the only policeman we know and a damned good one at that. He knows how to be discreet. It wouldn't be suspicious asking him down to stay for the weekend. Everyone knows we're friends. We can ask his advice. Do the police do private commissions – you know, sub-contract work?'

'No, I don't think so,' said James. 'Once you get them officially involved I think you'll find they are obliged by law to investigate to the fullest extent on behalf of the state.'

'But they can only start an investigation if they receive a complaint.'

'That's one trigger.'

'Well, maybe we can ask him to have a nose around but not make a complaint.'

'I don't know,' said James pensively. 'I don't think it works that way. By anyone's book, I've been assaulted. That's a crime. Once it's been reported, off they go full of enthusiasm to boost their clear-up rates.'

'Hmm, well, why don't we invite him down for the weekend anyway and see how it goes. I've been meaning to call him for some time now, just to catch up.'

'Was he promoted after the case?'

'Yes, but he may well have retired now.'

'He's not that old, surely.'

'Always difficult to tell Wilf's age,' said Celeste. 'And don't call me Shirley!'

Detective Sergeant Wilfred Thompson was on the path to retirement. This path had not been triggered by age nor by the accumulation of sufficient funds – and it was certainly not being followed voluntarily. Rather, he had been prodded and poked on to it by his superior officer who had suggested in no uncertain terms that Wilf leave the force under his own steam and with the benefit of a good pension, instead of being forcibly ejected by the disciplinary board.

The reason for this draconian action was simple. In the two years since his promotion, Wilf had driven Detective Chief Inspector Tristram Yates to the point of volcanic frustration, sending his blood pressure through the roof and contributing significantly to his accelerating rate of premature baldness. The focus and energy that had seen Yates bound effortlessly up the police corporate ladder had been diverted from his desire for promotion and channelled almost entirely into handling Wilf – and Wilf had worn him down. Crikey, had Wilf worn him down. Wound up to breaking point by that exasperating combination of Wilf's peerless detective skills, coupled with his smouldering insubordination and open resentment of authority, Yates had finally pulled the nuclear trigger.

As for Wilf, he'd rather enjoyed the past couple of years. Promoted after the Gordon burglary case with its extraordinary and devastating consequences, he'd strolled through his workload like a hot knife through butter, gathering in all manner of obnoxious miscreants and packing them off to court. He had one of the highest conviction rates in the Met and was admired greatly across the force for his unruffled approach and unconventional methods.

Except by Yates.

Yates didn't like unconventional methods. Yates liked convention. His mind worked on order. On precision. Meticulousness. The Book.

Wilf's intuitive approach was not covered by The Book. He drew on his vast experience, dogged determination – and contempt for convention. He and dear Tristram were like poles on a magnet, forever being forced into closer and closer contact, but never to actually touch. In this competition, the smart money around the station was on Wilf, but Yates possessed the ultimate power and had finally used it. Ruthlessly.

And so Wilf was now working out his last week of retirement notice on gardening leave. He still carried his warrant card and remained a serving officer, but Yates had taken a leaf out of Canon Law and excommunicated him, banning him from the station and effectively destroying his ability to carry out his job. If Wilf hadn't equally exasperated his Police Federation representative, he might have had recourse, but it all now seemed utterly pointless. Pity, he wasn't yet ready. He had plenty more stomach for the fight, but Yates had finally snapped.

Yates.

The trouble had always been Yates.

What a tit!

And now, as if all that wasn't bad enough, here he was experiencing an acute attack of Pie Dilemma.

Wilf stood in the local Co-op armed with his bachelor's basket and burdened with an impossible choice. Steak and kidney versus chicken and mushroom in a shortcrust topping Death Match. Which should he have in a sandwich when he got home? He hefted one in each hand, balancing them in a moment of uncharacteristic indecision. Ham and leek had already been rejected on the grounds that he liked neither of the constituents. Ham he found too salty and leek too slimy, which really only left the pastry, and even Wilf, as seasoned a bachelor as he was, even he couldn't face a pie without a filling, especially between two slices of bread. He sighed sadly, a bitter twist to his lips. How had it come to this, when the most important decision of his day was pie-based. Thankfully, mercifully, wonderfully, his phoned chirruped. The theme tune to *Z Cars*. Now, that had been a good programme, and the real reason he'd originally joined the force. For a young lad eagerly anticipating each new episode, the wonderful world of policing proved irresistible – even in black and white! Both pies were tossed back on the shelf. He peered at the screen, saw the caller ID and all the sourness that stained his face evaporated in an instant, leaving a rare smile.

'Ex-Detective Sergeant Wilfred Thompson,' he said crisply. 'Macaw recoveries a speciality, governments brought down to order!'

'Hello, Wilf,' chuckled a familiar and still very lovely contralto.

'Well, I'll go to the foot of our stairs, Celeste Gordon, now Timbrill.'

'Haven't forgotten, then?'

'Now that's not very likely, is it?' he countered with his usual heavy dose of sarcasm. He was feeling better already. Quite chipper, actually. 'God, it's great to hear your voice again.'

'Ex-Detective?'

'Gardening leave and on the path to enforced retirement.'

'I can tell from the tone of your voice you're really happy about it,' replied Celeste, matching his sarcasm. Wilf had missed her dry wit.

'I had a minor disagreement with a senior officer,' he said bluntly. 'It was either retirement with full honours and a pension, or the disciplinary board and a ritual casting out into the wilderness.'

Celeste guessed he had only been given the choice in grudging respect for his professional qualities and, more importantly, to keep the press from turning him into a martyr – after all, Wilf had been instrumental in solving the case of the decade.

'That's a shame,' said Celeste. 'You have a real gift.'

'Others don't think so.'

'Ah, yes, the less talented officers in the Met. Sorry, I meant to say your superiors.' Celeste paused and Wilf caught on straight away.

'You in trouble?'

'Maybe. Yes. I don't know.'

'Indecision? That's not the Celeste I knew.'

'I've not been in this situation before.'

'Is Bertie all right?' he asked suddenly.

'Yes, but why do you ask?'

'Well, we've all seen the consequences of his actions. He seems to have the knack of stirring things up, so I just wondered.'

'Not this time. It's James who has the problem.' Celeste noted obliquely that Wilf had asked after her pet but not her husband. She tried not to read too much into that. 'We were wondering if you could come down to Gloucestershire to see us. I guess you have time on your hands so why not stay for a couple of days.'

Wilf's mind was already working away, looking at angles, at motives. He couldn't help himself. 'So you think your phone's not tapped because you called me, but the situation is serious enough to warrant a face-to-face discussion, yet because of our previous association and friendship my appearance at your home would not arouse any undue suspicion just in case you're under surveillance. My, Celeste, what have you been up to?'

'That's the Wilf I remember,' she cooed in admiration. 'I've come over all goosebumpy.'

'I have that effect on women. And, oddly enough, llamas.'

'So are you available?'

'Let me consult my diary. Hmm, it's so full. How about tomorrow morning, the first off-peak train into Gloucester from Paddington.' Without looking, Wilf grabbed the nearest pie off the shelf, tossed it into his basket and headed for the checkout with a new spring in his step. It was only when he got home he discovered it was ham and leek.

'I've never been this far west,' said Wilf, standing at the bottom of the garden and looking out across the Severn Vale. The Malverns swept upwards in the distance, a roller-coaster silhouette of bald hills all in a line, a uniquely dramatic panorama found nowhere else in England. 'It's lovely,' he added. 'I can see why you gave up London.'

'Yes, we like it a lot,' replied Celeste.

'Big trees,' added Bertie. 'Very nice.'

'That's all right, then,' nodded Wilf, peering with affection at the big macaw. Bertie sat on a fence post protruding from the thick hawthorn hedge separating the garden from a field full of Gav's finest milkers. One separated herself from the herd and ambled over for a nose, udder swaying. She blinked coquettishly at them, chewing her cud with methodical deliberation.

'Hello, Buttercup,' said Wilf. 'Blimey, haven't you got gorgeous eyelashes.'

'That's the most disturbing comment I've ever heard you say.'

'And you're so big as well. I could get a lot of chops out of you.'

'Chops come from pigs and sheep.'

'Oh, sorry, I thought they came from Asda. I've had my mind on other things recently.'

'So I gather. We had no idea you were leaving the force.'

'Neither did I.'

65

'When do you actually finish?'

'Next Wednesday.'

'That soon? Would you like to stay with us until then and we can celebrate?'

'I'm not celebrating,' snapped Wilf.

'Now don't you go all bitter on me, Detective Sergeant,' said Celeste brusquely. 'We can do without that, thank you very much.'

Wilf shrugged. 'Sorry. Old habits die hard.'

'Time for new ones, then.' She and Wilf stared out again, drinking in the glorious view. He breathed in grass-scented air. It was considerably more pleasant than the pervasive whiff of diesel so often found in London. 'So what's on your mind, Celeste?' he finally said. 'Skip the bits that have been reported in the papers over the last few years. I've been keeping a distant eye on you both, just in case of … repercussions.' They both knew what he meant.

'James was attacked in London day before yesterday. This was no ordinary random assault. He was targeted because of who he is and what he's doing at Westminster. Three men roughed him up a bit, told him he would be contacted from time to time with specific instructions, that he would be required to comply with these instructions and that Bertie and I would be in danger if he didn't toe the line. As an indication of their goodwill, they left a holdall containing a large amount of money. Actually, a very large amount indeed.'

'Hmm, a financial inducement backed up by the threat of violence. It's always the same. These people show no imagination because they themselves would find the cash impossible to resist. Naturally he was also told not to contact the police,' said Wilf.

'Naturally.'

'Which was why you called me.'

'Not my idea. It was Bertie's suggestion.'

They both turned to stare at the macaw. 'Guilty,' he said in a sonorous Highland accent immediately identifiable as Mr Justice Alistair Cruikshank's.

'Bloody hell, he's as sharp as ever, isn't he?'

'Yes he is,' said Celeste, with conviction. 'You have no idea.'

'I have, actually. I'm really rather fond of him, you know.' Wilf gently stroked Bertie's neck, then smoothed down the feathers along his broad back. 'So, back to your problem. Do you still have the money?'

'Er...'

'Of course you don't,' said Wilf, rolling his eyes with professional weariness. 'What happened?'

'James was taking it back to his office in Westminster when he stopped to help out a beggar.'

'Let me guess.' His tone expressed sarcasm on a truly biblical scale.

'It was only when he got back to his office he found he'd forgotten to pick up the cash.'

'And you believe that?'

'Of course I don't,' retorted Celeste with a sunny smile. 'My husband is a qualified accountant. From Gloucester. He is not the sort of man who idly leaves a quarter of a million pounds with a bag lady by mistake, but he is the sort of man who would help someone less fortunate than himself with a generous act of kindness, regardless of the consequences. This is one of the reasons I love him so much.'

Wilf sighed. 'That could have been a major error. Evidence like that is a forensic dream and can often lead to a conviction. Also, and I'm going out on a limb here, those masterminding the attack just might be a tad upset he's given the lot away.'

'Tough. Too late now. I completely support my husband's actions.'

'So you're worried about possible repercussions. What do you want me to do?'

'I'm not an expert in these matters, but it seems to me we have two alternatives.'

'Next Wednesday figures significantly in one of these alternatives, doesn't it?'

'Detective Sergeant, I've always been most impressed with your perspicacity,' purred Celeste. Wilf liked it when she purred. He rather liked it when Bertie purred as well. This was a family that had been working diligently on its purring. 'Firstly, do you think we should report the incident and get the police officially involved?'

Wilf gazed into the distance again, eyes narrowed in thought. 'Chances are, of course, that the brains behind these thugs are in unassailable positions of power. Only those in power would be worried about the waves your husband's making – or have the resources to fill that holdall.'

'Makes sense.'

'Such people will certainly have influence in the higher ranks of the Met.' People like Hugo Chaplain, for instance. Wilf made a mental note to check up on Chaplain when he got back to London. Make sure he's behaving himself. 'They would know immediately if you told the police. Defying those specific instructions would certainly expose you and Bertie to the danger James is so keen to avoid.'

'My thoughts exactly. Besides, if we take that course then it's out of your hands. You would have to go back to London and do whatever it is you're planning to do in retirement while the police investigate. Sound attractive?' Celeste knew her man. 'Or, and this is my second alternative, you stay as our guest for as long as you like and keep an eye on things here at home. I've never felt vulnerable before, what with Bertie always on hand and my own particular skills with weapons of defence, but this is a fairly secluded location and the men James described were pretty hefty guys. I'd feel happier if you'd stay as my muscle.'

'I've been called many things in my life, but never "muscle",' chuckled Wilf. 'I'm rather flattered.'

'Obviously, I prefer James to be here as well, but he

feels he can't deviate from his normal routine. He's under almost constant press scrutiny at the best of times so they'd soon notice his absence at Westminster and start digging. I'm sure you'll agree it's best if he carries on as normal, show these people he's not intimidated, even if this does provoke a response. The threats made to him were very clear. Bertie and I have almost certainly moved up to target status, and that's a worrying thought.'

'I can understand that, Celeste, but having someone here will greatly reduce the chance of something unpleasant happening. Any policeman will tell you these characters always prefer to wait for the moment when you're at your most vulnerable, and that's when you're on your own. Why do you think they nabbed James in the loo? Still, we can take some simple but effective measures to beef up security. I'll have to accompany you wherever you go, of course.'

'No you won't. You'll stay with Bertie. He's more vulnerable.'

'There's two scarred ex-cons who'd disagree with that.'

'I don't care, Wilf.' Celeste's tone brooked no argument. 'I can look after myself.'

'Previous experience tells me he can as well,' observed Wilf dryly. 'Do you have an alarm?'

'Don't be ridiculous. I don't even lock the doors.'

'Right, well, that's going to change, starting now. What's in your appointments book for the next week?'

'I have an appointment at the hairdressers in Tewkesbury on Friday, and I'm sure I can handle that on my own. You can stay with Bertie and spend your time making preparations, laying the groundwork so to speak, for a smooth transition from serving officer in the Metropolitan Police to your new career as a concerned citizen privately engaged in solving our problem.'

Wilf ruminated. Like Buttercup. Then she farted. Wilf didn't follow her lead. He could have sworn a contented grin spread across her vacant bovine features.

Celeste Timbrill was a difficult woman to resist. On every level. He had to admit, of all the cases he'd handled in his long and largely undistinguished career, he'd never had so much fun as he'd had with her, despite the ever present risk of severe testicular damage, and the thought of just fading away into obscurity filled him with dismay. They both knew she was throwing him a lifeline. 'All right, I'll do it,' he said finally. 'For old times' sake.' The alternative was another Pie Dilemma.

'Now we're cooking,' said Bertie.

CHAPTER SIX

Doreen looked at her watch. Not long to go now. She checked the salon diary for the following morning. Blast! Her first appointment was Seraphina Truscott. Old Snotty Totty herself. The damned woman was never satisfied. Thought she was better than everyone in town since she snagged Sir Gerald last year. Gerry was the local aristocrat who lived up at Sodbury Grange. Seraphina went for the title, but didn't do her research – Gerry was boracic. Snotty found out soon enough once they were married and was not at all impressed. She'd carried a face like a spanked arse ever since. Still, Doreen was confident she'd have no trouble handling Snotty after her recent conversations with Moaning Maria. Now, there was a woman who could effortlessly grumble her way to an Olympic final.

The day had been busy and all three of them were tired. Sandra, her assistant stylist, and Maggie, the apprentice, made up Doreen's modest staff. Both revered their Gaia. In fact, both were absolutely essential in helping her juggle her twin careers of popular provincial hairdresser and Ruler of the World. Now, that was an odd mix, but whereas one of her roles was shrouded in absolute secrecy, Doreen's hairdressing history was well known.

After studying at Gloucestershire College and serving an apprenticeship in Thornbury, Doreen had saved her pennies and opened her salon in Chipping Sodbury – and things hadn't exactly got off to an auspicious start. Her choice of name, *Panache*, needed to be painted above the front window, but unable to afford a proper signwriter she'd engaged Bernie's brother. This was an unfortunate choice because Doug was dyslexic – and he'd also been out on the cider the night before, so the salon became *Pancake*. And it stayed that way. Doreen was genuinely surprised how few people noticed.

The salon struggled at first, as all new businesses do, but she was a determined woman and not afraid of hard work. Her little empire grew slowly and on occasion took priority over motherhood; Bernie often had to mind the kids in the evening while she made home visits, but her reputation spread and Pancake transformed itself into a little pot of gold, after all, she'd tapped into an inexhaustible market – hair is always growing!

Then *she* came – and brought Sandra with her to help out.

Although possessing one of the three classical names forever associated with hairdressing, Sandra proved universally abysmal at her new job. Customers avoided her if they could and Doreen often had to step in to save a cut which was heading off the rails at terrifying speed. Sandra's approach was more akin to logging, as Maggie once observed. Despite numerous complaints, Doreen always stoutly defended Sandra. Her talents lay elsewhere. Her colouring may have been questionable, but she was a first-class political analyst. Her poodle perming was once likened to coiled barbed wire clogged with tufts of windswept lambswool, but she was an incisive and talented administrator, fully justifying her position as Doreen's Number Two, a sort of Assistant Goddess. But for all those incredible talents, a razor-sharp mind, long auburn hair, warm brown eyes, a great figure and lively personality, she was miserably unlucky in love. Popes put on the Fisherman's Ring more often than Sandra had sex. She was well known in the Sisterhood for the paucity of her love life and its associated frustration, and this resulted in much good-natured ribbing. She needed a right old rogering, but somehow, bizarrely, there were never any takers. The eligible of Chipping Sodbury were, to a man, intimidated by her fearsome intellect, but for all that, she devoted herself to the Sisterhood and worshipped Doreen.

Doreen looked up from the diary. The last customer had professed herself happy and paid. 'Thanks, Julie, see you in six weeks. Don't forget to try that new conditioner!' The front door was closed and locked, the Open/Closed sign turned appropriately. Maggie emerged from the kitchenette with coffees and started to sweep the floor.

'So, have you sorted the Paraguayan debacle?' asked Sandra.

'Hope so. Maria wasn't too happy.'

'Sod her. She's quick to enjoy the benefits of being a President's shag basket. Make her work for the privilege. Sexual denial is just about as potent a weapon as you can get. Got to be careful with the Bolivians, mind you. They've always been a bit twitchy.'

'I don't anticipate any real problems. We'll see how it goes. Maria's got a real incentive to pull it off – I've offered her a day's shoe shopping in London.'

'Christ, expect peace to break out all over South America.'

'For all her complaints, she is *very* good at her job.'

Sandra consulted the diary. 'I see you've got Snotty first thing tomorrow.'

'It's an exercise in patience.'

'Want me to have a go at her?'

'Tempting.'

The phone rang. 'Panache, Sandra speaking, can I help?' She listened for a moment, then beckoned furiously to Doreen. 'You'll never guess who's on the line,' she whispered, covering the mouthpiece.

Doreen shrugged. 'Sixty-odd million people live in this country. You'll have to give me a bit more of a clue.'

'It's the Ginger Ninja!'

Instantly alert, Doreen took the receiver from Sandra and composed herself with a deep breath. 'Hello, Alice,

73

this is a rare treat,' she said carefully.

'Gaia. Not much time. Agnes needs feeding.'

'How is she?'

'She's a pigeon, Gaia. She doesn't talk much,' came the testy reply.

'And you? Are you looking after yourself?'

'Life is hard, Gaia.'

'You make it hard, Alice. You could come home to us. There's always a welcome for you here. You can rest, perhaps.'

'Impossible. Too much to do.'

'Still worried about those pesky mobile phones?'

'Yes, but that's not why I'm calling.'

'Oh?' Doreen's heart sank. Poor Alice Prothero. The Ginger Ninja. Once so intimately involved with the Sisterhood, she had suffered a major mental episode and taken to the streets of London, living under the radar and a large red bobble hat, convinced of a colossal global conspiracy to cover up the fact that global warming was caused by microwave emissions from mobile phone networks. This obsession had driven a schism between her and the few friends who still cared. Now it seemed there was something else to fret that extraordinary mind. 'What's bothering you this time?'

'James Timbrill.'

Doreen froze, unable to say anything. Alice cackled. Not a good sound over the phone. 'There, I thought that might catch your attention.'

'What about him?' asked Doreen carefully. The subject of James Timbrill – and his wife – was very close to her heart.

'I've been keeping an unofficial eye on him. You know, when I can spare the time from my research.'

'Thank you, Alice. I didn't know that. I do appreciate your concern.'

'I remember his potential importance. I haven't forgotten everything,' she added peevishly.

'Of course not. So what's happened?'

'He's been attacked.'

'Is he injured?' asked Doreen. 'No, of course he isn't,' she added, 'otherwise it would have been on the news.'

'Oh, he was hurt all right. Nasty testicular damage, by the looks of it, but nothing lasting, nothing that should worry his wife. It took three men to injure him. Professionals. Real nasty sods. Odd sort of a mugging, though. Nothing was stolen, but they left him a gift. A very generous gift, actually.'

Doreen was no fool. Neither did she underestimate Alice's intelligence. 'Someone's trying to corrupt him.'

'Yeah, I thought so, too. I don't think they're going to be too happy with him.'

'Let me guess.'

'Two hundred and fifty thousand pounds in used twenties. It took me ages to turn all the notes so the queen could look at me while I counted. He wanted to help someone less fortunate than himself. I touched his hand and looked into his eye. He's a very fine, honest, generous, good-hearted man.'

'Alice, you have to hand the money to the police.'

'And get arrested on suspicion of theft? Who would feed Agnes?'

'She's a pigeon. They're not fussy. They've perfected the art of pecking.'

'No, I'm keeping the money. It was a gift. It'll help my research.' The thought of the Ginger Ninja having access to sizeable funds made Doreen feel more than slightly uncomfortable. Her instability bordered on super-villainy. 'One thing concerns me, though.'

'They will target his wife as retribution,' Doreen said.

'Yes, and her weakness is the parrot.'

'He's a macaw.'

'His species is immaterial. Unfortunately, the potential threat to them isn't. You have to help, Gaia, if not out of simple compassion, then because of her heritage.' Alice changed the subject abruptly. 'How's the girl coping?'

Doreen glanced at Maggie, concerned that Alice's mind was doing that darting around thing again. It wasn't a good omen. 'She's not as focused as you are.'

'Give her time. She has the gift. I know she doesn't like to go up to the Hall, but see if she can help. Meanwhile, I will try to keep Timbrill under observation whenever he's in London, but my feet aren't so good nowadays. Thank heavens he's a man of disturbingly regular habits so I don't have to walk very far to find him.'

'You don't have to do this.'

'I'm still a Sister, Gaia. I have my duty.'

'Alice, please come home,' pleaded Doreen softly. 'We all miss you so much.'

There was a long silence. 'I can't, Doreen. I just – can't,' she whispered, voice wavering. 'Please, don't ask …'

The phone went dead.

Doreen slipped the receiver back on its cradle and stared at Sandra. 'Someone's attempted to corrupt James Timbrill.' She recounted the conversation in full. Sandra and Maggie listened intently.

'Alice won't return, then?'

'No. She doesn't think she needs any help.'

'How did she sound?'

'Tired. Thankfully, not so crazy.'

'We could find her, you know. If she's tailing Timbrill, we could do the same. Our paths are bound to cross.'

'And then what? Forcibly detain her? There's no easy answer. I'm just glad she's still alive. That's the first word from her in nearly three years.' Doreen looked at Maggie. 'What do you think, Mags?'

'She's right. We must to go to Temple Hall,' said Maggie. 'The Ninja always disturbs me. I need to take a look, see if anything comes to me.' A young woman in her early twenties, Maggie was slight of build, with spiked pink hair and a nostril stud. She wore dark eyeshadow to give a little depth to her wan face. Punk still ruled in Chipping Sodbury, even though it had swept through the rest of the country decades ago. It was the sort of place that set its own trends.

Despite her apparent lowly position at the salon, Maggie was a critical figure in the Sisterhood. She was Doreen's Pythia, her priestess and oracle, a position previously held by Alice until her breakdown. Because of this, Maggie had been thrust into the position prematurely, and openly acknowledged she was unprepared, but the Sisterhood had never been without an oracle and Doreen needed guidance. She felt a great deal of sympathy for her predecessor and was very conscious of the psychological pressures, but Alice was by far a more capable psychic – and therefore more susceptible to instability.

Helen herself had lived in an age where much store was laid on the mystical power of the Gods and the complex relationships between themselves and mankind. Oracles were valued above kings, so she naturally wanted to ensure the newly-formed Sisterhood was well provisioned in that direction. The inclusion of a Pythia at the heart of the Sisterhood had become an unshakeable tradition over the centuries and to simply discard such a tradition for the mere sake of modernity was unthinkable, even though today's society now almost totally rejected the unscientific notion of prophesy as hippy-dippy, a bit suspect, even a complete load of old mumbo-jumbo. Can't get an app, you see.

But for all that, it still worked.

The following morning found them driving slowly through the Cotswold village of Temple Guiting. Maggie peered out of the window. 'I see Mrs Jenkins has castrated her laburnum again,' she said absently. 'The poor thing's sure to die now.'

'Still hacking off the good growth and leaving the canker?'

'Uh-huh. It'll be down this winter or I'm Carmen Miranda.'

'She'll be upset,' said Doreen, craning her neck as they passed the doomed tree. Or large stick, to be more accurate. 'But I'd like to see you with a fruit bowl on your head,' she added. 'Very healthy.'

'You can wear your five a day,' observed Sandra. The lane twisted past the last few straggling cottages and just beyond the edge of the village they turned into the grounds of Temple Hall, gliding between stone pillars topped with statuesque stag heads, their age-old foreheads pocked and stained. A single-track gravel driveway meandered around several stately beeches before nuzzling up to the front of the old house. The car scrunched to a halt and they got out.

Temple Hall was, quite simply, breathtaking. The beautiful Cotswold limestone, once fresh and golden, had mellowed into a soft misty grey. The Hall sprawled comfortably like a corpulent elderly aunt after a heavy lunch. Its gables were tall, its roof a lichen-spotted expanse of stone slates sweeping up to the gently undulating ridge. Mullioned windows peppered the walls, peeping out from behind a rampant honeysuckle that looped and trailed around and over the central entrance porch. Inquisitive green shoots fingered upwards on a leisurely exploration towards the first floor bedrooms, laden with scented clusters of cream and yellow flowers, while 'S' braces of black iron corseted the old building, firming it up, countering the spreading forces of gravity which had tugged steadily at it for half a millennium.

The Hall stood in extensive grounds with formal gardens wrapping around the building like a colourful petticoat of shrubs and flowers. Neat, undulating, tree-dotted parkland radiated out beyond, seeping into the surrounding countryside. To one side, behind a high wall dripping in red and yellow climbing roses, the vegetable garden had provided generations of Sisters with carrots and onions, cauliflower and sprouts, potatoes and cabbages, broccoli, beetroot and beans of broad, runner, kidney and French extraction. This sumptuous produce was renowned locally and had been a staple at the village fete WI stall for as long as could be remembered. Doreen was looking forward to her lunch. She turned away to gaze down the shallow valley towards the village nearby. Temple Guiting was little more than a hamlet nestling in a fold of soft green hills, the fields jigsawed by dry stone walls. The tower of St Mary's could be seen rising above a stand of beech off to the left. Sunlight glinted on the ponds.

An aura of peace enveloped them all. There was no sound but that of sparrows arguing noisily on the roof and the muted buzz of bees busily visiting the honeysuckle, labouring from flower to flower in a determined quest for nectar, their legs clad in oversized pollen jodhpurs. The windless morning was warm and sunny, with just a few fluffy white clouds floating serenely overhead like cotton buds scattered carelessly on a blue table. All was tranquil and timeless on this lazy early summer's morning, the quintessential English landscape, forever calm, forever dreaming.

It was, truly, lovely beyond description.

Maggie closed her eyes and inhaled deeply. 'I adore the smell of this place,' she said softly. Doreen nodded in agreement. The Hall had been the home of the Sisterhood for centuries. There was something very special about the house and the astonishing secret it concealed. She looked up to where the land rose behind the roof in a low hill, a gentle dome covered in short grass, its rounded summit just visible between the ornate Elizabethan chimneys. A few unfeasibly woolly sheep grazed with the lethargic indifference for which their species was noted. As always, she smiled. Such secrets indeed!

'Come on, girls, let's have a cup of tea with Jenny before we get going,' she said, entering the porch in a scented swirl of sweet honeysuckle. Maggie was right, the place smelt divine, a mixture of heady perfumes, waxed wood and distant cooking. The entrance hall was impressive, as befitted such a grand residence, with a galleried balcony leading off to the first floor bedrooms. Light streamed in through the leaded windows to splash diamond patterns on the old oak floors. Portraits lined the panelled walls. An observant guest would have noted they were all paintings of women. Some were grand indeed: a Reynolds here, a Gainsborough there, a dreamy Fragonard between the windows, and above the ornate fireplace, dominating the entire room, an extraordinary, vibrant, brooding portrait of Helen of Troy by Sir Frederick Sandys.

A woman was waiting for them. 'Welcome, Gaia,' she said with a warm smile, kissing the back of Doreen's hand and each cheek. She was in her late twenties, willowy and slender, fresh-faced, with a tanned and healthy complexion, huge, luminously brown eyes and a dainty snubbed nose. Long, wavy, wheaten hair tumbled to the small of her back. She wore a simple white cotton dress, sleeveless, unbuttoned at the front to display a shallow cleavage and decorated with embroidered swirls around the open neckline. A polished black stone hung on a leather thong around her throat. She would have looked the epitome of sophisticated elegance but for the clumpy pink, purple and lime green floral wellington boots and supple leather utility belt slung low around her hips, its pockets and pouches stuffed with gardening tools, balls of twine and assorted horticultural paraphernalia.

'Hi, Jenny. Been rooting around the veggies again?'

'Of course. You don't think they grow that big without help, do you? Hello, Sandra. Had any cock recently?'

'Jenny Clarke, the state of my sex life is not on today's agenda,' observed Sandra with a sniff.

'So no change there, then,' sniggered Jenny. 'Have you thought about trying a girl? Might have more luck.'

'Men may be idiots, but women are completely insane,'

Sandra declared irritably, unappreciative of Jenny's radical suggestion. 'I think I'll stick with the idiots.'

'Hi, Jen,' said Maggie, hugging her friend briefly. 'Leave her be. She'll never bat for the other side. Take it from me.'

They walked through to the kitchen. 'Right, let's get the important things out of the way first,' said Doreen 'What's for lunch?'

'I've some broccoli and roasted almond soup on the go with fresh crusty bread.'

'Sounds great. I'm going to need some feeding.' Maggie's occasional sojourns into the mystical realm always left her feeling peckish, particularly since she never ate beforehand, to intensify the effect of the experience.

'Time for tea first?'

'Of course,' said Doreen firmly. 'Is the Oracle prepared?'

'We always keep it ready, Gaia, you know that. A new batch of branches arrived last week.'

'Good. It's a bit quiet around here. Where's the rest of the gang?'

'Downstairs – where else?'

'No need to disturb them for the moment. You know how engrossed they get. They'll be up for lunch.'

'They will,' agreed Jenny. 'Are you staying all day, Gaia, or do you need to get back?'

'We'll see how it goes. Sophie and Bex are covering the salon.'

'I'm doing sea bass and roasting some vegetables fresh from the garden for supper, if that'll help make up your mind.'

'Tempting. I suppose I could spare the time. I'll call Bernie and let him know.'

'Grand. That'll be all six of us!' Jenny loved her cooking.

Opulent sixteenth-century country residences were invariably provided with extensive kitchens, and Temple

Hall was no exception. The high-ceilinged room was long and filled with sunlight which fell in through tall, curtained windows. A massive fireplace filled the end wall, with iron-fronted ovens of varying sizes and complexity arranged on either side of the hearth. Copper-bottomed saucepans hung from thick bars set above the huge grate, but these were now more for show than practical use. Jenny preferred to cook on a modern six-burner gas range which stood incongruously amongst the old-fashioned oak kitchen cupboards, their blue slate work surfaces polished smooth from decades of scrubbing. She washed her hands in a gigantic granite sink inscribed in Latin around the rim and put the kettle on the range, her wellies scuffing against the stone-flagged floor as she shuffled around the large oak dining table that dominated the room. It was a substantial piece of furniture, plain and unadorned, with six sturdy legs and an accompanying harem of simple, spindled chairs.

Sandra sat while Maggie and Doreen inspected the pantries, poking, prodding, sniffing. She always sat in the same place, towards one end of the table. In front of her, the smooth surface was interrupted by a curiously lopsided diamond recess cut into the wood. An insert of red mahogany filled this shallow recess like a misshapen domino slotting into a hole. Sandra reached across the table and, pressing on one end, tipped it slightly, enabling her to lift the insert out of its snug home. She toyed with the flat diamond absently, turning it over and over before putting it back in place. The carpenter who had constructed the table had removed a disfiguring knot from the oak plank and shaped the insert to fit the resulting hole, a neat trick which preserved its flush surface. The imperfection had always fascinated Sandra. Maggie nudged Doreen and nodded over her shoulder. 'She's at it again,' she whispered. 'What is it with that piece of wood?'

'Beats me,' breathed Doreen, 'and if you don't know

then how the hell would I?'

The kettle began to sing, summoning them from the pantry. Jenny brewed the tea in a white china teapot and they all sat at the table, mugs in hand. Conversation flowed freely, as it always does when four intelligent women gather to drink tea. Doreen's new shoes were greatly admired, Jenny grumbled about a plague of slugs rampaging through her seedlings and Sandra anticipated a satisfactory resolution to the Paraguayan crisis, but Maggie sat quietly, as she always did before entering the Oracle, preferring to take comfort from the joviality of the others. Jenny noticed her pensive look.

'You OK, Mags?' she asked.

'Yeah, I guess. Make sure you've got plenty of strong coffee brewed. I don't want to be so wrecked I miss lunch.'

'Sure thing.'

There was an awkward silence. Each appeared wrapped in private thought, but Maggie knew they were all watching her discreetly, hoping for some clue as to what was about to happen. She didn't need to rely on her powers too much to perceive Doreen's sudden uneasiness or Sandra's quiet agitation. Alice's unexpected call had been disturbing. At least Jenny seemed unaffected. Although intimately involved with the administration of Temple Hall, her world was not so much dominated by political intricacies and subtle policy, as compost and rain and earthworms. There were times when Maggie envied Jenny's simplistic outlook on life, yet she was no fool. A born and bred country girl from Moreton-in-Marsh, she'd been with the Sisterhood these past ten years and there was no doubt the quality of the catering at the Hall had improved immeasurably since her arrival. Her intentions to remain there for the rest of her life were heartily endorsed by everyone who visited – Jenny's comestibles were legendary!

Maggie looked at her friend and, as always, sensed her

serene contentment. Jenny was unfailingly cheerful. Happiness cloaked her like a glowing aura. It was soothing to be in her presence and normally she would have enjoyed a little banter, some inappropriate double-entendres or a few pointed remarks about Sandra's dormant sex life – but not today. Maggie drained her mug and peered out of the window, a distant look in her eyes. Something white and woolly ambled past in the distance, bleating forlornly.

'You ready?' enquired Doreen gently.

'Sure, let's go see if we can get anything.' Maggie scraped back her chair and, leaving the kitchen, threaded her way through the house and down the rear stairs to the cellar. Sandra and Doreen followed. There, beneath the Hall, was a place that pre-dated the medieval building above by over a thousand years. The Oracle was the place where the Pythia entered her trances, the place where she saw.

Maggie had been clairvoyant since childhood, worrying her parents with her strangeness and uncanny ability to glimpse the future. Naturally, as any caring and responsible parents would have done, they totally misdiagnosed their daughter's uniqueness and consulted an endless succession of doctors, specialists and child psychiatrists, searching for an answer to their problem. Maggie assured them there was no problem, but she still had to endure scans and tests and experimental drug therapies and something unpleasant involving jelly and electrodes. It was only after saving her parents from certain death in a car crash that they finally accepted their daughter's unusual gift. With the love they poured into her, Maggie blossomed. One day, just before her nineteenth birthday, she calmly packed a small bag, kissed her mum and dad farewell and took a bus to Malmesbury. She sat in front of the abbey, waiting in the sunshine until a complete stranger with gorgeous hair and very nice shoes walked past. 'Hello, Gaia,' she called after Doreen. 'I

don't think you'll find Alice here.'

The shock on Doreen's face made Maggie smile. 'Sorry to surprise you like that, but I just thought you might like to know what you're dealing with here. You can deny it all you like, but I know you've got something to do with a woman called Helen, that your real name is Doreen and that you are going to sit down next to me because you desperately need a medium!'

And that was how it had started. Maggie's arrival had been a godsend for Doreen. Alice was an extraordinarily accomplished clairvoyant, but the pressures had taken their toll and one night her mind had shattered in the Oracle, fragmenting horrifically, and she'd fled into the darkness. The Sisterhood had never been without a Pythia, so when Maggie made her dramatic approach, Doreen accepted immediately. She then turned to the problem of finding Alice, but by that time she'd gone to ground in London, living off the streets and befriending pigeons.

Now Maggie stood before the entrance to the Oracle with Doreen and Sandra on each side. She hesitated. 'Do you know, I can see why Alice didn't like this place. It really creeps me out,' she said softly.

'Me, too,' murmured Doreen, 'so we'll keep it as short as we can.'

'Don't let me dribble too much.'

'We won't.'

'And I'll need coffee. Lots of coffee. I definitely don't want to miss lunch.'

'Jenny's already grinding the beans,' said Sandra. Maggie nodded. Doreen pushed the heavy wooden door open and stepped into the Oracle.

The place was old. Properly old! At well over four hundred years, Temple Hall was itself old in the traditional sense, but the Oracle beneath the Hall was ancient. The modest chamber where the Pythia made her pronouncements exuded age. Time had laden the atmosphere with a heavy aura of history. The Oracle was a

subterranean Roman crypt built on a knotted confluence of ley lines, and Temple Hall had been constructed over it, protecting and incorporating it, absorbing the masonry into its own structure, but the Oracle was not an original part of the house and had stood alone for centuries before the Hall foundations were laid.

It was not a large chamber – only the Pythia and a few attendants ever entered – and in construction resembled an early Romano-Christian baptistry, windowless, bare, ascetic and rough, with a few plain circular columns here and there to support the arched roof. This was fortunate. Archaeologically inclined visitors, although few, needed to see the Oracle as something else and there was no greater disguise than to hide it in plain view as a small private baptistry. The Sisterhood had spun a yarn that it was the original temple for which the village of Temple Guiting was named, but the actual truth was far more astonishing and carefully hidden away from prying eyes. However, such structures were occasionally attached to houses of elevated status and so it excited no undue interest to find the Hall had been built over the site of the original chamber.

Maggie followed Doreen, ducking her head as she passed under the low lintel, her gaze already distracted. The Oracle smelt musty and faintly aromatic. Doreen lit several bronze oil lamps of exotic design, their dim light casting wavering shadows. Sandra closed the door behind them and stood guard. Doreen squeezed Maggie's arm reassuringly. 'You OK, honey? You look anxious.'

'Anything to do with the Ginger Ninja disturbs me. I can feel it already without the smoke and booze.' Maggie knew she was only a fraction as talented as Alice and frequently questioned her abilities. This self-doubt made her nervous.

'You'll cope. I'll start the fire.' She handed Maggie a stone pitcher. 'Get this down your neck, girl!'

The sweet smell of apples rose from the pitcher.

Temple cider, made from apples picked from the Hall's own orchards, was potent enough to floor a charging hippo! Maggie sipped while Doreen busied herself building a fire.

The flagged floor of the chapel was bare and unadorned but for a small circular pit in its centre. This was passed off as the font to any outside visitor, the heart of the baptistry, but the stonework was charred and blackened, signifying the use of fire rather than water. Doreen piled dry branches into this pit and soaked them in oil. A match ignited the flames with a muted whoosh. The wood crackled and slumped as the fire settled. Smoke rose in a swirling column, strong and pungent from the sappy timber. The wood was juniper, cut from the upland forests of ancient Lycia in south-west Turkey. Sandra and Doreen waited for the initial surge of flames to subside, then brought forward a tall iron stool and placed its tripod feet into small recesses carved into the stone lip of the fire pit. Maggie shimmied herself up onto the crude seat and relaxed with her eyes closed, wreathed in smoke as the green juniper needles hissed and spluttered beneath her feet. She took another long draught of the strong cider. Then another. Smoke filled the Oracle, billowing back and forth before finding escape up the chimney above. The stones surrounding the chimney throat were blackened from centuries of use.

Doreen waited. Maggie needed to fall into her oracular trance, coaxed there by the narcotic juniper smoke and gut-rot cider. Frankly, there was nothing scientific about the process, nothing that could be quantified or corroborated by measurement. It would without doubt fail the most basic empirical test and to any reasonably rational mind was a load of old hokum.

Like bending spoons, watching water flow uphill and charming warts, it shouldn't work – but it did. Spectacularly.

The Pythia drained the pitcher with another long swig

and handed the empty to Sandra. She wiped her lips delicately. 'That's a strong one,' she muttered. 'Jenny must be spiking it with gin!'

'Better not,' replied Doreen.' I don't want you falling off that stool again.'

'I can hold my drink, Gaia,' she retorted. 'Well, most of the time, anyway.' She composed herself and closed her eyes. 'Remember, I'm not as plugged in as Alice. Something might come my way, but it might not.' Maggie had a healthy respect for Alice's gift. She saw where Maggie couldn't – and she was very aware that Doreen knew this as well.

They waited. Minutes passed. Sandra put another branch on the fire, even though the atmosphere inside the Oracle was already thick. She coughed behind her hand. 'That's nasty,' she whispered to Doreen. Maggie was almost entirely obscured within the rising column of blue-grey smoke. 'I don't know how she stands it!'

Maggie groaned softly and Doreen silenced Sandra with a flick of the wrist. They both leaned forward, instantly attentive. The Pythia spoke only once and, for some reason Doreen could not fathom, electronic recording instruments only ever picked up static inside the Oracle, so it was important to listen to every word Maggie uttered.

'We must move with care,' she intoned, her voice entirely flat and empty. 'Men are plotting.'

'Here we go,' breathed Doreen. The Pythia dived straight in, no messing. This was about James Timbrill. 'Tell me of these men,' she asked in a louder voice.

'There are five. They are avaricious. One lies close to death.' There was a pause. 'One of the others is responsible.'

'Are they near?'

'Lingfield.'

'Yes?'

'12.15. Dirty Laundry.'

'Thank you, Pythia,' Doreen said gravely. This was a reliable and useful extra source of income for the Sisterhood. The only trouble they had was finding a betting shop within a fifty-mile radius that had not banned them for life. 'And the five men?'

'Look to the rising sun.'

'The sun rises in the east,' said Doreen.

'Yes, to the east. Not far. I see glass towers beside a winding river.'

'A city?'

'Yes.'

'Tell me more.'

'A bridge that rises and falls.'

'London?'

'Perhaps.' The Pythia was invariably enigmatic. As always, this required precise questioning.

'Is the bridge old or new?'

'Many say it's old. We would say it's new.'

Doreen considered this. The Sisterhood had such a long history that they more or less regarded anything later than the sixteenth century as still under warranty. The ambiguous answer probably meant the bridge was at the very least Victorian. 'Can you see more?'

'A strong place of many walls filled with brightness.'

'The Tower,' murmured Sandra. 'The Crown Jewels.'

'Yes.'

'The men are in London.'

'Yes. They control the lives of many. They own much, they desire even more.'

'Businessmen?'

'Their power comes from money. Money is their god. They seek more. Foolish, foolish men, but very dangerous,' warned Maggie ominously.

'What has changed? Why have they stirred? Why now?'

'Something new disturbs them, something we must protect at all costs.'

'Will there be conflict?'

'Yes.'

'When will the conflict come?'

'It has already started. They have attacked once, they will again. The man has already suffered. His woman is next and those dear to her. She needs our help.' This confirmed Alice's assessment. It seemed certain that Celeste Timbrill was in peril.

'How can we help?'

There was a long silence. Maggie's eyes suddenly opened despite the stinging smoke, but her gaze was dull and distant. She inhaled the acrid vapours without coughing, even though Doreen and Sandra gasped asthmatically and fought for breath. Her trance was deep and of an intensity Doreen had never seen before. Wary of the potential for disaster after Alice's catastrophic breakdown, she was prepared to shove Maggie off the stool at the first sign of distress, but the Pythia remained serenely calm. 'I cannot say what I see. The visions are so strange,' she murmured eventually.

'Try again.'

'It darts here and there like a feather in the wind. It speaks like a child. It has no guile.'

'Is it a child?'

'No.'

'What is it?'

'It tells the truth.'

'A man?'

'No.'

'A woman. It must be a woman.'

'It is not human.'

'How can that be?' protested Doreen, nonplussed at the unexpected answer.

'I cannot say. It has no place in my memory.'

'No place in your memory?'

'It is not human!' repeated Maggie. 'Yet somehow it is. So strange,' she whispered again, closing her eyes. 'So very strange.'

'Not human.' Doreen's brow furrowed in concentration. 'Yet it has human qualities?'

'The very best. How valuable it would be to us. How precious. It wields much power, even though it knows it not. That is why the men of the lights desire to control it. They cannot be allowed or much will be lost.'

'Is it a machine? Some kind of computer, perhaps?'

'It is not made by the hand of man. It springs from Mother Earth.'

Doreen nodded. She'd heard such a pronouncement before. The Pythia was telling her that whatever it was, it was certainly natural. 'Look again, Pythia,' she urged. 'Tell me what you see.'

There was another pause. Maggie swayed slightly on her iron stool, hardly surprising since she'd just downed a quart of Jenny's wicked rhino-flattening cider in record time. Alcohol infused her mind, liberating the visions within, but there was only a limited time before the booze welled up to overpower her trance. She groaned softly, then hiccupped with surprising violence. 'I cannot see,' she mumbled. 'Its mind is so strange. There is no connection. It is not human.'

'Guide me, Pythia,' pressed Doreen gently. 'You have never failed us before. I am Gaia. Show me the way.'

'It purrs.'

'It purrs?' exclaimed Doreen, in a state of some considerable confusion. 'Is it a cat?'

'No, it does not have enough legs, yet it purrs.'

'I do not understand. I need to know more.'

'It has a child's love for its mother.'

'But it is not a child.'

'No. It is not human,' reasserted the Pythia firmly.

'Can you see a shape? Is it large or small?

Maggie inclined her head slightly, as if listening intently to a distant whispering voice. 'A colour! I see a colour.'

'What colour do you see?'

'Blue. So blue!' Then, with increasing wonder. 'Yes, so beautifully blue.'

Doreen caught her breath, a sudden blaze lighting her eyes. Her face flushed with excitement. 'Is it an animal?' she asked firmly.

'Yes.'

Sandra turned to Doreen, puzzled. 'What kind of an animal is blue and purrs?'

'Yes, I have it,' said Doreen, smiling for the first time since entering the Oracle. 'You say it darts here and there like a feather. Like a feather, Pythia. Is it a bird?'

Maggie swayed again, fully immersed in her visions, even though the smoke was dying down now. The Oracle stank of burnt juniper, a scorched, rank, aromatic pungency. Her closed eyes fluttered and rolled continuously beneath their lids as if she were in deep REM sleep.

'No. Yes. Maybe.'

There was no doubt she was sitting on the fence with that one.

Doreen persisted. 'I ask again, Pythia, do you see a bird?'

'Yes, I see now. It is a bird. A big bird.'

'And it is blue?'

'As blue as the sky. Find it and you will find salvation.'

'Of course, it had to be. I know exactly where to find this bird,' said Doreen, relaxing with a small smile of triumph.

'The macaw,' muttered Sandra, nodding.

'Yes,' said Maggie firmly. 'Yes, Gaia, she is nearing her time at last. Salvation for us will come through them both, the blue bird and the woman. The two are as one, like mother and son. Look for the blue bird and you will find all you seek, but you must find it quickly. These men will attack very soon. Before the next full moon. You must hasten. Much will be lost if she falls.'

'What is the nature of this attack?'

'Violence. Be careful, Gaia.'

'What must I do?' asked Doreen decisively.

'Have courage. All is not yet lost, but the bird and the woman must be gathered in quickly. That is your part. Your action will set things in motion, like the tiny drop of rain that starts a thunderstorm. It is your only hope against this wickedness. They will follow her to their doom. Here, it must be here, where we can help, but it is very dangerous. Stray only a little and the Sisterhood will be destroyed. Take c-courage and, and you –' she suddenly pointed at Sandra. 'You are going to have such … such a lot …' Maggie's words became increasingly disjointed as she finally wilted under the relentless alcoholic onslaught of the cider.

'Yes, Pythia, what am I going to have?' asked Sandra urgently, but it was too late. Maggie began to emerge from her trance, coughing and hiccupping. Her head snapped up and her eyes suddenly popped open.

'That's your lot, Gaia! No more! Hope it wasn't too bad,' she slurred in her normal voice, then sniggered helplessly. The Pythia of the Sisterhood of Helen was now completely and hopelessly blootered.

'Damn,' muttered Doreen. 'I needed just a few more seconds.' The nature of these things defied any logic. It was pointless Maggie re-entering her trance; the visions pertaining to the attack would not be repeated. If Doreen persisted in her questioning, then the Pythia would simply sink into silence, a sort of grumpy oracular sulk. She only ever pronounced once.

Doreen could not help but feel disappointed. Had it been Alice on the stool, then the information would have poured in, but Maggie had done her best. Self-doubt plagued her, clogging her mind, affecting her vision. Most of what she'd said was already known. However, Doreen was now aware of several new facts. There were five men ranged against them and these men were already weakened by their own internal strife. That they will very soon make their move against Celeste Timbrill and her famous macaw had already been guessed by Alice, but it looked like Doreen would now have to intervene personally, which was a little worrying. Doreen was not a woman of action. Unless it involved curling tongs, of course. Then came the intriguing prophesy about Sandra. Now, what was going on there? Was it to do with the coming conflict or something completely unrelated? Experience had taught Doreen not to discount anything said by the Pythia, however seemingly trivial.

'Yeah, yeah, OK, so we're in for a choppy ride, but what about me?' Sandra was almost hopping from foot to foot in exasperation. 'Come on, Maggie, you can't leave me hanging like that.'

'My, is the world spinning or is it me?' Maggie slid off the stool and collapsed in a giggling heap at Doreen's feet, embracing her legs. 'No, I've had a think about it and decided it's definitely me. God, that cider has some punch. Take some home for Bernie. He'll love it.' The Pythia sighed happily, a dreamy smile of contentment on her rubicund face. 'I do love you, Gaia,' she mumbled, 'and you always wear the most gorgeous shoes. Very comfy. Oh, yes, and Sandra, you're going to have sex. Lots and lots and lots of sex! About bloody time, too.' Moments later, she was asleep, snoring gently with her cheek resting on Doreen's burgundy and tan Mary Janes.

CHAPTER SEVEN

How quickly hair grows.

Philosophers and academics worldwide occasionally gather to debate really important questions, to ponder weighty matters, and these admirably lofty intellects sometimes amuse themselves by considering those professions without which humanity could not survive, professions for which there will always be a demand, and the greatest minds on earth always boil it down to just two; undertakers and hairdressers. Celeste mused upon this, the subject of the last Royal Institute Christmas Lecture, as she drove from Prior's Norton to Tewkesbury. She had no immediate plans to engage the former, but the mirror revealed a need to employ the latter. Her hair remained as it always had been: long, wavy, thick, a glorious sweep of the most gorgeous tint of vibrant copper, a colour which unfailingly turned heads each time she walked down the street.

Celeste's route could frequently be determined by the breadcrumb trail of men lying concussed at the bases of lamp posts across town. Just join the dots.

The hue remained completely natural and she'd still, after all these years, never met anyone who had exactly the same unique shade. She'd let it grow since marrying. James liked it that way. He adored the way it was now long enough to sprout from the crown of her leather hood and still cascade in flowing tresses over her shoulders and breasts.

However, as all women will testify, there is an importance to visiting the salon which almost all men simply fail to comprehend. This is one of the basic incompatibilities between the sexes and those few men who actually make the effort to bridge that divide, to show even a fraction more understanding than the grudgingly obligatory, 'Yes, dear, your hair looks lovely,' are whisked immediately into a nirvana of gastronomic and sexual ecstasy.

Occasionally, if they're really lucky, both at the same time!

When a woman announces in irritation that her hair is a mess and that she needs – no, it is more than needs – that she is compelled by a deep-seated psychological necessity to get down to the salon, then there is no power in heaven nor earth capable of deflecting her determination – and for that the manufacturers of brushes, combs and mirrors will always be eternally grateful.

And shampoos.

And conditioners. Especially conditioners.

Once, many years ago, shampoos contained – well, shampoo, but nowadays, with a multi-billion pound industry driven by the planet's most powerful corporate chemical companies and guided by slick advertising campaigns feeding on feminine paranoia, there is a positively kaleidoscopic range of available products, all containing something impressively exotic guaranteed to make your hair as irresistible to men as hot double chocolate fudge cake to a class of dieters. Even the most rudimentary browse along the supermarket shelves will reveal serum with coconut, honey, orange peel concentrate and kiwi fruit, or extra-hold conditioner with molasses, rosemary, lemon, marzipan, jojoba and sesame seed butter. There's even a super new ethical green shampoo containing essence of vanilla, hempseed oil, cloves, a light seasoning of thousand island dressing and a soupçon of rhino dung extract, all blended with the distilled tears from poverty-stricken children living in countries still unable to reliably generate electricity.

And that's just the natural substances. Matters become exceedingly interesting when chemists grin and rub their hands together. Now we're in an entirely different ball game. Take polyquaternium, for instance, a substance found in shampoo which sounds like it could easily double up as the exciting ingredient in a weapon of mass destruction. A supervillain's dream.

'I will use the polyquaternium bomb, have no mistake!'

'You bastard!'

'Mr President, such language. The Pilgrim Fathers would not approve.'

'But the children – have pity on the children!'

'Rest assured they will all arrive at the pearly gates with unfeasibly shiny hair.'

Little wonder the ozone layer quietly gave up the ghost.

Some products now have so many active ingredients that an abandoned bottle, given sufficient time at the back of a warm bathroom cabinet, contains all the necessary chemical compounds to propagate a new form of life. A mini-world where nature weaves her magic wand, where the progression through single-celled creatures to more complex organisms gallops along at a merry pace until tiny mammals appear, and if they are by chance hirsute then they will develop new shampoos of their own – and so the universe proceeds in stately splendour, driven ever onwards by the twin unstoppable powers of evolution and hair care products.

Tewkesbury was a pleasant little town, Y-shaped, with the War Memorial at its heart. Cars hurtled around it like rampaging Cherokees around a wagon train. The main streets were lined with many timber-framed buildings, giving the centre a nostalgic, chocolate-box, medieval feel. Numerous alleyways plunged off to either side, veins branching from the main arteries to penetrate deep amongst the jumbled houses behind. It was here the Avon and Severn met, and both were notorious for flooding, the locals accepting this annual deluge with typical

Gloucestershire stoicism. Every year the town became surrounded by creeping brown waters, every year the news crews turned up to pester the locals and every year they were told to mind their own business and shove off back to London in no uncertain terms.

Celeste left Wilf back at the cottage playing one of Bertie's favourite games – Hide the Nut. Her baby was very good at this. He always found the nut, wherever it was hidden. Knowing that should keep them happily occupied for a few hours, she parked up and took a coffee and Danish pastry in a quaint tea shop adjacent to the Abbey, then strolled along the High Street. Despite her worries, the day was so fine she found herself in a really rather good mood, as any woman normally would be with such beautifully painted toenails and so pleasurable a sex life. Goodness, had that been a wonderful evening. She smiled at the memory and tossed her head, hair swinging luxuriantly. Behind her, a man fell over a litter bin.

Yes, it was a lovely morning.

Although she liked Tewkesbury very much, to her mind the town lacked a really first-class leather fetish boutique. But that wasn't too much of a problem, she had an excellent relationship with a London specialist who helped her in that direction. She visited the bank, had a new battery put in her watch, and generally nosed in shops, all to cheerful greetings. People here were always happy to pass the time of day, to chat, to smile. She was reminded very much of the friendliness of Manaus. That town, too, was located at the confluence of two rivers, although she had to admit the Negro and the Solimoes had a bit more punch than the Avon and Severn.

Finally, it was time for her appointment. She had been using *Snippets* since moving from London. The salon was small and friendly, with just three chairs. The girls were very good, the prices reasonable, the tea and biscuits excellent and the conversation entertaining. What more could you want from a hairdressers?

She did not notice a man leaning casually against a lamp post on the opposite side of the road, a man whose eyes missed nothing. A notebook came out and information was duly recorded. Good, past experience told him the target would be occupied for an hour at the very least. Plenty of time for a pee, tea and bun before resuming surveillance.

'Where's Terry?' asked Celeste as she sat. Teresa Green had been her stylist for two years and knew Celeste's mind. The relationship between client and hairdresser was deeply symbiotic and based on a profound mystical connection of which male psychologists were blithely unaware.

'I'm sorry, but Terry is unwell this morning, Celeste. I'm filling in for her. My name's Doreen. Don't worry, I've spoken to Terry and she's told me you just have a minimal cut and blow dry.'

'Exactly.'

'Want to try a poodle perm?' enquired Doreen mischievously.

'Heavens, no!' exclaimed Celeste. 'With this lot frizzed up I don't think I'd be able to get out of the door.'

'And definitely no colouring required.'

'None needed.'

'So she said. I have to say, Celeste, I've never seen such a fabulous flame.' Doreen stood behind Celeste. They communicated via the large mirror on the wall in front of the chair, as demanded by strict salon etiquette.

Celeste smiled. 'I'm very proud of it.'

'I would be, too,' replied Doreen. 'Incidentally, sorry about the scarf. I know, a hairdresser who covers up her own hair must have something to hide. Seems a bit suspicious, like a doctor who's ill, but I'm recovering from chemo-hair at the moment. I look a bit like a patchy Betty Boop.'

'No problem. I'm just glad to hear you're getting better,' said Celeste. Doreen was perhaps a few years older than she was, a comfortably built middle-aged woman with pale green eyes. She was dressed all in black, trousers and blouse, with a contrasting multi-patterned headscarf of bright primary colours completely covering her hair.

'The nice shoes do help though, don't they?' commented Celeste. She'd noticed Doreen's very smart floral print satin courts.

'They do indeed.'

'That's quite a heel as well. Don't you find your feet ache after a while?'

And so the conversation began. It ranged widely, covering such topics as scones (plain versus fruit), fashions for women who possessed a hip girdle actually capable of accommodating babies, the many delights of chocolate (preferably smeared over naked firemen), whether toilet paper rolls should be over- or under-hung and the genetic inability of men to load a dishwasher in the correct manner.

All amusing and accompanied by tea and busy scissors. Doreen had a dry sense of humour which appealed to Celeste. At no time did she ask where Celeste was going on holiday.

'I remember you from the TV a few years ago,' she finally said.

'Yes, but I'm living the quiet life now. I've no ambition to be a celebrity. The intrusion is unbearable.'

'I can imagine. You married James Timbrill, didn't you?'

'I did. We're very happy.'

'Is Bertie well?'

'Thank you, yes. He enjoys country living very much.'

'Haven't met a bird yet that doesn't like a tree. Except perhaps a penguin, but you know what I mean.' Doreen paused for a moment, looking thoughtful. 'I guess your husband finds life difficult at Westminster,' she said finally. 'Especially after the last election. The political elite doesn't like independent thinking as much as the

100

people of Gloucester.'

'They don't like independent anything.'

'I can imagine. That's why it's so important James continues to expand the group of IMPs.'

'I think you'll find he's happy as he is.'

'Yes, he does strike me as an extremely contented man. I'm sure much of that is because of you.'

Here we go again, thought Celeste, now well experienced in anticipating the probable course of the conversation. 'Will the word "meditation" be included in your next sentence?' she enquired mildly.

'None of my business,' chuckled Doreen. 'What you decide to do in private is up to you. I personally like to have my husband suck tinned peach slices from between my toes, but then I live in Chipping Sodbury. We like to live life on the wild side down there. I guess in principle, it's no different. Uses a lot less rope, of course,' she added thoughtfully.

'I've always found rope to be useful in any situation. I recommend it to you.'

'A girl should always play to her strengths,' observed Doreen. Her instincts were not wrong. Celeste Timbrill was a compassionate, strong-willed and consummately capable woman. Fearless, too. It took guts to attack two armed burglars. Admittedly, it was Bertie who'd done the most damage that night, but reports in the press had praised her courage in taking on Pritchard and Coberley.

And then there was her hair!

The hair confirmed Celeste's importance to the Sisterhood. It seemed unbelievable, but there was no doubt in Doreen's mind that future global stability depended entirely on the colour of Celeste Timbrill's hair. Time to draw her in. Delicately. This needed careful handling.

'The changes James has forced at Westminster are impressive. He's always cropping up on the news. What's happened in Gloucester is spreading. His new ideas of fully inclusive politics have struck a chord. Have you noticed ordinary people are beginning to stir all over the country?'

'Oh, yes. James finds it deeply rewarding. You should see what turns up every morning in his email inbox. His poor fingers are wearing away.'

'I don't know much about these things, but I would imagine there are plenty of characters intent on stopping him.'

'My husband is a determined man,' said Celeste neutrally. Now then, what's this Doreen angling after?

'If organised properly under his leadership, I can see a dramatic shift in power coming. There's a change in the air, Celeste, and it's being driven by an awakening electorate.'

'Our conversation suddenly seems to have veered away from kittens and embroidery,' observed Celeste carefully. 'Why is that?'

Around them, the salon had slowly emptied of customers. To Celeste's surprise, the door was locked, the closed sign put up. The other members of staff quietly melted away, leaving her alone with this intriguing woman.

'I'm afraid I have to press you on this, Celeste. The immediate future of this country is in peril. Politically, the way forward is through James, but there's a lot of people in the establishment who'd be quite content to see him fail.'

'I'm sorry, Doreen, but you've lost me. Terry usually chats about celebrities and holidays.'

'James can do his bit in London, but he's going to have to be a lot more careful.'

'Meaning?' Celeste's tone of voice betrayed her sudden caution. What was going on?

Doreen paused from her cutting. 'I know about the attack on your husband,' she said softly. 'I'm so sorry he was hurt.'

Celeste stiffened. She stared at Doreen for a long time.

'Discounting my husband telling you, and I know he hasn't, there are only two ways you could have known about that. Either you're working for those people who are attempting to corrupt James – and I warn you, I will take a very dim view if you are – or ...'

'Her name is Alice.'

'Ah. The Bag Lady.'

'She wasn't always like that. I know her well. Alice suffers from delusional paranoia. In a way, her condition is my fault. She was, once, an employee of mine.'

'I didn't realise hairdressing was such a dangerous profession.'

'It's normally just about the most benign job in the world, but I'm not just a hairdresser.'

'Really? I wonder what gave me a clue as to that,' said Celeste with more sarcasm than intended. Well, Wilf had been staying for a while now. She was obviously beginning to adopt some of his cynicism.

Doreen sighed sadly. 'Poor Alice. Her breakdown has haunted me for years. I haven't heard from her at all until she called last week to tell me of the attack.'

Celeste was struggling. 'Why would she call you? Why was she there when those men beat up my husband – and why are you here telling me about all this now?'

'Those are three very good questions. Fortunately, they're also simple to answer.'

'Well, Doreen, whoever you are, you better start talking now or I'm off, locked door or not.'

'Celeste Timbrill, you and I both know you're not going anywhere until I've finished your hair. No woman would willingly walk out of a salon half-cut on one side,' said Doreen firmly. 'Think of the ignominy!'

Celeste pursed her lips. 'Yeah, that's true – you've got me there. Captive to my own vanity.'

'Likewise,' muttered Doreen, waving at her headscarf. 'Still, at least now I've got the time to answer your questions. Firstly, Alice called me because she knows of my interest in you and your husband, and by extension, Bertie. Like you, I regard him as an equal member of your family and the events of the next few weeks may well concern him. I can't explain why, but it appears he's got an important part to play in this.

'Secondly, Alice was there because, unknown to me and entirely of her own initiative – and, I have to say, at great personal cost to herself – she's been keeping a watch over James for some time now. She may have a few screws loose, but there's still a first-rate mind stuck under that bobble hat. She understands and values his importance.

'Thirdly, I'm telling you this now because you're going to need help. I have some information on the men who orchestrated the attempted corruption of James. They're wicked, but powerful. They need to be stopped. If they triumph, James will be unable to continue at Westminster and the best chance we've had of curbing the malignancy of these dreadful people will be gone. They will gain strength until they become our masters. I don't think you'll fancy that and I sure as hell know I don't.'

'You don't strike me as a person intimately acquainted with the subtleties of politics,' observed Celeste.

'Like I said, I've got two jobs.'

Celeste chewed on her lower lip. This hairdresser was the oddest person she'd met in a long time – and there was some pretty stiff competition in that area – but she was also strangely compelling. There was something about her that Celeste saw in herself. It was almost as if she and this woman were related in some way, even though Celeste knew she was an only child and had no cousins. Doreen was certainly intelligent. Significantly intelligent, in fact, and she clearly saw the growing conflict at Westminster that she and James had been discussing on and off over the last two years.

But then she'd mentioned Bertie, and that was a mistake. Celeste was zealous in her protection of her beloved. Admittedly, Bertie had played an unwitting but vital part in the downfall of the last government, but in the end he was just a macaw and had simply been responding to an unlikely series of coincidences. She'd done everything in her power since to give him as stable, quiet and uneventful a home life as possible. He was a pet, and yet here was this obviously serious woman telling her quite openly that it appeared he was about to play a vital role in some new adventure. As she was herself. Celeste did not court vital roles in new adventures. She actively avoided them, yet deep down, buried far below many layers of maturity and sensibility, there still lurked the little girl who'd plotted Martin Shufflebottom's downfall, who'd lived in Brazil and ridden river boats through teeming jungles, and who'd stood in her jim-jams and whipped the living crap out of two black-clad burglars – and enjoyed it!

Something tugged at her. A seductive finger beckoned. Oh, how it beckoned. She stared with intense concentration at the reflection in the mirror. Doreen continued patting, preening and pampering, combing gently, snipping here and there. She seemed fascinated by Celeste's glorious copper hair, almost as if she couldn't resist running her fingers through the long wavy tresses, and was seemingly oblivious to the scrutiny.

'So tell me, who are you, Doreen?' Celeste asked finally. 'Who exactly are you?'

'I'm Gaia,' came the simple reply. 'The Protector. I'm the Supreme Goddess of the Sisterhood of Helen, Defender of Knowledge and Mother of Blessed Lycia.

'Sounds impressive? It should do – I control this bloody ridiculous planet!'

CHAPTER EIGHT

'You look surprised,' said Doreen calmly, comb in one hand.

Celeste pursed her lips and shrugged non-committally. 'Frankly, it's not every day I'm confronted by a goddess, especially one working in a hairdressing salon. Forgive me if I seem inclined to disbelief. I would have laughed, but you're obviously serious and I didn't want to appear rude. Perhaps I could suggest a modest increase in your medication.'

Doreen chuckled. 'Don't worry, it's just my official title. Rather grand, don't you think, but I have no supernatural powers. I don't wear my knickers outside my tights and I can't heat a ready-cooked meal with my super laser sight. Sadly, I'm just a tubby mother of two in her late forties with a plumber for a husband.'

'That sounds refreshingly normal, so where does the planet-controlling bit fit in?'

'It's quite a story.'

'Well,' said Celeste, 'as you've already pointed out, I'm trapped here by my own vanity until you've finished my hair. And unlocked the door,' she added pointedly.

'You can leave any time you like.'

'Good. I'd like to keep that option open.'

'Sitting comfortably? Good, then I'll begin.'

'Please do. I'm rather intrigued now. I hope it's not boring.'

'Believe me, by the time I've finished, boredom will be the last emotion you'll be feeling!' Doreen paused, as if choosing her words carefully. 'It all started with Helen of

Troy, our founder and first Gaia, on Midsummer's Eve, 1176 BC. Now, that definitely was a flicker of a smile, wasn't it?'

'Yeah, sorry about that.'

'Don't apologise. I think I'd do the same in your position. In fact, at the time, I think I did,' added Doreen thoughtfully. 'Well, no matter, I did tell you it was going to be quite a story! I'll try and skip through some of the boring bits, but it's one of those stories where the boring bits are actually quite important. Anyway, Helen had just returned from the carnage of Troy in a foul mood, appalled at the pointless loss of life. Men had died in their tens of thousands, a dreadful waste, and all because of a petty lovers' tiff. She pledged herself there and then to do all in her power to prevent such stupidity ever occurring again and, with her daughter and a few other notable women, established the Sisterhood of Helen at Patara, a city in ancient Lycia, now a region of south-west Turkey. The Sisterhood had one aim only, and still does today: to moderate the stupidity of men – and believe me, have we had our work cut out for ourselves!'

'Can't argue with that.'

'Helen was an astonishing woman. We all know about her fabled beauty and the number of ships her face was supposed to have launched, which is, incidentally, an entirely apocryphal tale, but coupled with her unquestioned physical uniqueness was a penetrating mind and far-ranging vision. She realised right from the very beginning that the human race could only truly advance through pursuit of understanding and knowledge. This was a major revolution in thinking for the time since deities and religion supplied all the explanations for the natural workings of the world. The ancients believed in the Gods because it was expedient to do so, and kings could control their populations by claiming they had been instructed to invade this country or that by divine messages from the Gods themselves, which can be a bit tricky to corroborate.

'Making an extraordinary leap of intuition, Helen, although publicly as conservative as any Spartan woman, had the foresight to see the value of natural philosophy – what we today call science. So, right from the outset, the Sisterhood concentrated its resources in two directions: the subtle control of political leaders to stop them engaging in endless wars, and the encouragement and preservation of science. Each was inextricably connected to the other – without periods of peace and social stability, science could not really establish itself and advance, and if catastrophe did fall and civilization failed, the knowledge to start all over again had to be preserved. So, on the one hand we discouraged war while on the other we nurtured and preserved scientific thought wherever we found it, from Egypt to Greece and later, to the Islamic world.

'However, although natural philosophy was barely embryonic in Helen's time, there was one science that was already well developed. Astronomy. The ancient Greeks believed the earth was the centre of the universe. This was logical because no one could feel the planet move, and such a notion neatly fitted their religious views, but key philosophers and mathematicians questioned this assumption. A bright young man called Aristarchus upset a lot of people by suggesting the sun was the centre of the universe and that the planets all revolved around it in circular orbits. Seems logical to us now because we know that's actually the truth, but back then, well, what a fuss. His mistress was one of ours. She encouraged him in the face of ferocious conservative opposition. Pillow talk, one of the most formidable forces known to man! With her backing, he published his ideas while she, naturally, reported everything to the Sisterhood.

'Sadly, he was before his time and religious dogma crushed his ideas for eighteen hundred years. Organised religion held absolute power during that time, forever dragging mankind back into the mud. Orthodoxy is the sworn enemy of both intelligence and curiosity and our civilisation floundered in nearly two millennia of intellectual darkness. Science was actively discouraged and only the great Islamic philosophers made progress. This was a bad time for the Sisterhood – especially after the fall of the Roman Empire. Not for nought were they called the Dark Ages. Heresy was punishable by death and any woman attempting to challenge the authority of the church was simply burned as a witch.

'So we tinkered here, persuaded there, watching and waiting as the centuries rolled on by, frustrated, frightened, but still quietly encouraging where we could, failing on many occasions, as war after senseless war continually ravaged societies across the world, but a single success here and there amply compensated for the numerous failures. And, of course, we preserved as much knowledge as we could. Then, eventually, as is always the case, a few remarkable people were identified and subtly directed. We were the force that urged a brilliant man called Nicholas Copernicus to re-ignite the astronomical debate. Astronomy was always the key. All other branches of science were at that time either non-existent or at best, very basic, but if we could start an astronomical revolution then the other sciences would be drawn along it its wake.

'Copernicus came through, bless him. He proved the sun was the centre of the solar system despite intense pressure from the authorities. We then found a ready and eager convert in Galileo, even though he was cruelly persecuted and forced to recant by the Inquisition. The Inquisition, by the way, was one of the most lethal forces we have ever encountered. They delighted in burning many Sisters, but none gave away our secret.

'And all the time we accumulated knowledge, safeguarding it against loss through war and destruction. We already had ample evidence of how the destruction of such knowledge can cripple mankind for centuries. Have you ever heard of the fabled Library at Alexandria?

'Yes, of course. Wasn't it burned and everything lost?'

Celeste suddenly caught her breath at Doreen's gentle shake of the head. 'No? You're joking!'

'I'm not joking, Celeste. The burning of the library was the greatest disaster of the ancient world. Hundreds of thousands of documents were destroyed, an irretrievable loss – but the women who cleaned the library and stacked the shelves were all Sisters, and each night, as they cleaned and tidied, they also copied. For decades, they copied, and when the flames came it was the copies that were lost; over five thousand of the rarest, most precious and most remarkable scrolls were spirited away right under the librarians' noses. Original works by Aristotle, Euclid, Pythagoras, Ptolemy and Archimedes, all safe, along with originals from every philosopher and scientist since, spanning the entire history of Western culture.'

'But this is extraordinary!' exclaimed Celeste, then remembered she was supposed to be a sceptic. 'But only if it's true, of course.'

'It's true all right.'

'Then these relics must be absolutely priceless.'

'They are all very precious financially, but to an infinitely greater degree as landmarks in the intellectual development of mankind. We treasure them all greatly and take great pride in preserving this knowledge.'

'Where do you keep all these books? Not here, surely.' Celeste couldn't help glancing around. A hairdressing salon in Tewkesbury seemed an awfully incongruous place to house a library worthy of the Gods themselves.

'All in good time.'

'But surely other historians should be allowed to examine them?'

'Perhaps, but there are two vital dangers to consider. The first is simple – to reveal what we keep would be to reveal our existence, and that would be fatal to us. Our political effectiveness would be destroyed. How do you think a Prime Minister or President would react to the knowledge that he'd been manipulated – by women! They would surely move against us and without the Sisterhood there would then be no check on their future idiocy.'

'Yes, I can see that,' admitted Celeste.

'The other danger is far more subtle. There are accepted beliefs so entrenched in our society that to reveal them as utterly false would be catastrophic. There are books and scrolls in our possession, for instance, which could raise some extremely awkward questions for some of the main religions of the world. These religions would certainly survive because many people need spiritual support in their lives, but an awful lot of people would have their faith shaken to the core. It's one of those paradoxes that although we've been struggling against religious orthodoxy for so long, we actually have in our possession the evidence to severely undermine many aspects of those religions. The fact that we've not done so is a powerful argument in favour of our benevolence since we have no wish to shatter the beliefs of millions of people.'

'Don't tell me Jesus never existed!'

'Of course he did. We have his diary, in which he laid out the theological framework for the book that eventually evolved into the Bible, but when you compare his extraordinary writings in original Aramaic with the earliest copies of the Bible, there are significant differences that can only be attributed to an agenda by those who had a vested interest in promoting the new religion. For example, the Bible has sanitised a considerable number of characters whose real behaviour was a little less saintly than generally accepted.'

'Oh dear.'

Doreen shrugged her shoulders nonchalantly. 'Ever been to Padstow?'

'No. Why?'

'There's a woman in Padstow who's related through ninety-six generations to Christ! He was a human being, after all, with urges and passions. Actually, he was a bit of a scallywag. Knew he had only a few years left and used them to good effect. He was a handsome man and on a mission, two things irresistible to women. His aura of serene virtue was added later to conceal the existence of his three children.'

'I'm not sure if I want know all this.'

'In fact we have first-hand, cast-iron evidence of the actual existence of all manner of prophets, all of whom were compassionate, inspiring and remarkable people, but let's just say that for political expediency, the later official biographies of some were at considerable variance to what we know as the truth.

'So, with the slow passage of time, we watched, influenced and tinkered where we could. Many Gaias were unknown to history, but some were not. Eleanor of Aquitaine was one, followed by her daughter-in-law, Berengaria. She was the wife of Eleanor's son, Richard the Lionheart. Now then, how's this for a chivalrous tale of derring-do. Richard was already on the Third Crusade when Berengaria was instructed to exert some pacifying influence on him and so she sailed for the Levant. Unfortunately, her ship ran aground in Cyprus where she was threatened by the island's ruler. When he heard of this, Richard booked a short holiday from the Crusade, hopped over to Cyprus with an army, beat merry hell out of the locals, rescued Berengaria and married her in the Chapel of Saint George in Limassol. How's that for a romantic knight in shining armour story!'

'Wonderful. Did they live happily ever after?'

'No. He was as gay as a pair of pink leather jodhpurs!'

'Hey, don't knock 'em,' retorted Celeste. 'I've got a pair and they're lovely.'

'I might have guessed,' sighed Doreen. 'Anyway, there were no kids from that union. Berengaria did her best to mollify him when she became Gaia herself, but to no avail. We tried desperately to influence the kings and princes of the day not to go on the Crusades, but were unsuccessful.

We're still reaping the bitter consequences of that little catastrophe, even today.'

'How do you know all this? All these people and dates?'

'I'm Gaia. I've learned. It's my duty, but also my pleasure. How can you not be interested in something as wonderful as this?'

'Well, one thing's for sure, I'm going to have to rethink my entire knowledge of history,' muttered Celeste, then again remembered to be sceptical. 'If it's true, of course.'

'Girl, I haven't even started! This has been going on for well over three thousand years – the entire duration of our civilization, and it's still going on at the moment. I'm endeavouring to avoid an unnecessary and potentially nasty little war developing between Paraguay and Bolivia. You have no idea how exasperating it is trying to massage the egos of two colossally stupid presidents!'

'That should be easy enough,' said Celeste. 'One of them's bound to have a mistress – that's the only reason for becoming so important. Get your girl to deny him sex. Then again, he's probably impotent, so the humiliation of having the press reveal that Captain Inert is now lodging in his presidential trousers should be sufficient to deter even the most warlike of dictators.'

'Already done. Nice to see you're thinking along my lines.'

'My pleasure. Let's get back to the Sisterhood.'

'Oh, so now you want to know more! Curiosity getting to you?'

'I have to say there is a compelling side to your story,' admitted Celeste coyly. 'What happened after Galileo?'

'Well, the next great breakthrough came with Sir Isaac Newton. Now, I definitely know you've heard of him.'

'Apples in orchards. Bump on the head resulted in concussion, during which he invented gravity, or so I believe.'

'More or less. Isaac was a remarkably intuitive man,

uniquely talented, gifted beyond measure, possessing a profound insight and a penetrating, incisive mind, capable of outstanding clarity of thought rarely seen throughout our entire history.'

'You like him, then?'

'He was stellar, in every sense of the word. Cleverest man that's ever walked the planet, bar none. Centuries before his time. His talents attracted our attention from very early on and we were on the point of recruiting his half-niece, Catherine Barton, but there was no need. Isaac had already deduced our existence, the only person to do so in our entire history. To him, it was obvious that someone had to be saving the knowledge of the ancients, someone had to be quietly influencing world leaders, and having pondered on the problem, came to his conclusions on sheer intellect alone. From the few scattered sources still available, he followed our path across Europe to Britain and somehow figured out where we were based.

'You should read the account made by the Sisters of the day he cantered up to their front door on his horse and calmly asked to see the works of Aristotle! How could we refuse? He was so overcome by the sight of all those great books that he knelt and kissed the Temple floor, weeping uncontrollably. He pledged himself there and then to the Sisterhood, heart, mind and soul, and never wavered in his loyalty. In fact, he cultivated his well-known irascibility to fend off friends and colleagues, fearful that he would let his great secret slip in some moment of idle conversation.

'Once he had access to our records, he was galvanised into action, and the results we all know today. Incidentally, have you ever heard of Fermat's Last Theorem?'

'Sorry, that one slipped through without me noticing.'

'Understandable, it is a little arcane, but basically it's an unsolvable mathematical equation. Pierre Fermat preceded Newton by a few years and left a cryptic message in a book of mathematics declaring that he'd solved the problem, but mischievously gave no details of how. This caused enormous perplexity and frustration amongst mathematicians until finally, the theorem was solved in 1993.'

There was a telling pause. 'It wasn't really solved then, was it?' said Celeste at last.

'Er, not quite. We have a full account of what happened. Isaac and Catherine were staying with the Sisters at Christmas. They always did – his birthday was Christmas Day. That particular evening is well documented. Having enjoyed a meal of roast goose, and after helping the Sisters chase a wilful cat outside, only for it to appear at the window yowling to be let in again, he settled himself beside the fire and while the Sisters played games, roasted chestnuts and sang songs, Isaac sipped hot mulled wine and spent an enjoyable few hours tinkering around with Fermat's Last Theorem, scribbling his elegant solution in the back of the very first copy of the *Mathematica Principia* which he'd donated to the library. Signed by Uncle Isaac, dated Christmas Day 1689 and dedicated to Catherine, this is one of our greatest treasures, indeed, without doubt it remains one of science and literature's most magnificent works – and next to his solution for Fermat's Last Theorem is Newton's original sketch for the design of the world's first cat flap. Not bad for an evening's work!'

'A cat flap! No, I'm sorry, but that's stretching things too far. I'm becoming sceptical again.'

'Nonetheless, it's true. I've seen it myself. Catherine Barton eventually became Gaia and helped her uncle to the end of his days. She was rewarded for her services to the Sisterhood by being buried in Westminster Abbey to the right of her beloved uncle and beside her husband, and one of the very few actual physical indications of the existence of the Sisterhood can be seen on their memorial – a tiny cherub carved in the image of Helen of Troy. Catherine is still revered today as one of the most successful and accomplished Goddesses since Helen – and from that time we've always kept cats at the Temple.'

'That's extraordinary – or at least it would be to a mathematician. I suspect the average football supporter would be less interested!'

'You're quite right, of course, it is extraordinary, but only to a few. However, revealing just this one small fact would certainly turn science on its head. It would be profoundly disturbing and would fairly upset most of the world's mathematicians, so just imagine what would happen if we started to dispel some of the more treasured religious beliefs.'

'Why are you telling me all this?'

'To try to get you to understand just how important an influence the Sisterhood has been over the centuries, how it has continually strived to promote scientific advance to counter the blinkered dogma of ignorance while at the same time attempting to ameliorate the stupidity, arrogance and pomposity of those in charge of our lives.'

'You mean men?'

'Well, yes. Mostly. I love men as much as the next woman and I'm blessed with a wonderful husband and son, but let's face it, they do so often come up wanting in the brains department, especially when they get in control of a country. This two-pronged approach was decreed by Helen and we've been following her teachings ever since.' She patted and preened Celeste's hair one last time. 'There, my lovely, I'm done. What do you think?'

Doreen had finished styling Celeste's hair and a wonderful job she had done as well. Her burnished tresses were beautifully cut, and shone like polished copper, falling over her shoulders in luxuriant waves.

'Thank you,' said Celeste faintly. She had almost forgotten her hair was being cut. Doreen's quiet recitation was mesmerising!

'Let's have a nice cup of tea. You look like a girl who could do with a fruit shortie!'

Celeste would remember that extraordinary

conversation for the rest of her life. She and Doreen communicated through the mirror. Doreen stood behind the padded chair with a mug of steaming tea in her hand and they looked at each other in the glass as she calmly destroyed Celeste's fundamental understanding of – well, just about everything!

'Moving forward a century or so, we come to another important example of our influence. We were the driving force behind William Herschel. He discovered the planet Uranus using a home-made telescope in his back garden in Bath. He and his sister, Caroline, built their telescopes together and they were without doubt the finest of their day. Bath is just down the road from here and Caroline, having joined the Sisterhood some years before, eventually became the two hundred and twenty-second Gaia. Smart woman – discovered eight comets!'

'I'm beginning to wonder if there's any discovery that can't be traced back to you. Surely someone noticed it was the women doing all the work?'

'They did notice. Sometimes. Actually, speaking honestly, they only noticed very rarely. Men are so gloriously egotistical! Almost all were quite happy to take the glory and have their names recorded for posterity.'

'And the Sisters were content with this?'

'Entirely content. Our philosophy has always been one of discretion and Sisters were satisfied in the knowledge that they had effected real change. Besides, the prospect of being burnt as a witch is a pretty powerful argument for keeping your mouth shut.'

'Did anyone else figure out what was going on, apart from Newton?'

'Only one other, and I know you've heard of him as well. Edward Jenner, the country doctor who discovered the principles of vaccination. His remarkable story is inextricably entwined with the Sisterhood. He's a Berkeley man, you know, got a statue in Gloucester Cathedral.'

'Yes, I've seen him there. So what happened?'

'In the late eighteenth century there was a smallpox epidemic in Gloucester, so Jenner was familiar with the scourge of the deadly disease when some years later a young milkmaid named Sarah Nelmes visited him suffering from a bout of cowpox, which she had contracted from her cow, Blossom. Jenner took samples from her sores and infected other patients, who he then exposed to smallpox. This was a real gamble because if his ideas proved incorrect, these patients would have almost certainly died. However, they didn't catch smallpox and Jenner headed for the history books. That's how it's taught at school.'

'And the truth?'

'The truth is almost exactly the same as the accepted version. Edward married a local lady called Katherine Kingscote, who had already been inducted into the Sisterhood. We had long pursued a policy of recruiting intelligent and capable Gloucestershire women as a protective buffer around the Temple.'

'I notice you keep mentioning this Temple,' observed Celeste.

'Nothing gets past you, does it?' nodded Doreen. 'I'll explain it all in good time. Meanwhile, returning to Jenner, you have to realise the Sisterhood had spent centuries encouraging the development of medicine – many of our members had suffered the agony of a high infant mortality rate, so Katherine was ideal material for us: clever, capable, Gloucestershire-born and married to a gifted physician.

'Katherine knew Sarah well. While delivering milk to the Jenner household, Sarah commented to Katherine that she'd noticed all her milkmaid friends, once they'd contracted cowpox, seemed to be spared the ravages of smallpox. Katherine thought this worthy enough to mention to Edward and encouraged him to investigate this oddity when Sarah contracted cowpox herself later that year. Edward conducted his risky experiment on volunteers from the Sisterhood and vaccination was born. Although he is attributed with the discovery, our records indicate he fully recognised the contribution of his wife, Sarah and those very brave volunteers, and only on their firm insistence did he reluctantly accept the entire credit for his breakthrough.

'The subsequent eradication of smallpox by vaccination is regarded by the Sisterhood as its single most important contribution to the welfare of mankind, and as a result, both Katherine Kingscote and Sarah Nelmes are considered Goddesses, and Blossom, bless her hooves, in recognition of her selfless contribution to medicine by a grateful public, bequeathed one of her horns to the Jenner museum in Berkeley – we have the other in our care!'

Doreen paused, looking thoughtful. She drank the dregs of her tea and looked out of the window to the street outside. Yes, that man was back again, nonchalantly loitering on the far side of the street in an entirely unsuspicious manner that made it plainly obvious what he was doing. It was clear Celeste Timbrill had no idea she was being shadowed. Mags was right, the enemy were already on the move. She watched him discreetly through another mirror, allowing her to observe without looking directly at him. He was whiling away the time browsing the window of a shop opposite the salon which sold Turkish carpets. It suddenly struck her as one of those strange coincidences – Troy, Blessed Lycia and Patara, all vital to the Sisterhood, all were to be found in modern-day Turkey. The thought made her wistful. There were so many subtle coincidences connecting our lives. She pursed her lips. 'I was once like you,' she said softly. 'Happy with my little life, totally oblivious that much of my knowledge was based on complete fabrication, a mother of two – a hairdresser, for God's sake – until *she* came!'

'I've been meaning to ask you about that,' said Celeste. 'What happened? When were you first approached?'

'Now this'll make you smile,' said Doreen. 'Believe

me, events really don't get more unlikely than this. There I was, working in my salon – not this one, by the way. This one I've commandeered for the morning just to talk to you. Anyway, I was on my own finishing up for the day. Thinking about it, she must have been waiting for the others to go home, watching me from across the road, I guess. I'd given Jeanette Hough's hair a final blow dry and shooed her out, when in walked this very tall elderly lady. She had a refined air to her. Elegant. Classy. Her hair was beautifully cut and she wore dark glasses, which I thought a bit odd for a February afternoon in Chipping Sodbury. She sat down as bold as brass, took off her glasses and fixed me with quite a stare.

'"Doreen Coddle," she said in a husky Yankee twang, "Ah'm Katherine Hepburn and ah want to talk to you about saving the world!"'

'Good God!' exclaimed Celeste, suitably open-mouthed.

'Do you know, that's exactly what I said! Kate just laughed at the look on my face. "You'll never make an actress," she said, "but you will make a superb Goddess." Well, after that I just had to learn more. Our conversation was very similar to the one we've just had, but I seem to remember I was even less inclined to believe her and said so in no uncertain terms, after all, what on earth does a Hollywood legend have in common with a little old hairdresser like me? I even suspected Bernie had called up one of those spoof actresses to play a trick on me.'

'Bernie? The plumber?'

'Uh huh. That's just the sort of thing he'd do, but somehow in my heart I knew she was the real thing. There was an air about her that was quite simply majestic. She patted my hand, told me to sit down and when she'd finished her story it was well past my bedtime. I was dumbfounded. Even though history had not exactly been my favourite subject at school, I still knew enough to realise nothing would ever be the same. I think it's the enormity of it all that draws us in. The Sisterhood transcends mere individuals, it appeals to women on an almost genetic level, to our natural urges to protect and nurture, our abilities of persuasion and our willingness to sacrifice ourselves for the sakes of our children.'

'And don't forget our unwillingness to put up with crap,' added Celeste.

'How could I have overlooked that,' replied Doreen dryly. 'Once the existence of the Sisterhood has been revealed, it sort of makes everything else look a bit petty. So you see, it's just the very biggest thing ever. There has not been a single notable event in western history that has not been influenced by us, and we carry on today as we've always done in the past, moving quietly behind the scenes, diluting the stupidity of men down the centuries, encouraging the expansion of reason and science, fighting the terrible curse of ignorance and preserving knowledge as best we can.'

'But why you – of all people, why you?'

'I know, how come a hairdresser ended up as Guardian of the Earth – apart from being chosen by Kate Hepburn? Well, to answer that properly I'm afraid we'll have to take a drive. There's a place not too far away from here that you must see. It is a place of great age and it contains a remarkable secret. You're looking worried again. I don't blame you. Imagine how I felt when Kate walked into my shop and told me my career path had just changed direction!'

'How far away?'

'Fifteen miles, no more. Why?'

'Sorry, but I can't come. I have a house guest at the moment who is no doubt being tormented mercilessly by Bertie. I don't think it's a good idea for his sanity to leave him alone with my baby for more than a few hours.'

'May I ask who is this guest? Is it someone you trust?'

'It is someone I trust implicitly, and if you've done your research you should know who he is.'

Doreen drummed her fingers on the back of the chair, deep in thought. Who would this resourceful woman turn to for help? 'Ah, yes, of course. The policeman from the court case.'

'Impressive deduction, Doreen.'

'Thank you.'

'His name's Wilf Thompson. Bertie suggested I call him. James and I thought this was inspired. He's an accomplished and experienced detective and will be staying for as long as this situation remains unresolved. I certainly feel more comfortable knowing he's around – our cottage is a little remote. Could be useful in a pinch.'

'Sensible precaution – however, it's important that Bertie comes with us.'

'Bertie! Why? What's he got to do with all this?'

'Not all is clear yet, but our Pythia insists, and I've learnt over the years to implicitly trust our Pythia.'

'What the hell's a Pythia?' Celeste frowned in perplexity.

'The Priestess of the Oracle. Our psychic guide.'

'You use a Priestess?'

'No, we use a twenty-three-year-old girl I met in Malmesbury called Maggie, who has the gift of prescience. She actually doesn't like being called a Priestess. Thinks it evokes images of enthusiastic chanting and nervous goats. She's the one who's foreseen Bertie's importance in all this and, as I've said, I've had ample reason in the past to trust her judgement implicitly.'

'Frankly, this sounds like a complete load of old baloney to me,' muttered Celeste, frowning. 'I can just about get my head around you being a scissor-wielding goddess, but clairvoyance? Come on, Doreen, you're asking too much.'

Doreen looked at her watch. 'Would a small practical demonstration convince you?'

'What do you mean?'

'How much money do you have in your purse?'

'That's a bit personal, but if you really want to know, I've just drawn a hundred pounds out of the bank.'

'Ample. There's a betting shop two doors down. Put all the money you have on Dirty Laundry. To win. 12.15, Lingfield Park.'

'You're kidding! What if I lose? I won't be able to pay for my hair.'

'You won't lose. This is one of Maggie's specials.'

'But I've never been in a betting shop in my life. I wouldn't know what to do.'

'Just walk in and look helpless. The staff will pounce like vultures. Then you can stiff them like a pro.'

'Can't you come with me?'

'Sorry, I've been banned from every betting shop south of Birmingham. Now, that should tell you something, shouldn't it.' She looked at her watch again. 'Better hurry, Celeste, you haven't much time.'

Celeste stared at Doreen for a few moments, still hesitating. 'Go!' she urged, so Celeste grabbed her purse and scampered out of the salon. Doreen tidied up as fifteen minutes ambled past in a very agreeable manner.

'Well?' she enquired when Celeste reappeared. She didn't really need to ask – the look on Celeste's face told it all. 'What were the odds?'

'Thirty-three to one,' she said faintly, holding up a fat envelope.

'So you've won just shy of three and a half grand.'

Celeste nodded, still apparently in considerable shock.

'Well, my lovely, we win every month. Without fail. All because of Maggie. Still think it's a load of old baloney?'

'How the hell did that happen?' murmured Celeste. 'I can't believe it.'

'This is nothing. Wait until you see her really fly. You'll soon change your mind – and remember, Maggie is not a patch on Alice.'

'But this is extraordinary. You could all become

fabulously wealthy.'

'Yes, we could, but we won't. Someone would eventually notice so we only take a modest amount when we need it and no more. Don't forget, we're sworn to do no harm, even to the bookies. Now then, shall we go and fetch Bertie?'

'That could be a problem. There's no way Wilf is going to let me swan off on my own with him,' said Celeste. Especially now he was officially her 'muscle'. She was in no doubt he would be taking his new duties seriously.

'Sorry, but this is Sisterhood business. No men allowed.'

'Then I'm afraid I'll have to decline. I had a devil of a job persuading him to let me come into town this morning and he certainly won't let me out of his sight if I have Bertie with me. There's no way I can give him the slip.'

'You sure? Come on, Celeste, we're two bright women – we should be able to run rings round him, detective or not.'

'I suppose so, but I don't like to deceive him. He is on our side, after all.' She considered for a moment. 'I'll just have to see if I can coax Bertie out of the house without Wilf noticing.'

'Good. We'll drop by to pick him up – Prior's Norton isn't really out of our way.'

Celeste started in shock when Doreen said this, then realised the Sisterhood must have been gathering information about her for some time. 'You seem to know an awful lot about me,' she said suspiciously.

'Of course we do. You and James are important to us and so is Bertie.'

'Your Priestess come up with that?

'No, I figured it out for myself. Listen, you've been extraordinarily patient, more so than I was with Kate. Despite a calm exterior, I suspect you're bubbling inside with a good old healthy dose of scepticism and, frankly, I don't blame you at all. But, more than anything I can say, I know that just seeing this place will convince you I'm speaking the truth. Shall we go?'

'How much do I owe you for the hair?' she asked, checking herself in the mirror again. 'I can pay cash,' she added with a grin.

'You owe me nothing, but it would be nice to contribute something to the salon. They still have their business rates to pay – even the Sisterhood can't change that!'

Celeste put the envelope behind the counter. 'Well,' she said in answer to Doreen's raised eyebrow, 'if my husband can give Alice a quarter mill then I'm sure I can afford three grand for the cut. Unexpected money's for impulse spending, isn't it?'

The two women left the salon.

The man followed.

CHAPTER NINE

Twenty minutes later, Doreen pulled into the small church car park at Prior's Norton. 'Which house is it?' she asked.

'The thatched cottage through the trees. We can get into the field behind through that stile. Watch for the nettles. And the cows.'

Buttercup lowed a cheery welcome as they crept along the hedge until they could peer into the garden. The cottage sat with chocolate box perfection amongst its colourful flowers. 'This is very nice,' murmured Doreen, 'but how are we going to lure Bertie away?'

'Shouldn't be a problem – it looks like Wilf is having a snooze. Some bloody guard he turned out to be!'

Through the open sitting room window, the distant rattle of his steady snore wafted out across the garden. Wilf slumped on the sofa, head back, eyes closed, book open but abandoned on his chest. Bertie sat at his shoulder preening what few hairs remained on his sparsely-covered crown. The sight was rather comical. With roles reversed, it appeared the guarded was doing a substantially better job than the guard. To Doreen's surprise, Celeste whistled shrilly – and Bertie's head instantly came up at the sound. She flicked a hand signal and he jumped off the sofa, disappearing from view.

'Now what?' asked Doreen.

'Just wait. You'll see.' Moments later, a blue head appeared in the cat flap. There was a lot of pushing and squeezing before he managed to lever his bulk through, and, once in the garden, scampered his way to Celeste, his long tail swishing from side to side. A powerful thrust of leg and casual flex of wing brought him up onto the fence post poking through the top of the hedge, one of his favourite perches. 'Mummy!' he chirruped happily. 'Hello, Mummy!'

'Hello, Bertie. Have you missed me?' Celeste ruffled his neck feathers affectionately.

'Missed? Yes. I'm hungry.' This was a fairly common response from Bertie, ever the optimist. He suddenly spotted Doreen standing behind Celeste and peered at her with great interest, head tilting first to one side, then the other. 'Hello,' he said cheerfully. 'My name is Bertie and I'm very pleased to meet you.'

Doreen, although somewhat prepared for her first encounter having studied the numerous news reports featuring the big macaw, still found herself gaping. The bird was nationally famous – it was like meeting a celebrity – but this one had casually brought down the last government with a single sentence. Even so, she still could not believe her ears. His level of intelligence was astonishing.

Celeste chuckled. 'You've spent all morning destroying the foundations of my world, so please forgive me if I say it's nice to return the compliment. We've both had a day of surprises, haven't we? Go on, Doreen, introduce yourself. He won't bite.'

'Hello, Bertie, I'm Doreen,' she said rather self-consciously, very aware the macaw looked alarmingly large now his face was at her own level. That wicked bill was long and curved like a scimitar. She hesitated for a second, then bowed her head respectfully.

'Doreen,' said Bertie ruminatively. 'Hello, Doreen.' He regarded her with that steady stare which unnerved so many people, then dipped his head in what could only be a return bow. Celeste raised her eyebrows in surprise. 'Doreen. Yes, I like you. Do you have any nuts?'

Doreen and Celeste stood in the library at Temple Hall.

Celeste wore a heavy leather falconer's glove, Bertie's powerful claws encircling her wrist. He had been surprisingly docile in the car. Normally, he disliked travelling by road – he found the constant changes in motion disturbing – but to Celeste's relief he displayed an unusual tolerance. Fortunately, Temple Guiting was a mere twenty miles or so from Prior's Norton and he seemed to spend most of the time staring thoughtfully at Doreen. She could sense Celeste's scepticism growing again and the two women barely exchanged a word during the brief journey. Doreen concentrated on her driving, but glanced in the mirror constantly, as if more interested in where she'd been than where they were going. On one occasion, a slight smile twitched her lips, but she said nothing to Celeste.

The library was a long, low-ceilinged room with heavy oak beams overhead, each carved with flowery garlands dancing merrily along the timbers. Mullioned windows marched down one wall, the panes criss-crossed in leaded diamonds. The hand-made glass was very old – each pane was a subtly different tint of pale bluish-green. A fat black cat lay on one sill, curled up fast asleep in the sun, its long tail hanging limply over the edge. Bertie dismissed it with contempt.

Panels of oak covered the walls, the wood polished to a sublime sheen, with a goodly number of bookshelves indicating the purpose of the room, all plain in construction but evidently sturdy. The books they contained stood to attention like disciplined warriors, their spines of finely tooled leather lined up in formal ranks. There were hundreds of volumes, big and small, thick and thin, pristine and moth-eaten. The overall impression was of a rather dark and serious room, with the exception of a large, exquisitely patterned Persian carpet spread over the uneven oak floorboards between several comfortable sofas. Thick and soft underfoot, it brightened the sombre atmosphere with a wildly exuberant splash of reds and creams, ochres and golds.

However, the real focal point was a massive and solidly constructed stone fireplace bulging out of the panelling like the buttress of a mountain. The heavy lintel was charred black in the middle and stood shoulder-high above a deep grate, the stone beautifully carved with curlicued garlands of flowers to match the beams above. The fireplace was obviously used regularly and was certainly capacious enough to mount a respectable conflagration, one worthy of the attention of the local Fire Brigade. Even though a bright early summer sun now warmed the house, Celeste could still detect the faint aromatic acridity of wood smoke lingering in the air, a comforting smell which, when combined with the exotically bright carpet, seemed to subtly alter the character of the library, turning it into a homely and snug place, a room where one could curl up on the sofa with a good book or enjoy conversation and conviviality on a cold winter's evening in front of a roaring fire. She liked the library's serene, old-fashioned charm and comforting atmosphere. Doreen had referred to the Sisterhood's library several times in the salon, but somehow Celeste sensed this was not what she had been brought to see.

A door opened and two women walked in, one soberly dressed in long dark skirts and a matching knitted twin set, a frumpy, matronly figure with greying frizzy hair – a goodly portion of which appeared far too unruly to remain incarcerated within her bun and sprung outwards in all directions like excitable radio antennae. Her eyes, though, were sharp and icy blue, her cheeks cherubic, her lips firm. She looked like an old-fashioned, archetypal schoolmistress, someone who forced recalcitrant young ladies to learn physics or chemistry at a time in their lives where all that consumed them were boys, the latest mascara and learning how to light a cigarette without setting fire to their hair.

The other, by way of complete contrast, was

surprisingly young, perhaps no older than eighteen or so, a thin slip of a girl, skinny, leggy and angular, with no apparent hips or breasts to interfere with her boyish silhouette. Two long, braided, dusky ginger pigtails fell to the small of her back where a black scrunchy bound the ends together as one. Her clear, pale face was spattered with spectacular freckles, as if she'd been involved in a drive-by incident with a jar of Seville oranges. A smile hovered on plump lips. She wore no make-up when, in Celeste's eyes, she really needed to, especially around her wan eyes. A good meal would probably do her no harm either, something with lots of fat and carbohydrate, followed by a giant pudding. Frankly, she looked as if she'd not seen any sunshine for months, but then as a redhead she had the skin type that didn't appreciate exposure to ultra-violet light, as Celeste knew well herself. She wore shiny black patent slippers, patterned black tights under a red check miniskirt and a white T-shirt proudly bearing the immortal logo, *Cover Your Boobs in Snopake*.

Not that she'd need much to achieve such a noble goal.

Bangles glittered on each wrist, loops of silver-chased beads hung around her neck and silver rings occupied every finger and thumb, so she obviously appreciated jewellery, but not enough to have her ears pierced. Two more disparate figures could not be imagined, yet in one way they were identical – both she and her middle-aged shock-haired companion wore half-moon glasses perched on the ends of their noses.

'Hello, Gaia, always nice to see you here,' said the young girl.

'Hi, Cutie. How's it going?'

'Pretty good.' She pecked Doreen on each cheek and kissed the back of her hand. Cutie's companion tutted at the informality shown by her companion and chose to curtsy respectfully. Doreen nodded in response, looking suitably grave. Cutie giggled at her obeisance and turned

131

to Celeste. 'This has to be her. Celeste Timbrill, née Gordon. Welcome to Temple Hall, and welcome to Bertie as well. Gosh, he's a lovely boy, isn't he?' Bertie seemed to swell with pride at her admiring praise.

'Celeste, I'd like you to meet Geraldine Pye, known to all, inevitably, as Cutie.'

'Hello, Cutie, pleased to meet you.' Celeste used her left hand to shake Cutie's right. Bertie occupied the other arm like a giant blue gargoyle.

'Likewise. This is Martha, our very own Scrabble champion. A word of warning – do not engage her in a Sudoku challenge! Don't be intimidated – she has been known to smile once in a while. She's my assistant.'

'Your assistant?'

'Your confusion is natural,' interposed Doreen as Cutie giggled behind her hand. It seemed she did a lot of giggling. 'Cutie has been in charge of our library these last three years.'

'Since I was sixteen,' said Cutie proudly, 'but I couldn't do my job without Mama here.'

'I'm not your Mama, you cheeky girl,' tutted Martha irritably. Celeste had a suspicion she did a lot of tutting.

'We make the perfect team,' said Cutie. 'Mama knows everything about everything.'

'And you're good at computers, I guess,' said Celeste.

'Computers?' Cutie was momentarily nonplussed. 'Oh, no, we have no computers here. None at all.'

'Pardon?'

'Of course we don't have any computers. Computers can be corrupted, they're too unreliable, too delicate, too temperamental and are really excellent at losing information. Besides, they can be hacked by any spotty geek half my age. They are just too – too ephemeral. Around here we have a deep and healthy suspicion of anything new, like this latest generation of electronic books that's being so aggressively marketed. I don't like them at all. The great thing about a traditional book is that you can put it on a shelf, leave it there for five hundred years, take it down again, open it and start reading. All you need is light, conveniently provided by the sun every day. Could you do the same with an eBook? Don't think so. Modern computers have only existed for thirty years and yet we all rely on them so totally that a simple software failure can bring a company to its knees in seconds. Can't have that now, can we?' said Cutie with a frown. 'Oh, no, that would be catastrophic.' It seems she did have a serious side after all.

'I don't understand,' said Celeste. 'You're a librarian, but you don't have any computers. How do you find anything?' She peered around the room, surprised at just how many of the books appeared identical.

'We use a good old-fashioned card system, cross-referenced against author, title, subject, age and language. It's very simple and therefore extremely reliable, and still operates if the power goes off.'

'A card system?' exclaimed Celeste, obviously surprised.

'It works for us. Actually, it's worked very well for quite a while,' she added with a mischievous twinkle in her eye.

'Sounds to me like you need to move with the times,' observed Celeste.

'But we do – we no longer use Latin!'

'But surely a computer would help enormously.'

'No,' said Cutie decisively, shaking her head. 'It wouldn't, and you'll soon see why. Shall we show them, Gaia?'

'That's why we're here, Cutie. Do your thing, babe.'

Cutie walked to a large oak panel beside the smoke-stained fireplace. An oval brass plate set into the floorboards at her feet marked the spot where Isaac Newton solved Fermat's Last Theorem and invented the cat flap. She grinned over her shoulder at Celeste and reaching high above her head with both arms, pressed simultaneously on two innocuous wooden bosses. There was a heavy, well-oiled clunk and the panel unlatched, springing outwards an inch or so. Cutie pulled it back on great iron hinges to reveal a short stone passageway beyond. The floor was perfectly level, the walls perhaps an arm's span wide, the ceiling a graceful arch overhead. Warm light glowed off golden walls.

'Spooky! Scared of ghosts, Celeste?'

'No, but I do want to make sure Bertie won't be alarmed. What's down there?'

'Wonders beyond your imagination,' whispered Cutie theatrically.

'Do we really have to go in?'

'Yes, we do, but don't worry, the passage doesn't get any smaller. It's neither damp nor dark and there are no spiders. There's a landing, then some stairs further in, but they're straight and shallow and very easy to negotiate. We have a lovely sunny day as well so there'll be plenty of light. Now, before we enter I have to ask if you have anything combustible on you?'

'Combustible?'

'Anything that can burn. Matches, napalm, pocket-sized tactical nuke, Boeing Dreamliner, anything like that?'

'No. Why?'

'We take nothing in there that can burn and you'll soon see why. Gaia?'

'Thanks, Cutie. Before we go down, I want to impress on you that what you're about to see can never be discussed or revealed. We're going to show you something truly remarkable, something so amazing that even though I've seen it many times before, I'm still totally overwhelmed each time I come here. It's important you see this because it will help you understand in a way I cannot explain with mere words. I'm placing absolute trust in you, Celeste, but I'm supremely confident my trust will be vindicated, even though you and I met only for the first time this morning. You have to give me your word you'll never talk about this except to the people who you see here in this room, and even then you'll always need to be discreet in case of wagging ears.'

'I don't know if I can give such a promise. It depends on what I'm about to see,' said Celeste carefully.

'There's nothing bad or evil here. I'm not asking you to promise anything beyond your abilities. This is a good secret to keep. You'll understand when you've seen.'

Celeste hesitated for a moment then nodded, and having committed herself suddenly felt a powerful surge of curiosity tinged with bone-deep excitement. A tingle skittered down her spine. Something at the end of that passage called to her on a visceral level. She stroked Bertie's head and muttered a few words of comfort to him, but he was craning his neck, peering into the tunnel with a steady stare, his interest already consumed. Celeste followed Doreen through the open panel and into the passageway with Bertie on her arm. Cutie stepped in behind her and Martha brought up the rear.

The panel closed with a snick and Celeste looked around in surprise. The tunnel was sealed yet remained bathed in light, but she could see no windows or lamps of any kind. Instead, bright shafts of sunlight poured in through circular apertures set in the roof and walls. The women descended a short flight of stairs into a small hexagonal chamber, each wall perhaps ten or twelve feet wide. More openings in the vaulted ceiling provided illumination, each dazzling spot of brilliance about a foot in diameter and regularly spaced.

The masonry around her was still as fresh as the day it was cut, the sublime honey-cream Cotswold limestone glowing warmly in the golden subterranean sunshine, the joints between each carved block barely visible. The floor was black marble and worn smooth down the centre from the shuffling of thousands of feet. She became acutely aware that this place was old beyond measure. A further passage led off to the right. An inscription was carved into the arch overhead.

Non nobis solum.

'That's Latin,' she said, looking up at the chiselled words.

'It is indeed,' replied Cutie. 'What do you think it says?'

'I haven't a clue. My languages are English and Portuguese.'

'It was put there by the master mason who made this place. He knew his Cicero. It's part of a longer quote and means, "Not for ourselves alone". Quite appropriate, I think you'll find.' They passed under the arch and proceeded down the tunnel. Celeste peered into one of the wall apertures as she passed, shielding her eyes against the brightness. Intense light was funnelled down a long polished metal tube set in the rock before streaming out horizontally across the passage. 'This is amazing. Where does the light come from?'

'Just you wait,' Cutie murmured conspiratorially, 'just you wait!'

They reached another flight of stairs after perhaps fifty yards or so. Again, a number of tubes clustered in the arched ceiling provided ample light. Celeste could easily see to the bottom of the stairs as she began to descend. 'There are ninety-nine steps,' said Cutie. 'Never figured out why, but I guess the Sisters had a sense of humour. However, we do know from our records that the master mason argued for a nice round hundred. Romans, eh, always so conventional!' They negotiated the stairs carefully and proceeded along another identical passageway. Celeste had a good sense of direction and guessed they were directly under the low hill she'd noticed rising up behind Temple Hall. They were now easily several hundred feet below ground.

The passage ended and they stepped out into a huge chamber, an enormous subterranean cavern. Light flooded in through scores of tubes set in the domed ceiling high above their heads. The space was vast, well over two hundred feet across. It was such an astonishing and totally unexpected sight that Celeste simply stopped dead in her tracks, gaping uncontrollably. Cutie scampered past and twirled across the floor as if dancing, her arms spread high and wide, her eyes closed, a dreamy smile on her face.

'Welcome, Celeste! Welcome, Bertie!' she called, her girlish voice echoing. 'Welcome to The Temple, the library of the Sisterhood of Helen and beyond all doubt the greatest repository of knowledge on this good planet Earth!'

CHAPTER TEN

It took some time before Celeste was able to gather herself. Eventually, the numbing plateau of shock receded and she began to take in details. The Temple was cloverleaf in shape, with six identical apses radiating out from a central domed rotunda like petals around the heart of a flower, each with massive, curving limestone walls. The blocks were cut square and true and finely chiselled to produce a rough but pleasing effect. These curving apses were themselves of significant size, with great hemispherical ceilings and colonnaded entrances, while the heart of the Temple was circular with the domed roof above supported by a ring of smooth grey granite columns. Arches sprang in all directions, leaping from column to column overhead. Over the ages, small white stalactites had formed in some of the joints high above, but the building was still sound and the roof looked solid enough to support mountains. The craftsmen who had assembled this structure were seeking strength and longevity, but had still managed to create a building of simple grace and elegance, even though the entire interior was devoid of any decoration but for a line of bold inscriptions running around a frieze at the base of the central dome: Latin, Greek, Arabic and other ancient tongues Celeste did not recognise. There was a quiet heaviness that spoke of centuries, but Cutie's happy humming seemed to breathe life into the ancient stones.

The walls of each apse were lined with shelves, thick slabs of the dark marble supported by heavy pillars of masonry. Further simple shelves of English oak, identical to those in the Temple Hall library above, stood in concentric circles radiating out from the centre like waves formed when a stone is dropped into a pool of knowledge. These stacks were a later addition, Celeste could see, necessary because the library had slowly filled over the centuries. At the very centre, right in the heart of the Temple, were several desks and workbenches, all positioned beneath the greatest concentration of light tubes. Sunlight poured down like spotlights in a theatre, illuminating every corner of the ancient building, but the light was brightest in the centre.

And books! There were books everywhere – tens of thousands of books. The marble shelves were stacked high with documents and ancient tomes of every description: codices, tubes containing scrolls of papyrus and leather, engraved metal sheets, carved ivory folios, clay and stone tablets, wax boards, parchments, vellum and medieval leather-bound volumes almost too heavy to lift.

Compelled by wonder, Celeste slowly wandered forward in amazement, for once totally overwhelmed, and after gazing around and up at the massive dome well over a hundred feet above her head, found herself meandering aimlessly towards the desks, perhaps drawn by the pool of warm light, perhaps by a sudden need to sit down. Bertie stirred and before she could stop him, leapt from her arm. He soared upwards, chattering and whistling, flitting from apse to apse as he explored eagerly. The Temple was large enough for some serious flying and he swooped between the columns like a scrap of blue paper blown by the wind.

'Cutie, can you please stop cavorting around like an infant and come here for a moment,' chided Doreen. 'I can see Celeste needs some answers to her questions.'

'Sure. I can do the tour guide act. No point in asking Mama – she can only talk to the books! What do you want to know, Celeste? Everything?'

Celeste nodded, then realised very quickly how Cutie had attained her position. The girl talked with a precision born of frightening intelligence and a profoundly deep understanding of her subject. It seemed utterly incongruous that such a youngster barely out of puberty could hold so much knowledge and present it in so clear and logical a way.

'Let's start at the beginning,' she said. 'This library is by far the oldest on earth. Its original home was in Patara in a building incorrectly identified by archaeologists nowadays as the Corinthian Temple. Patara was – and I suppose, technically, still is – a city in south-west Turkey and, although abandoned now, was once the main port of Lycia. Sisterhood policy has always been that the library should be distanced from centres of power since these proved too attractive to invaders and therefore susceptible to destruction. When Patara eventually fell into long decline through natural causes, the library was moved briefly to Rome, then to a country which at the time was on the very edge of the empire – Britain.

She swept her arms around in an all-encompassing gesture. 'This wonderful place was built between AD 310 and 321. The order came from Rome itself, along with sufficient silver to pay for the work, eight master masons to oversee the construction and a team of fifty skilled stone carvers. The design is based on The Pantheon, but without the fancy interior, and its only function is to provide a cool and dry repository for the thousands of documents, books, scrolls and parchments that were about to make the long journey from Rome. The library lies at the heart of the Sisterhood's philosophy and would never have been established had we not taken our ancient pledge to protect knowledge for the benefit of mankind.

'Yet, paradoxically, we cannot now reveal the existence of the Temple without compromising our secrecy and consequently destroying our political efficacy. *Non nobis solum.* You saw the inscription over the entrance. It reminds us of that conflict every day. How ironic that we, the sworn defenders of knowledge, now have to keep this astonishing source of information so secret in order to maintain our moderating influence on world leaders.

'This library holds many treasures and contains a true historical record of the last three millennia, as written every day by generations of impartial librarians. Here is knowledge that would destabilise religions, astound scientists, amaze philosophers, yet all must remain forever hidden.'

'But how was it built?' asked Celeste, still struggling to comprehend. 'How can you build something so big and then hide it so easily?'

'Simple. The long passage of time has done our work for us, obliterating all signs of the Temple. In the Apse of Arcturus I can even show you an account of the construction of the Temple itself. It's in Latin, of course, but I can translate if you wish,' she added mischievously.

'No need to show off, young lady. A short description in English will suffice, thank you very much,' said Doreen with that particular trace of sternness which comes as second nature to any mother.

'Sure, Gaia. At the time of its construction, this location was a remote and heavily forested area belonging to the estate of the Roman Villa whose ruins are now located in Spoonley Wood, south-east of Winchcombe. This precise location was chosen because it's on an intersection of many potent ley lines, the strongest running south-north from Carnac in Brittany, through Stonehenge, Temple Guiting and Holy Island on its way to the North Pole. This line is powerfully magnetic and has a wide-ranging influence, from impressive radio reception to annual migration patterns, and at this exact point intersects with a strong east-west line running from the Rollright Stones and out to Crug Hywel, a prehistoric fort in Wales.

'Once the precise location had been carefully divined, the Imperial masons recruited local labour and the site was cleared of timber. The structure was built into a natural declivity in the side of a low hill well above the water table, allowing free drainage. This bowl was enlarged by excavation and the quarried stone that was extracted provided the necessary materials for the masonry. The stonework was laid with great skill and care. The drum walls of the rotunda are fifteen cubits thick, or about twenty-two feet, ample to support the vaulted and domed roof above. The six apses are identical and were later named after the great stars of the northern hemisphere by Isaac Newton: Betelgeuse, Arcturus, Rigel, Vega, Sirius and Aldebaran. Once completed, the whole Temple exterior was sealed in the brand new wonder material of the age, concrete, and then coated in pitch. It was then covered in earth. Buried. Totally. Being underground, the temperature and humidity remain constant, the air is always cool, and cool air is dry, making it a perfect environment for the storage of documents.

'The columns around us were brought by ship from Rome herself, one per ship, and there are twenty-four in all. They're almost identical to the columns found in the entrance portico to the Pantheon. That building's original design was more flamboyant, but budget cuts made these two dozen superfluous to requirements and they were moved into storage. The Sisterhood acquired them at a very reasonable price, according to the accounts.

'The lighting is natural and comes via polished copper tubes, lenses and mirrors which were imported from Memphis in Egypt. We clean the mirrors and dust the light tubes every two years. There are no moving parts and the system works as perfectly today as it did two thousand years ago. As long as the sun provides light, it will last indefinitely. As well as providing us with an inexhaustible source of illumination, the tubes also ventilate the entire Temple, but heat from the sunlight, ingeniously concentrated by the lenses, also drives off much of the moisture in the air filtering down here, making the atmosphere unnaturally dry. Now, isn't that clever!'

'Seems fine to me,' ventured Celeste, sniffing

cautiously.

'Try spending a few hours down here and you'll understand exactly what I mean – you'll get a really rasping throat,' said Cutie. 'The bronze Lycian oil lamps you can see at the base of each column were brought from Patara. We still light them every Midsummer's Eve to celebrate the founding of the Sisterhood. They've been lit over three thousand times in all, and nearly two thousand times in this building alone. We allow no other sources of flame down here, no fire or electricity – the library is lit entirely by natural sunlight falling on mirrors that direct beams through lenses and along the polished copper light tubes set in the walls and roof. The idea came originally from the Pharaohs and much impressed Isaac Newton. Obviously, we do not work at night.

'The Roman masons were paid well and never revealed the Temple's existence, and the large numbers of local labourers were uneducated and could not read or write, so within a generation or two all knowledge of the Temple was lost. The roof of turf provided grazing for the Sisterhood's sheep and cattle and there remains to this day no evidence at all of the secret building below. The entrance was once inside the Oracle, disguised as a small Roman baptistry, but the Sisterhood accrued some considerable wealth through the woollen trade in the Middle Ages and the larger and more grandiose Temple Hall was built on the site in 1588, providing accommodation for the librarians, a new concealed entrance to the Temple itself and protection for the original baptistry which now lies beneath the Hall. The woodland was gradually cleared in the surrounding area and the village of Temple Guiting became established, growing very slowly over the centuries, however, the grounds of Temple Hall are extensive enough to prevent encroachment on the site, preserving our secret. The Hall now lies at the edge of the village, well above Saint Mary's church and the ponds.'

Cutie paused. Celeste began to understand exactly why Doreen had said what she had just before their descent into this astonishing building. The mere sight of the Temple, more than anything, made her realise the importance of the Sisterhood. She looked around again at the enormous structure and its priceless contents. Cutie eyed her speculatively. 'You keeping up with all this?' she asked.

'I think so.'

'Good, because Mama will be asking questions at the end!'

'You cheeky young thing!' scolded Martha. 'Now don't you go listening to her, Celeste.'

'Cheeky! Cheeky!' piped Bertie, latching on to a word he liked the sound of and repeating it to himself. He liked this place very much. It was light and airy and reminded him of vast spaces beneath the forest canopy back home in Brazil, but much quieter, of course.

'Cutie!' warned Doreen.

'Sorry, Gaia. Anyway, to return to my story.' Clearly impervious to admonishment, she resumed her explanation with impressive clarity. 'The Temple was built on the orders of Prisca, wife of Diocletian, fifty-fourth Emperor of Rome, in the last spring of his reign. Sisterhood records were held for a short while in Rome, but she was a far-seeing Gaia and her Pythia had foretold the increasing decadence of Rome could only lead to its complete destruction. Prisca decided to move the records to the furthest point in the empire, which at that time happened to be the distant, chilly and wholly unattractive barbaric province of Britannia. The books were packed into four ships which sailed through the Pillars of Hercules, around Iberia and Gaul and up the Severn estuary to the busy outpost fort of Glevum, now Gloucester, docking at a quay still lying a dozen feet below the County Shire Hall in Westgate Street. From there, the books were taken to the villa at Spoonley Wood for temporary storage while the Temple was under construction nearby.

'The library has remained at Temple Guiting ever since, with generations of librarians gathering, conserving and storing all this knowledge as an archive on behalf of our species. All work is done manually. Always has been, always will be. We regard every modern form of electronic data storage with great suspicion. It's far too temporary, too flighty. Our records need to withstand the test of time. However, collectively, the human race now has many diverse methods for the storing and retrieval of important information and so our prime function is no longer the protection of knowledge. The other great libraries, safely scattered across the world and too numerous to be destroyed all at once, have now taken on that mantle. The modern age of instant media has rendered much of our traditional work obsolete so we are now engaged in a programme of recording all the old and fragile scrolls onto thin slate sheets, engraving onto a medium that will last more or less indefinitely, rather than the hundreds of years for paper and mere few decades for digital documents.'

Cutie showed Celeste the workbench next to her desk. It was bathed in an aura of brilliant light. 'This is where Mama and I work. These slates are from North Wales, and the language is Latin. The book we're currently engraving is the only surviving copy of the *Algamest* by Ptolemy. This dates from the second century AD and is a mathematical and astronomical treatise. We're on volume seven of thirteen, so plenty still to do. This is the original, signed by Ptolemy himself. This actual book was copied into Arabic before we took it into our care and scholars in the West were then only able to study the work again when the Arabic copies were retranslated back into Latin in the twelfth century. These volumes alone are – well, utterly and completely priceless. If they came on to the open market I'd be surprised at all if they didn't fetch at least a hundred million pounds! Like so many of our books, they are the sole examples and therefore totally irreplaceable.

'Medieval Muslim scholars were easily amongst the finest that ever lived, and preserved much of the old knowledge at Cordoba and Toledo in Moorish Spain. Fearful of loss after the destruction of the library at Alexandria, they were avid collectors of knowledge from all over the known world and made huge advances in medicine, maths, physics and astronomy while the rest of Europe foundered in war and mud and squalor during the Dark Ages. I cannot stress enough the staggering impact of these early Islamic philosophers. They translated Egyptian hieroglyphs seven centuries before the Rosetta Stone was discovered, produced the first anatomical drawings and performed effective surgery a millennia ago. Even Isaac Newton admired them, and it took a lot to impress him!

'Come with me. I'd like to show you a few more of our star exhibits.' Cutie showed no diffidence, no nervousness in the presence of her Gaia and guests. She was in charge down here, amongst her beloved books. They walked across the rotunda into another apse. *Aldebaran* was inscribed into the keystone above the arched entrance. Cutie placed her hand on each scroll and volume, strolling slowly along the stone shelves, reaching up for some, down for others as she spoke. 'Here's the original notes on the discovery of Uranus and Neptune, and these are Galileo's first drawings of the moons of Jupiter. Down there are some sketches made by Leonardo da Vinci on the recurring theme of the spiral in nature, which led him to ponder on the possibility that the helix, or even an entwined double helix, capable of storing huge amounts of information in a compact area, may have an important part to play in the structure of life. He was a bit before his time, that one!

'This volume here is the only surviving copy of the *Cypria*. It's part of the Epic Cycle – you can see we've all eight parts safely tucked away alongside each other, including the *Iliad*, *Odyssey* and even the *Aethiopsis*. That's a rare one – even our copy is a bit tatty!

'Let's see now, all these copper scrolls come from the library of Rameses the Great. No cheap papyrus for the great Pharaoh. Oh, no, he was wealthy enough to be able to shell out for the high-end market!' They moved on into another apse. 'Here we have all our Islamic volumes, including major works on astronomy and mathematics by al-Khwarizimi. He was brilliant, bringing Greek geometry and the Indian numerical system together to create the algebra we still use today. He was also the first to use algorithms and adopt the concept of zero as a number. Incidentally, any scientific name beginning with 'al' almost invariably derives from one of these Muslim scholars. Now, that was one really clever man – I'll bet he was cracking at crosswords! What's wrong, you look puzzled?'

'These books open the wrong way!' exclaimed Celeste.

'No they don't. Arabic script is read from right to left, therefore the spines are on the right. It's very peculiar, isn't it, but no more peculiar than an Arab trying to read Mills and Boon in English. That calligraphy, though! Astonishing, isn't it.'

Celeste finally managed to open the book and thumbed carefully through the pages – backwards – admiring the beautifully flowing script and detailed illustrations. 'Why have I never heard of these men?' she asked.

'Let's just say our Western culture has been a little slow in coming to appreciate the contributions to science made by Islam. I'm ever hopeful that one day soon the situation will be rectified,' replied Cutie. 'Knowledge, whatever its source, should be treasured, and we're so thankful to have such a wonderful collection of early Islamic works here in the Temple. Aha! This is one of my favourites.' She pulled out a small volume that was obviously made from gold. The gleaming cover was pristine, totally untouched by any signs of tarnishing, and was inlaid with precious stones. She opened it up, stroking the thin gold pages gently. 'This is Persian, a personal account by King Darius of how he established an astronomical observatory at Pasargadae to celebrate consolidating the Persian Empire. Look at this Cuneiform – have you ever seen anything so delicate. This is simply gorgeous, magnificently illuminated in his own hand, too. Loved his diaries, did Darius.' She replaced the beautiful book and indicated the rest of the shelf. 'All these works are original, but as a precaution, as I've already mentioned, we're now copying the more valuable and fragile documents by inscribing onto slate with a diamond-tipped stylus to ensure their preservation for all time. That's what good old Mama and I do most of the time – when we're not reading, that is.'

'Surely you don't keep the copies in the same building as the originals?' asked Celeste.

'Not even I'm that much of a numpty,' replied Cutie. 'No, the slates are returned to the same mine as they came from in North Wales and stored underground in the abandoned caverns. We still like to keep ourselves as distant as we can from centres of importance and, let's face it, you can't get any more desolate than North Wales.'

'You've never been to Swadlincote, I take it?' observed Celeste wryly.

Cutie giggled again and Bertie copied the chuckle expertly.

'Oh, God,' muttered Martha in despair, 'now there's two of them!'

'What's in there?' asked Celeste, pointing to an ordinary, yellow cardboard box. Rather incongruously, there were bunches of bananas printed on its exterior and a florid sign announcing the contents were the proud product of Ecuador. 'Surely you're not storing bananas as well?'

'Might have held them once,' said Cutie, lifting down the box and opening its flaps, 'but not now. Have a look at this.' She pulled out a large white satin sheet and shook it open. Figures marched across the cloth in black ink, meandering tracks of arcane symbols connected by a plethora of arrows and herded between brackets. 'The writing is Albert Einstein's and this tablecloth belonged to the wife of his friend and fellow physicist, Freundlich. Once she'd finished scolding their guest for ruining her finest linen, she thought it might be of interest to us and so it found its way into our care. She told him she'd washed the cloth when he came back to check his maths the following morning. Now, there was a night of alcohol-fuelled genius. The poor man was most upset because he was convinced he'd solved the Unification Theory, but couldn't remember how.' There was an almost hypnotic beauty to the equations. 'Looks kind of important, don't you think?'

Cutie folded the unique cloth, put it away and popped the box back onto its shelf. 'Come over here, Celeste. You might find this more interesting.' There was a single wooden case with a glass lid standing alone in the centre of the apse floor. Beneath lay a very old leather-bound volume.

'What is it?' asked Celeste, thankful to be spared the arcane intricacies of Albert's work. All she'd ever wanted to do whenever she saw pictures of the iconic physicist was pin him to the floor and run around his wayward hair with a pair of clippers!

'Just about one of the most important books ever written,' replied Cutie brightly. She opened the case and lovingly caressed the rough, cracked hide of the front cover with her fingertips. '*De Revolutionibus Orbium Coelestium*, by Nicholas Copernicus, signed by the author and dated 24th May 1543, the day he died. A rebel to the very end, he scrawled in Latin below his signature, "The Holy Mother Church, although most blessed and wise in matters spiritual, is not wise in this matter." Had a bit of trouble with the Pope, did our Nicky Boy! His sister, Katharina, was one of ours. Her support for him was vital in his long struggle against religious zealotry.'

Celeste turned to Doreen. 'You mentioned Copernicus

earlier.'

'Yes, I did indeed. He proved beyond doubt that the earth orbited the sun and so ignited the astronomical revolution, shattering the dogmatic stranglehold of the church that had lasted for fifteen hundred years.'

'Ah!' sighed Cutie, clasping her hands to her heart theatrically. 'My hero! I want his babies! Lots and lots of babies!'

'Stop fooling around, you young minx!' growled Martha, unable to take any more of Cutie's horseplay. 'This is a serious business.'

Cutie put on a mock face, pulling the corners of her mouth downward. 'This is a serious business,' she repeated, dropping her voice an octave, then scampered off, beckoning for them to follow her into the next apse.

'She's not usually this disrespectful,' muttered Martha. 'I can only apologise, Gaia.'

'Martha, she's just turned nineteen and has spent almost every day of her life for the last three years studying in this cave. Give the girl a break, will you.'

'I think she's lovely,' said Celeste. 'A bit cracked, but lovely.'

'I like Cutie,' announced Bertie firmly.

'That's settled, then,' murmured Doreen. Martha threw up her hands in dismay and scuttled away as if to make sure Cutie wasn't causing any damage. Celeste glanced up at the inscription over the entrance. *Betelgeuse*. Scrolls were neatly stacked in ordered lines along the stone shelves. Cutie took them down one by one and displayed them to Celeste. 'Works by Anaximander and Anaxagoras – mustn't get those two mixed up – Pythagoras, Hippocrates, Thucydides, Diogenes, Tacitus and Livy to name but a few.'

'Sounds like a boy band,' smiled Celeste. A really smart one.'

'Somehow, I can't see songs in Latin taking the charts by storm,' said Doreen.

'But these are in fantastic condition. How on earth have you managed to keep them from deteriorating? I'm no librarian, but even I can see these are still fresh. I thought parchment had a sell-by date after which it falls apart.'

'Normally it does,' replied Cutie. 'You'll get maybe a thousand or fifteen hundred years from a really good scroll before it crumbles into a dust bunny, but we discovered the perfect preservative centuries ago. Tell me, Celeste, what food was found in Tutankhamun's tomb that could still be eaten? What popular breakfast spread contains natural antibacterial properties and never goes off, even after millennia?'

'Er … marmalade?'

Cutie giggled again at Celeste's stab-in-the-dark answer. 'Not quite. It's honey. We soak all our ancient documents in a special honey mix. The papyrus is absorbent and the honey keeps it supple and resistant to ageing.'

'Surely that makes the pages stick together?'

'If you used normal honey, yes, it would, but there are one or two other natural ingredients added into the mixture which prevents that from happening, including olive oil. All you have to do is wait a few years for the solution to cure and Bob's your uncle, and let's face it, a few years down here mean nothing! This also allows us to handle documents without the need for gloves and all the other assorted paraphernalia that normally restrict archivists when dealing with really old and fragile documents.' Cutie cast around for a second and then eased a scroll off a nearby shelf. 'Let me introduce you to one of the giants of science,' she said. 'Although this document is reasonably robust, I'd appreciate you showing a little respect, after all, it is the thick end of two and a half thousand years old!'

Celeste accepted the honey-soaked scroll and unrolled it very gently. Although the papyrus had darkened over the aeons, the writing was still clearly visible, the angular symbols indicating the language was Greek. She marvelled that she was actually touching something that was truly ancient, yet it seemed almost as fresh as modern paper. The papyrus was soft and supple to the touch, as flexible as a damp chamois cloth. She held it to her nose and inhaled cautiously.

'Most people prefer to read Archimedes, not sniff him!' observed Mama with a rare smile.

'There is a faint sweetness to it, I must admit,' said Celeste, handing the scroll back to Cutie.

'Not all of our documents are so fragile,' she said. 'We have diptychs made from ivory, for instance, and before you ask, a diptych is a pair of wooden plates hinged along one edge like the covers of a modern book, with the text protected inside. Now, let's see if we can find one to show you.' She scanned the shelves and picked up a flat box that looked uncommonly like a slim-line backgammon set. 'Here we are, this is Greek and from about the second century BC, which makes it an extremely early example. See how the opening edge can be tied shut with twine to keep the contents from prying eyes.' Cutie opened the two wooden halves of the diptych to reveal the interior. Inside, the age-old ivory writing surface was covered in line after line of finely tooled geometric symbols. It was an exquisite piece of work, complete with tiny etched diagrams.

'What does it say?' asked Celeste out of sheer curiosity.

'Why, Celeste Timbrill, are you trying to test me?' said Cutie with the indignant air of a professor confronted by an upstart, long-haired student, but then she winked, pushed up her half-moon glasses into their operating position and peered at the script, her mouth working silently. 'Hmm,' she said after a minute or so. 'Yes, I've got it. This is a treatise by the Greek mathematician and inventor Ctesibius on hydraulic engineering, and on this sheet of ivory is the first ever explanation of the concept and mechanics of the siphon. Interesting and important, particularly if you're planning the water system for a city. There's still a really impressive siphonic aqueduct just outside Patara that's over fifteen hundred feet long and would work today if the stones were realigned. Siphonic aqueducts allow water to flow uphill. Very clever. All our modern toilet cisterns work on the siphonic principle, so it's a good example of how the ancients helped make your trips to the loo more pleasant and stopped you getting typhus.' She carefully closed the diptych and replaced it on the shelf. Celeste wondered how long it would be before it was opened again.

Cutie moved on. The Apse of Sirius beckoned. She skipped in and gave an exaggerated flourish, like a magician's assistant relieved at the unexpected but welcome return of the white rabbit. 'In here we have the history of the Sisterhood, an accurate and unbroken archive from Helen of Troy to Doreen of Chipping Sodbury, over three thousand years of meticulous records, all preserved by us women. We're mentally suited to the job, you see. We're methodical and careful. This is why most librarians have always been – and remain to this day – women. It's our legacy to the world. We protect knowledge with the same intensity as we protect our children. Most people think librarians just boring old biddies, but we have helped control the destiny of mankind for millennia! Of course,' she added thoughtfully, 'Mama is continuing the fine tradition in boring old biddies!'

Martha hissed sibilantly, but Doreen placated her with a touch on the shoulder. Cutie blew a kiss at her seething companion and forged on. She waved her arms around again, as if unable to encompass everything in the Temple. Her excitement knew no bounds. She was really fired up now, her face flushed, her eyes shining. She spoke with an intoxicating passion that reached out to Celeste. 'Once it had assimilated the library of Pergamum, the great library at Alexandria was the only other to ever rival ours, but whereas that library was renowned throughout the ancient world, the Sisterhood's has always been shrouded in secrecy. We spirited the originals away and left copies in their place, so when the library burnt to the ground, thousands of the most significant documents were saved, thus preserving the ancient knowledge. Snuck 'em out right under the nose of Eratosthenes, the chief librarian. He's the chappie who measured the size of the Earth using a stick, a well and a bit of simple maths! Clever man – I'd have liked to have met him. We've also got many Aramaic scripts that recount the life of Jesus and the Apostles, scripts that were mysteriously omitted from the Bible. Even the Vatican library has no idea they exist. Contrary to a whole raft of recent popular adventure novels, there never was any conspiracy at the advent of Christianity, no super-secret organisations vying for power. Jesus most certainly did live and was a great prophet, even though he wasn't quite the saint the Bible makes him out to be!'

'So I believe. What treasure's kept over here?' Celeste wandered into the next apse, walked up to the case at its centre and peered in through the glass cover.

'These three volumes are Uncle Isaac's own handwritten *Philosophiae Naturalis Mathematica Principia*,' smiled Cutie fondly, 'the Mathematical Principles of Natural Philosophy. These journals contain the first really important and mathematically sound laws of nature. In here you'll find Newton's three laws of motion and his universal law of gravitation.' She lifted the glass lid and opened one of the books. Latin text interspersed with lines of equations marched across the yellowed pages, with later marginal notes added in English. 'Without doubt, you are looking at the greatest single feat of intellectual achievement in the history of our species,' murmured Cutie, gently thumbing through the pages. 'Look at the elegance of the calculations and wonder! This was published in 1687 – over three hundred years ago, and yet here we find an explanation as to why the planets orbit the sun, a method of calculating gravitational pull just about anywhere in the universe and equations to determine the motion of all objects. The laws set down in these books are all pervasive, from influencing the design of pinball machines to allowing Neil Armstrong to stroll around the moon!' She turned to the back. 'And here's Isaac's solution to Fermat's Last Theorem. Even today there are almost certainly more fingers on one hand than mathematicians alive who can truly understand this, and I'm certainly not one of them, but I do recognise that!' She pointed at a little sketch down in the bottom corner of the page.

'Well I'll be damned – it's a cat flap!' laughed Celeste. 'Doreen, you were right, and I apologise for my earlier scepticism. The cat flap has swung it for me! That's so unlikely it has to be true. I'm in!'

'I'm in!' repeated Bertie immediately.

Mama caught her breath at the pronouncement and Doreen's eyes blazed. Cutie clapped her hands and grinned. 'There, Gaia, woman and bird, together as one, just as the Pythia predicted.'

'Is there nothing this bloody Pythia doesn't know?' muttered Celeste. 'I feel trapped, like I'm on a runaway train.'

'You'll get used to it.'

'I'm not sure I will.'

'Actually, you're going to have to get used to it whether you like it or not,' said Doreen firmly.

'Why? What's going on?' Celeste's suspicions instantly surfaced again. 'What do you mean? I want an explanation right now!'

'She doesn't know yet, does she?' said Cutie. 'You've kept it from her so she could make up her own mind, come in of her own free will. Clever, clever Gaia!'

'Tell me!' demanded Celeste. 'Now!'

'Calm down, Celeste, there's no need for anger. You're going to need our help to defeat those awful men who are attempting to destroy James's career, and you're going to need our help to promote this refreshing new democracy that he's ignited. You've already figured out that these men will now target you and Bertie after their failed attempt at corrupting your husband, and there's every chance they're already moving against you.'

'I know all that, so what's Cutie talking about?'

'You have to understand that the complete genealogical record of Helen's descendants is held here,' explained Doreen. 'We can trace her bloodline through one hundred and sixty-four generations, mother to daughter, to the present day. In all that time the line has never failed in its strength and although many Gaias have been related to Helen, in one of those historical oddities that occasionally occur, our most recent Gaias have not. Kate Hepburn was not of Helen's line. Neither was Clementine Churchill before her, nor Agatha Christie before Clem, but Annie Scott Cook most definitely was, and although she is unrecorded by history, she worked wonders restoring the Sisterhood after Emmeline Pankhurst's aggressive leadership. We were nearly discovered then, and Em had to resign when her radical politics contradicted Sisterhood policy. We've always worked behind the scenes, you see, but the poor woman was far too feisty to take a back seat. As I said, most Gaias in our long history have been descended from Helen, but not all, and when there is doubt in the succession, the Pythias have always advised the Sisterhood to go back into the bloodline to select our next Gaia.'

'Don't you see? That's why Kate Hepburn came to see me,' said Doreen firmly. 'I am Gaia because of my ancestry, and when the time comes, I shall step aside and you will take my place!'

'Me? Why me?' exploded Celeste, a look of dumbfounded outrage on her face.

'Because we need you as much as you need us – and now you'll see why.' Doreen loosened her colourful scarf and pulled it from her head. Her bobbed hair fell free.

There was no thinning caused by chemo; the thick locks shone with copper brilliance in the subdued light. It was identical in hue to Celeste's.

'This colour is the fabled Flame of Sparta. You and I, Celeste, we're both True Daughters of Helen of Troy!'

CHAPTER ELEVEN

'Now wait just one minute,' exclaimed Celeste, shaking her head from side to side in vehement denial, more shocked than angry. 'I'm not liking this. I'm not liking it one little bit.'

'Why not?' asked Cutie with all the innocence of a child. She may have reigned supreme amongst her books and possessed a deep knowledge of classical languages, but she was still inexperienced in many ways. 'What could be more thrilling than to find you're related to the greatest woman who's ever lived?'

'The girl is right,' interposed Martha unexpectedly, taking charge. 'I've made special studies of the lineage and there's no doubt. No doubt at all. Look at Gaia. Look at her hair. Have you ever seen such a distinctive colour? The particular gene that creates the Flame of Sparta is now incredibly rare, but when it does appear it is still strong and vital. Tell us, Celeste, have you ever, in all your days, met anyone with the exact hair tint you have?'

There was a long, telling pause.

'There you are, your silence is entirely understandable. That's because there are just nine women alive today who carry this gene in its purest form. Nine! Out of a total world population of over three billion women. The bloodlines bifurcate and recombine continuously, so as each generation is born there are only a very few who carry the true blood of Helen. Three of the nine are in this Temple right now: Gaia, yourself, and Little Miss Serious here!' Cutie grinned and waggled her fingers at Celeste. 'Of the remaining six, four currently live in Britain: two are still children, even younger than Cutie; one is a nun and therefore beyond reach and reasoning by us; and the last is Alice, who has unfortunately suffered a serious mental breakdown and now roams the streets of London accompanied by her pet pigeon. What a sodding tragedy!' Martha's suddenly bitter tone surprised Celeste. 'The remaining two who live outside Britain are twin sisters from Finland. We keep a close eye on them. Twins are always exciting genetically. We have high hopes for daughters from those two in the years to come.' Martha regarded Celeste with a steady eye. 'You're still not convinced, are you. Well, we can always show you the bloodline. Would you accept that as proof?'

Without waiting for an answer, she bustled over to one of the thick marble shelves, old-fashioned skirts swishing, peered myopically at the tomes through her half-moon spectacles while running a finger along a row of leather book spines, then pulled out a great volume and placed it on her desk under the pool of golden sunshine. 'Here's an abridged family tree of the House of Sparta. It follows the strongest line only, the primary line. The numerous branches are dealt with elsewhere and a surprising number reappear at a later date to combine once again with the dominant line. Here is Helen and her daughter, Hermione. Now follow the red path as I turn the pages.

'These are the centuries of Blessed Lycia, here we have Cleopatra, hair as red as blood and a strong Gaia, here the removal from Patara to Rome, then to Britannia. The Dark Ages follow. There's Eleanor of Aquitaine.' The pages turned one by one. 'The line's now passing through Tudor and Georgian England and eventually we reach your great-great-great grandmother. This is where it gets really interesting. Gaia?'

'Thanks, Martha. As I said before, Celeste, you and I are related to each other, but only very distantly. Five generations ago, in the middle of the nineteenth century, twin sisters were born, Sarah and Emily Blackwell. Here they are.' Doreen tapped at the page with her manicured nail. The details were recorded meticulously in copperplate. 'They both married and the bloodlines separated again, but you actually have a greater claim to be Gaia than I do since my branch of the family is descended from Emily and has the recessive gene, while the primary line followed Sarah. Yours is the dominant line. How do I know this? Well, unlike my hair, yours will not go grey. Ever!

'You will carry your colour to the day you die, you lucky, lucky woman. You can also see it in the eyes – yours are pure malachite green. They are Helen's eyes, whereas mine are much less … vibrant. A sure indication of the recessive gene. Cutie's likewise. Her hair is also a subtly different shade and, although she would undoubtedly make a fine Gaia, her real value to the Sisterhood is as Guardian of the Temple.

'So, from Sarah came the next generations of your family until we reach your mother, Barbara. I realise this has come as something of a surprise to you, but the archives cannot be doubted. We have a complete and detailed record of your family tree right here.' Doreen placed her palm on the page as if to emphasise her point. Bertie bobbed his head up and down beside her, craning his neck to see what was going on. Celeste had long ago accepted his need to be involved and, without thinking, stroked his violet blue crown and ran a hand gently down the blue feathers covering his broad back. 'Look, Bertie, books,' she murmured.

'Yes. Books. Old books.' His cogent reply startled Martha.

Doreen continued. 'Ray, your father, had an unusually high number of relatives on the distaff side who were secondary daughters of Helen, while Barbara, your mother, was a natural redhead and secondary daughter in her own right. We watched closely when they married, hoping for a girl, and were delighted when you were born.

161

The combination of two lines of secondary daughters always produces a pureblood True Daughter. Always! In you, the bloodline has emerged once again as strong and vital as ever. If you doubt what I'm saying just look at the colour of our hair. Even Cutie – a pureblood True Daughter of Helen herself – even she doesn't have the same rich tints you and I have. This is the extraordinarily rare red-copper Flame of Sparta, the bronze that drove men wild.

'Helen wasn't some ditzy blue-eyed blonde with big tits and pouting lips, like those favoured by Hollywood directors. She had red hair and blazing green eyes – why the hell do you think the Athenians went to war over her for ten years? Fair-haired women were two-a-penny in those days, no one would fight for a decade over some airhead with a peroxide mop, but a green-eyed redhead – a Goddess – now that was another thing entirely. Her blood flows in your veins as sure as spring follows winter, and you will be the next Gaia after I retire.' There was such passion in Doreen's voice, such daunting force, that even Celeste, accustomed as she was to exercising power herself, felt thoroughly intimidated. Doreen seemed to sense this and suddenly relaxed, a quirky smile hovering on her lips. 'It is your destiny, Luke!' she added mischievously.

'It might seem amusing to you, but I'm really struggling with this,' muttered Celeste. 'It's just too weird to be talking about history and destinies and priestesses. Will I have to wear hessian underwear or something?'

'Not unless you want to. Listen, I'm trying to make light of a matter so serious that most people would run a mile. It's only natural you should be disturbed, but that will pass. Running the world's not actually that complicated. Despite our joking, most world leaders are reasonably competent. They just need a nudge here and there to keep them on the straight and narrow. Despite what feels like crushing responsibility on that front, I still spend more of my time covering up grey roots or poodle perming. Kate also found she had plenty of spare time and continued to make films nearly right up to her death.

'Look, my throat's getting dry from the atmosphere down here so shall we go upstairs and have a nice cup of tea and we'll try to answer any more questions you have?'

'Yes. Thanks, that's just what I need.' Celeste slipped on her gauntlet and called Bertie. He sidled across the top of the chair and hopped onto her arm.'

'Hello, Mummy,' he said brightly. 'I love you.'

'I love you, too, Bertie,' replied Celeste, kissing his head. Doreen noted she did not patronise the bird by using an infantile sing-song voice. She spoke in a normal tone, replying as she would to any human. To Celeste, Bertie was an equal, to be treated with courtesy and respect – however, he did allow himself to enjoy some affectionate neck petting which resulted in something quite unexpected. Curiously, he began to purr. Loudly. Doreen nodded, remembering the Pythia's bizarre prophesy. 'The blue bird that purrs,' she murmured to herself. 'Well I'll be damned!' She opened her mouth, but Celeste cut her off.

'Don't ask! It's a long story and I'll tell you some time, but at the moment I'm the one who needs explanations.' They all headed for the tunnel leading back to Temple Hall above.

'There's another thing you have to consider as well,' mused Doreen as they crossed the polished marble floor.

'How can there possibly be more?'

'There's lots more, but this is a simple observation, one even a person as shell-shocked as you can appreciate.'

'All right. Go on.'

'It's obvious when you think about it – you've been drawn to live in Gloucestershire. This is not an accident. A convoluted path has led you here, from Oakham to Brazil to London to here. We thought we'd lost you in South America, but the Pythia urged patience and she was right, as always. Generations of Gaias have lived here, drawing comfort and strength from this Temple and its unique position within the Earth. Even Kate, as staunch an American as you could find anywhere, visited constantly, drawn back time and again to recharge her emotional batteries and watch you grow from that gawky ginger-haired adolescent into a confident, superbly capable woman. It's no coincidence the library ended up here and that I'm here. Now you. Why is that?

'This area of Britannia, the old Roman province, has always had a special attraction. The earth's magnetic field is strong here. Ley lines cluster in this part of the world. Huge amounts of energy flow back and forth through the land, drawing us even though we're unaware of it. Stonehenge is a mere stone's throw away and on the same ley line as this Temple, and there are more barrows and burial mounds around here than you can shake a stick at!'

'Sounds a bit too New Age for me,' observed Celeste, slowly climbing the long flight of stairs.

'Me, too,' agreed Doreen. 'But in today's modern, technologically developed society, just ask yourself one question. Why on earth do you think GCHQ ended up in Cheltenham? The answer is simple – the radio reception's phenomenal. Best in the Northern Hemisphere. If an organisation as important, committed, sane and clever as that acknowledges the influence of the area, then there must be something in it.

'Look, no one was more sceptical than I, but then I saw Alice at work was astonished at the results. Her oracular vision, clairvoyance, intuition, guesswork, call it what you will, is impressively accurate. For example, we've got an unblemished record on the turf. Bookies scream and bolt their doors when they see us coming – as you've already found out.

'Think about it, Celeste. We're all creatures brought to consciousness by this planet. Our ancestors were much more in tune with the natural world than we are now. Just because we prefer to rely on the internet, heated curling tongs, mobile phones and depilation cream, doesn't mean these natural forces have diminished.

'I could blather on all day, but once you're Gaia and see the Pythia in action, you'll soon change your mind. Pity you weren't with us when Alice was in her prime. She was one of the most powerful oracles since the time of Blessed Lycia. Until her breakdown, of course.'

'You've referred to this Blessed Lycia several times. What is it? I want to know more!'

'Cutie knows more than anyone alive. Let her tell the story.'

'Sure, Gaia, it'll be a pleasure. Of all the ancient societies, one of the most successful, prosperous and free was the Lycian,' said Cutie, slipping back into her role as narrator, 'and that was so because it was essentially matriarchal in nature. However, we have to go even further back in history to appreciate the reasoning behind Helen's choice of Lycia as the society within which to embed the developing Sisterhood. She was actually trying to emulate the Cretan Minoans, who were wiped out by the eruption of Santorini. Minoan civilization was also matriarchal and highly successful in itself. Did you know they invented air conditioning two millennia before Christ? Had that volcano at Santorini not popped, then the entire history of Western civilization would have been radically different. Greek culture would have been very strongly matriarchal, influencing the Romans afterward. There would have been very few wars and religion would never have been allowed to stifle scientific advancement. As a consequence, our race would likely now be cruising the galaxy instead of bumbling across the Atlantic in glorified tin tubes powered by spark plugs!

'The time of Lycia was actually the Sisterhood's most successful era. Women established the Lycian Federation, a loose collection of city-states strung out along the coastline of what is now south-west Turkey. Each city had a vote in the national assembly, and the larger ones had three votes each. The ruins of these cities can still be seen today – you can go on a package holiday jeep safari and drive through the ruins of tragic Xanthos, up to majestic Tlos or to dreaming Pinara in its mountain fold. This assembly then elected judges and other important officials, and the Lyciarch to be their leader. It was the earliest recognizable form of representational democracy and it was a good model, good enough for Thomas Jefferson to admire and acknowledge when he was writing the US constitution. It's still that influential, even today! The whole of European civilization and everything that's sprung from it can be traced back to the early democracy of Lycia. Their Federation survived under various occupations, knowing when to bend in the wind, welcoming Alexander the Great and, more notably, embracing the Romans, who were entirely happy to let the Lycians run their own affairs with the absolute minimum of interference. The Sisterhood's influence again.'

'So if Lycia was so successful, why are these cities now all ruined?'

'Earthquakes! Big bastards. They all went at the same time so they couldn't support each other. The population that survived could not rebuild and the only way they could avoid starvation was to return to the land.'

Celeste emerged from the tunnel into the low-ceilinged library again. It felt almost claustrophobic after the astonishing airiness of the massive subterranean Temple. 'You should have been a history teacher,' she said to Cutie.

'God, no,' replied Cutie. 'Don't condemn me, please! Knowing all our accepted history is wrong and having to keep it quiet would send me mad. Besides, I hate kids!'

'You're still a child yourself,' growled Miserable Martha, still apparently smarting from being likened to a boring old biddy.

'No I'm not. I've recently acquired the vote, which I fully intend to use at the earliest opportunity. How could I not, having just expounded the virtues of democracy? I also have an IQ that's indecently high, three-quarters of a degree in classical languages and a deeper knowledge of truth than any university lecturer will ever have. That's why I dropped out of Oxford the moment Gaia and the Pythia sought me out and asked me to be the Guardian of the Temple. The youngest ever!' she added with swelling pride. 'But I couldn't do my job without my lovely Mama.' Cutie kissed Martha on each cheek and draped arms around her neck, hugging her affectionately, an action that brought some considerable embarrassment to the older woman. 'There's Celeste thinking I do all the work around here,' she said, 'when Mama's just as clever as I am, so I'll let her finish the story – she gets really grumpy when I don't let her say anything.'

Blushing furiously, Martha gently disentangled herself from Cutie's embrace, fumbled with her spectacles and, recovering from her discomfiture, struck a formal pose. She thought for a moment, then launched into her subject with barely disguised enthusiasm, a lively spark in her eye. 'The Lycians fought in the Trojan war where, no doubt, Helen first became aware of the matriarchal nature of their civilization. After the war, she and Hermione visited Lycia on a number of occasions and were so impressed they decided to base the embryonic Sisterhood there. On Midsummer's Eve, 1176 BC, they stood on the sands at Patara accompanied by matriarchs of all the major cities. Under the stars, these women formed the Sisterhood, its aim to avoid at all costs a repeat of the disaster of the Trojan War. Basically, they pledged themselves to try everything in their power to moderate the blind stupidity of men, to mitigate, deflect, ameliorate, call it what you will, the urge men have to destroy and kill each other. They would use their guile and persuasion to influence kings, princes and despots away from courses of conflict. At the same time, they would attempt to preserve knowledge as a hedge against any potential catastrophe.

They established the post of Gaia to lead the Sisterhood, the Pythia to advise and help the Gaia, and they immediately began recruiting from every region in the ancient world. We've been at it ever since,' she concluded with a shrug, 'and sadly, history has shown we've only been marginally successful.'

'Don't be modest, Mama,' chided Cutie. 'Yes, there have been many wars, but there would have been many, many more without us.'

'Cutie is right,' added Doreen. 'We've done much that can never be acknowledged and sometimes we even have to force an aggression to prevent a greater disaster, but normally we are able to effect changes more subtly, as I've been trying to do in Paraguay. Sadly, there have been untold wars and the human race has suffered enormously, but believe me, things could have been catastrophically worse had we not existed.'

'Curious, isn't it,' mused Cutie. 'Popular literature is awash with numerous adventure novels all about secret organisations and cabals, all evil, all run by men – and all entirely fictitious. The only one that actually exists is the Sisterhood, it's run entirely by women and it's been extraordinarily beneficial to all mankind for the last three millennia. Now, surely that tells you something, doesn't it?'

Celeste considered this and realised the two women were speaking from sure knowledge. It was a sobering thought. She sighed. 'This is too much,' she said quietly. 'I need tea, a breath of fresh air – and I need to think.'

They took their refreshments in the flower garden, sitting in the shade of an ornate arbour dripping in heavy clematis blooms. Bertie sat on the back of a chair, preening and chirping to himself happily. Doreen and Cutie respected Celeste's silence, watching as Martha tended to several beehives dotted about on the far side of the garden, her protective clothing making her look like Miss Havisham out on the pull. An industrious humming filled the air.

'You've got a lot of bees,' Celeste murmured.

'We make a lot of honey,' replied Doreen. 'Martha wants to give you a jar as a present.'

'Thank you. Bertie likes a spot of honey once in a while.'

'Yummy honey,' said Bertie. He closed his eyes and started to purr in contentment as Celeste stroked him absently. Eventually, she shook herself out of her reverie, dunked her biscuit and took a sip of tea.

'Better?' asked Cutie.

'Considerably.'

'Good. The custard creams help, don't they?'

'They do indeed. Excellent dunking biscuits.' She looked around at the beautifully tended garden. 'So who else lives here? These flowers don't grow on their own.'

'Jenny looks after the gardens and grows our vegetables. She's also a very good cook. Then there's me and Mama, Maggie the demon turf-tipper and Gaia's assistant, Sandra. She comes over at weekends because she's not getting any cock and has nothing better to do.'

'Oh, dear.'

'It's a source of amusement to us all.'

'And how many abroad?'

'Sisters are close to the powerful in just about every country in the world,' said Doreen. 'You know what they say – behind every man is a great woman. There's more truth in that than you can imagine. In all, there's about four hundred. Also, because of our long association with Turkey, our chief historian, Jodi Taylor, is currently overseeing the restoration of Patara, and a fine job she's doing as well. Jodi has induced the authorities to commence a reinstatement of the old pharos, the lighthouse at the entrance to the harbour. The Turks have only recently begun to appreciate their staggering archaeological heritage and, unlike in this country, where we merely preserve our ruins, they've adopted an enthusiastic policy of reconstructing their ancient buildings using all the original stones, most of which still lie where they fell. It's a remarkable programme and we're proud to be involved, albeit in our usual subtle manner.'

'The Lycians established their national assembly in Patara and a bouletarion was built there, next to the amphitheatre,' added Cutie.

'What the hell's a bouletarion?'

'A council building,' explained Doreen. 'It's like a smaller version of the main theatre, but a bit grander. The Lycian Federation met there to vote on the issues of the day, but it also doubled up as the venue for the new Sisterhood. It's lost its roof now, but you can still visit Patara and see the ruins. I've been there myself. Got some photos somewhere of Bernie pottering around. You and I will have to go. Even we have traditions, and each new Gaia is dedicated inside the bouletarion at Patara.'

'I can't go to Turkey!'

'Of course you can. We'll drive to Birmingham and jump on an Airbus! We'll have a great time. It was in Patara that the fledgling concepts of democracy and representation were established. Lovely, bountiful, rich, peaceful Lycia had already proved democracy could work, and the sisters went out to spread the message throughout the world.'

Cutie nodded. 'Its matriarchal society was dedicated to nurturing and caring. The Lycians were peaceful unless threatened, strong in defence, generous in spirit, just in law and fair in judgement. We know all this today because the Sisterhood had long established itself at the heart of their society and our records are very clear – you can read them yourself if your Lycian and ancient Greek are up to scratch.'

'I'm hungry,' announced Bertie to no one in particular. It was one of his regular general requests for comestibles.

'There's some fruit in the kitchen,' said Martha, joining them. 'What does he eat?'

'Ask him yourself,' replied Celeste. 'Use simple words and you'll probably get a response.'

'Simple words?'

'Yes. Monosyllabic.' She paused, a mischievous twinkle in her eye. 'I've been led to believe you're good at Scrabble, Martha, so I'm sure you can think of a few.' She winked at Cutie, who was trying desperately to stifle her giggles at Mama's sudden discomfort. The situation appeared to be causing some considerable confusion for Martha. She glanced at Doreen, perhaps hoping for a word of encouragement from her Gaia, but all Doreen did was raise an eyebrow fractionally. Cutie, helpfully, slapped Martha hard between the shoulder-blades and she stumbled forward, suddenly finding herself face to face with the big macaw. Bertie regarded her with what could only be described as a withering stare.

'Bertie?' she asked, somewhat querulously.

'Yes,' came the response. 'I'm Bertie. Who are you?'

'I'm Martha.'

'Oh. Jolly good.' This was a new phrase for Bertie. He'd been waiting for the appropriate moment to use it. This seemed the time. It was delivered with all the haughty disdain of a dowager duchess encountering an unhygienic gentleman of the road while out walking her pompadoured Pekingese.

'Do you want some fruit?'

Bertie recognised the words and their pleasurable consequence. Perhaps this old grey woman was nice after all. Wilf was nice. He was old and grey as well. Perhaps this was something common to all old and grey people. He thought for a moment, then said, 'Yes.' There was another short pause. 'Please,' he added, remembering his manners.

'Not pears,' advised Celeste. 'Definitely not pears!'

'I think we have some apples and bananas.'

'Thank you, that will be fine.' Martha scuttled off to the kitchens, relieved to have survived the short interview.

'Mummy?'

171

'Yes, my love.'

'Fly?'

'Yes.'

With permission granted, Bertie leapt up and, with a powerful sweep of his wings, soared away over the gables. The conversation had been too quick and complex for him to understand so, with boredom setting in, he decided to explore while waiting for his food. The Hall swung around beneath him, surrounded by its fertile, kaleidoscopic gardens. The rounded hill covering the Temple was dotted with snoozing sheep. Another building nearby took his interest and he swooped in for a closer look. A pentagonal folly housed the primary mirror for the Temple's peerless lighting system. Visible only from the air, the structure was subtly camouflaged from prying eyes by a thick ring of holly trees.

Bertie took it all in. This was a very pretty place. The trees reminded him of the jungle back in Brazil. Not quite as dense, of course, but quite acceptable nonetheless – and the sun above was most agreeably warm on his back. He floated on air both warm and sweetly scented, drifting at leisure, then saw the old lady returning with fruit. He descended in a stately manner to land on the back of his chair again in a rush of air, then sidled up to the bowl and got stuck into an apple, trilling happily to himself as he peeled off the skin. Yes, perhaps she wasn't so bad after all.

Celeste stroked him gently. She stared around at the Hall and its exquisite gardens. 'How on earth do you pay for all this? Sorry to bring up something so mundane as money, but I just can't see how it's done.'

'Well, for a start we don't pay any salaries,' said Cutie, 'which is why Gaia still owns her own hairdressing salon. This is a vocation, not a career. Also, in an organization as old as ours, we have accrued substantial resources over the centuries by the simple process of natural accumulation – if you invested a few pounds each year starting at the end of the English Civil War then the compound interest over the best part of four hundred years would now make it many hundreds of thousands of pounds. In addition, the Home Farm attached to Temple Hall has always been extremely profitable, so that takes care of our everyday needs and gives us all a share of the surplus at the end of the year. None of us need much to live on. Our board and lodgings are free, the food is home grown and there's always the Pythia's betting tips to top up the kitty, keeping me in clothes and paying for Mama's weekly lessons at Grumpy College!'

Doreen gave Celeste a speculative glance. 'All these questions. Yes, I can understand your desire to know more, but I think you've been procrastinating. There's one question you haven't asked, yet it's the most important.'

Celeste nodded. She felt a growing admiration and respect for this Doreen. 'Why now?' she asked.

'Because we have to help you fight this conspiracy. You're family now, Celeste, and we protect our own. That attack on James was just the beginning. You and Bertie are now also under immediate threat and we can't allow that. You're too important, and not just to us. Your husband is on the verge of changing the political landscape of this country – and for the better. That process has to continue at all costs and this will be the only chance we have of stopping those who oppose him. Do not underestimate how far they'll go to preserve their influence and fortunes.

'There is also a danger to the Sisterhood. Should these men achieve their goal, then our influence in this country will be severely diminished. Left unchecked, who knows what catastrophes these idiots will lead us into. Consequences could ripple out across the world, setting us back for decades. There's a lot at stake here, Celeste, and we will do our best to help. Our resources may seem scanty, but my girls all punch above their weight, as you will find out when you're Gaia. However, it also appears we have a champion.' Doreen pointed at Bertie, who sat on the back of the chair opposite the table and watched proceedings with his usual lively attention, the half-eaten apple still in one claw.

'Hello,' he chirped conversationally, aware that he had suddenly become the centre of attention. 'Buy one, get one free!'

'Maggie's quite certain. Bertie has an absolutely vital role to play in all this, even though it's obvious we don't know what that role is precisely.'

'Bertie!' exclaimed Celeste, finally descending into a splendid state of total confusion.

'Yes. Bizarre, isn't it. Somehow, somewhere, and very soon, something is going to happen that only Bertie can resolve, and if he fails, it seems certain this resurgence in democracy, your life with James – and our legacy – will be utterly destroyed!'

Two hundred yards away, hidden in a copse, the man watched through field glasses. My, this target got about. All these locations she was visiting. This place was something else, mind you. Very pretty – but also nicely isolated. Miller would be tactically interested in that, but not as interested as knowing exactly why she and the bird were here. Something was definitely going on at this Hall.

His notebook was filling up fast.

CHAPTER TWELVE

'Where the hell have you been?' ground out Wilf as Celeste breezed through the front door, Bertie waddling along beside her, chattering happily to himself.

'At the hairdressers, where else – and I'll thank you not to take that tone with me,' she said primly.

'With Bertie?'

'Of course not. I found him perched in a tree down the lane. Didn't you notice he was gone?'

'I – er, well, he may have given me the slip.'

'I warned you about leaving windows open. Didn't do a very good job, did you. Fine minder you turned out to be, letting my baby roam around outside on his own. If I didn't know better, I'd say you fell asleep.'

'Um … I might have dozed for a while,' admitted Wilf with, it has to be said, a hangdog expression of guilt.

'Wilf, I'm disappointed. Surely you're not so old you need to have a catnap every afternoon.'

'I am certainly not,' he replied indignantly, then regarded her with a narrowed expression. She was uncharacteristically calm. Experience had taught Wilf that when it came to Bertie, Celeste veered towards passionate, to say the least. 'Have you been somewhere?' he asked suspiciously. 'Somewhere without me? You've been gone a long time.'

'Of course I've been somewhere. I visited the bank, shopped a little and had a coffee. I've spent the rest of my time at the hairdressers. Honestly, Wilf, you can tell you're not married. Any husband will tell you this is a serious business.'

'Anywhere else?' he probed. Her explanation, although reasonable, was not entirely satisfactory. Wilf had been around for long enough to sense when something didn't add up. For her part, Celeste was determined not to lie. Wilf deserved more, but there was no chance she would ever tell him of her trip to Temple Hall. She suddenly began to realise the enormity of the responsibility Doreen had laid on her and its implications with regard to her personal relationships. The thought of keeping this from James did not sit comfortably.

'You have to understand it takes me longer at the salon than most. I have my image to maintain.' She tossed her head in the manner she'd seen on those black and white shampoo adverts where moody models smouldered in wild and windswept locations, then threw in a generous amount of pouting for good measure. 'And you haven't even complimented me on my hair.'

Wilf sighed heavily, admitting defeat. 'It looks very nice,' he said wearily.

'Too late,' she sniffed. 'You had your chance.'

'Get that, would you, Wilf,' called Celeste from the depths of the cottage. 'Might be someone you recognise.'

Wilf considered this highly unlikely as he put down his newspaper, levered his lanky frame off the sofa and went to the front door. He was still in the doghouse from the previous day, but whether for letting Bertie escape or for not noticing her hair was difficult to tell. He knew precisely no one in Gloucestershire so had little confidence this situation was likely to change. 'All right, I'm coming,' he muttered in response to another heavy knock. 'Keep your hair on.'

If only he had been able to follow his own advice.

'Hello, Wilf. It's been a while.'

Wilf gaped, then grinned with delight. 'Colin! This is a surprise.'

Colin Kynes pumped his hand enthusiastically, a happy

smile splitting his narrow, restless face. 'How the devil are you? Still catching crims?'

'Fine and yes, or at least for the next few days.'

'Retirement, eh. Good man.'

'Not particularly happy about it, but there isn't a lot I can do.'

'You'll survive,' replied Colin unsympathetically. 'Great to see you again. Lovely place, isn't it?'

'Very nice,' agreed Wilf. Best keep his real reasons for visiting quiet. 'What on earth are you doing here?'

'It's a regular trip for me. And for her,' Colin added, stepping aside to reveal a large cage supported on a wheeled frame. Inside, haughty and aloof as ever, sat a magnificent hyacinth macaw.

'Milly?'

'That's right.'

'You're not going to bend my ear again, are you?' asked Wilf cautiously. He had first-hand experience of just how acid-tongued Colin could be, particularly when some randy bird flies in and vigorously shags his prize virgin macaw.

'Not this time, Wilf, but you may remember what I said to you at the time.'

'If I recall correctly – and I do – you said quite a lot of things to me, some of which could have got you arrested.'

'Yeah, well, I was angry.'

'You don't say. I'd never have guessed, and were you upset because hyacinths mate for life and that Bertie and princess here had tied the matrimonial knot? Till death do us part.'

'I was, they do, and yes, and as a result I have to bring Milly here for regular spells of love leave.'

'So Bertie's a dad.'

'Twice over. She and Bertie have been good parents and the chicks are strong and healthy. We're hoping for a third this year, which is why we're here.'

'Why doesn't she just come and live here with Bertie?

asked Wilf, helping Colin to wheel the cumbersome cage into the lounge.

'The zoo authorities won't allow it. Milly is far too valuable a specimen to simply give away. Besides, she's become a bit of a celebrity herself as a result of her association with Bertie, boosting attendance to the aviaries at Regent's Park.'

'Milly!' Bertie scampered into the room, his claws clicking on the old oak floorboards. He squawked discordantly, head bobbing, calling out happily.

'Dogger,' announced Milly in a distinct voice. 'Moderate or good, occasionally poor.'

Whether this was a comment on Bertie's performance was not clear. 'Never mind,' he replied.

'Hello, Colin. Lovely to see you again.' Celeste appeared, kissed the slightly embarrassed aviarist on the cheek and turned her attention to the cage. 'Hello, Milly, how are you?' She opened the cage door and drew Milly out on her wrist. Milly's claws were considerably smaller and less needle-tipped than Bertie's, but she was careful nonetheless. Milly was still quite capable of drawing blood. She was deposited on top of her cage and stroked affectionately.

'Shall we, gentlemen? Tea in the kitchen, I think. Let's give these two a little privacy. From past experience, this shouldn't take long,' she added wryly. The kitchen was typically country cottage, with a stone flagged floor and old-fashioned oak cabinets. An Aga the size of Doncaster dominated the room. Some of Celeste's unique mementoes had made the trip from London, including, perched up on a shelf, Brazilian Big Boy and his unfeasibly engorged fertility phallus. Wilf smirked. Now, there was a bloke who could boast proper wood!

They sat around the table listening to the muffled sounds of raucous squawking coming through the closed door. Bertie was doing his ten-second thing again. Celeste brewed and handed around the dunkers. Digestives. Plain ones. The supreme dunking biscuit, requiring skill to prevent soggy collapse, yet unsurpassed in texture and taste. The little ritual was held in silence, but much appreciated by all.

'Where's James?' asked Colin eventually.

'He's tied up in London,' replied Celeste, 'and before you ask, I had nothing to do with it this time. He's got an important vote in the House tomorrow afternoon.'

'Still observing the will of the people.'

'Absolutely.'

'I'm full of admiration. Wish we had an MP like him.'

'Well, Colin, if you feel that strongly about it why don't you stand at the next election. All it'll cost you is the deposit. You could join my husband's little band of rebels. What's your constituency?'

'Chipping Barnet.'

'That would make you a CHIMP.'

'Perhaps not,' he chuckled.

'Will you be staying long? You're welcome to join us for dinner.'

'I'd love to, Celeste, but I have to get back to work. I've an unwell military macaw that needs some TLC.'

'How long will Milly be with us this time?'

'We can spare her for a week if that's OK with you, although judging by the post-coital silence, I might as well take her home now.'

'At least give them some time together. Bertie does enjoy her visits. Well, he does most of the time, but I don't think it's wise to leave her any longer.'

'Why? Does he get fed up with her conversation?' asked Wilf, smiling.

'Yes!' replied Celeste and Colin simultaneously.

Miller drove up and down the lane, checking out the old timber-framed building partially hidden amongst the trees to supplement the information he'd downloaded in London. He loved these new mapping apps. As a cautious man, he'd always appreciated the importance of good information, but visiting a location vicariously was still no substitute for giving it a good old eyeball. Having pretended to visit the church next door, he now had a good idea of the lie of the land. He parked the nondescript Transit nearby, tucking it under the branches of an old chestnut overhanging the modest church car park. He got out and had a look around. Birds chirped happily in the hedges, a squirrel bounced across the road, tractors rumbled in the distance. Quite a change from London. There was no one in sight so he crept across Buttercup's field, slipped through the stile in the hedge and secreted himself in a furry part of Timbrill's garden, flitting from bush to bush. The cottage was less than fifty yards away across a striped lawn. He hunkered down behind a tree and peeped around the trunk, confident his camo gear made him virtually invisible.

He'd picked his time carefully. With Timbrill at Westminster for the vote tomorrow, the only occupant of the house should have been his wife. She of the eccentric sexuality. Never liked leather much, had Miller, apart from a good pair of gloves to protect the knuckles when fighting, of course. However, there was an unexpected vehicle in the driveway, a small van. He knew ginger's car would be there, but the presence of this other had not been expected. Still, he was a seasoned expert in field surveillance and refused to panic. Back to the trunk, relaxed and resting on his haunches, he pulled out his smartphone, scrolled to games and opened *Katapult Kanaries – The Yellow Peril*. He thought this an appropriate way to while away the time, considering the task in hand. Three figures could be seen through the kitchen window. Too many to tackle. Patience, my boy, he told himself. Give it half an hour. See what happens. Country folk are always popping in and out to borrow a cup of sugar. Why the hell they couldn't just put sugar on their shopping lists like everyone else was a mystery to

Miller. Unless it's a rural euphemism, of course. He pondered on that while running up a decent score on his game. Presently, Miller heard the van engine start. He glanced around the trunk and saw it crunch down the gravel drive and accelerate away along the lane.

One down, two to go. That's more like it.

Miller was a resourceful man. He'd been around a bit. Actually, he'd been around quite a lot. Mostly with the SAS, more recently on his own. He had a unique set of skills which, once he'd served time and been dishonourably discharged from the army for the attempted murder of a superior officer, had proven most attractive to certain employers in the private sector. Employers like Netheridge, for instance. Miller had taken to post-military life like a duck to water. The pay was great and as long as he remained discreet, he soon found he could get away with just about anything, but he never forgot his training. How to avoid FISHing, for instance. Fighting In Someone's House, to use the accepted army acronym. He could still do it if absolutely necessary, and always carried a lead-filled sap and blade for that purpose, but preferred not to if possible. Fortunately, those psychos up at Credenhill had taught him all manner of ways to persuade people out of a house without resorting to violence.

He paused his game and pulled another phone from his pocket. Unlike his own sophisticated, top-of-the-range mobile, this was a cheap, well-worn, no-frills phone, much used and, in the relentlessly advancing world of mobile telecommunications, about as ancient as the dinosaurs. For God's sake, it even had funny little bumps below the screen called buttons. Miller didn't care about that. All that concerned him was the unused pay-as-you-go SIM card inside. He always carried a number of these tatty old phones, all paid for in cash. He used each to make just one totally untraceable call, then threw it away. He remembered buying this one from a car boot sale in Huddersfield. He'd haggled hard and eventually got it for a pound. Bargain!

He tapped in a number. Faintly, muted by distance, he heard the phone ring in the cottage. Here we go. 'Mrs Timbrill?' he enquired in a cultured voice. 'My name is Dr Lucius Lancer. I'm calling from Cheltenham A&E Department. Do you know a Mrs Glynis Badham? Oh, good. Well, I'm sorry to say she's been admitted with a broken leg and concussion. Yes, a hit and run in town, an out-of-control mobility scooter apparently. She's a little delirious, but has been calling for you. Can you come immediately? Excellent, that's very kind of you, Mrs Timbrill. Please ask for me when you get to reception.'

There, that should do it. He removed the SIM card and stabbed it deep into the soft soil at the base of the tree, then threw the old mobile into the farthest corner of the hedge. He went back to his own smartphone and resumed playing *Katapult Kanaries* for a few minutes. Yes, that was surely the front door slamming. He peered around the trunk and saw Celeste get into her car. The other man didn't. He waved her off and disappeared back into the cottage. The car slid down the drive and away past the church.

'Damn,' muttered Miller. Bloody locals – haven't they got their own homes to go to? He thought for a moment, then shrugged. 'Oh, well, looks like I'll have to do this the old-fashioned way.' Miller liked the old-fashioned way. It always included violence. He was a man who enjoyed a spot of vigorous physical confrontation, especially when he knew the measure of his opponent. The man was tall and thin, much older than him, a bald, morose streak of misery. Miller immediately dismissed him as a local. They all looked so sodding weird. He should have just taken his cup of sugar and buggered off. Now the lanky old fool was going to get a headache. He saved his play, pocketed the phone and, emerging from the bushes, took a good look in every direction. With the coast clear, he strolled nonchalantly around the side of the house to the back door.

If you're going to assault and kidnap, do it in style.

The door was inevitably unlocked. He just loved rural folk. They were so trusting. He eased it open silently, waited a few seconds just in case, then padded into the kitchen, heavy sap in hand. A newspaper rustled in the next room. Miller closed in on the sound like a seagull homing in on an abandoned fish and chip supper. The man had his back to the door. Miller ghosted forward and tapped him on the back of the neck with the sap. He knew exactly how hard to hit someone, having done it many times before, and the man collapsed with a sighing grunt, falling into his open newspaper before sliding gracefully to the floor like an unset grey blancmange, face down, knees tucked up and arse pointing to the beamed ceiling.

'Exemplary! Give yourself a Mars Bar,' murmured Miller proudly. That was a perfectly executed blow. He waited for any repercussions, but the cottage remained silent. The only witness watched, but said nothing. Bingo! Miller knew he'd have no difficulty identifying his target and so it proved. A substantial bird cage stood beside the fireplace on a wheeled supporting frame, its wire door open – and beside it perched a large blue macaw.

A very large blue macaw.

Miller baulked for a moment. 'Jeez,' he murmured softly, 'you're big.' The two eyed each other up for a moment, then Miller tried the universally accepted approach. 'Who's a pretty boy, then,' he cooed soothingly, clicking his fingers. The bird considered this in aloof silence, then uttered one word.

'Biscay!'

Miller didn't have the time for social niceties. He drifted forward, increasingly aware of the size of his target and, keeping an eye on its claws, then lunged, grabbed it unceremoniously around the neck and swiftly stuffed it into the cage with little ceremony, thankful for his leather gloves. The bird squawked in loud indignation, wings flapping, but he ignored its shrill protest. A violet feather fluttered to the carpet in the struggle, saving him the trouble of plucking the damned thing. He picked up the feather and, taking a plastic bag from his jacket pocket, extracted a forensically clean note using disposable tweezers.

A careful man, was Miller.

Both were laid on the kitchen table. Miller liked a touch of the dramatic and with a violent downward sweep, stabbed feather and note to the table with Celeste's best Japanese boning knife. His favourite way to leave a message. He retrieved the Transit and reversed up the drive, then rolled the cage to the front door, bumped it over the sill and manhandled it into the back of the Transit, struggling a little with its weight and bulk. The double doors slammed, he strapped himself in and drove away in a manner entirely unsuspicious.

That was easy.

Had he bothered to look back at the cottage, he would have seen another blue bird watching from the bedroom window.

Bertie started out of a light snooze, aware of noises downstairs. Mummy must be home, he thought, and stretched a wing lazily. He'd been basking in a pool of bright sunshine on his favourite window ledge, the only spot in the house where he actually felt as warm as he'd done in Brazil all those years ago. Now, there was a country that knew a thing or two about heat. And trees. And rain. Yes, lots of rain. It rained out there almost as much as it did here in this chilly land.

He cocked his head to one side. Surely that was Milly squawking. She didn't sound at all happy. Odd, considering the circumstances. They'd mated not an hour ago and she seemed pretty happy then. Mind you, she could have been faking it. Bertie had been around humans long enough and seen sufficient TV to understand the unsettling concept of faking it. He also knew she was twenty-five years his junior, but he'd always known she liked the older, more mature macaw. Having never had a mate before, Bertie had no real experience in these matters to make comparison, but he had to admit that she appeared much more willing nowadays than she had done at their first encounter. That little incident at the zoo must have come as a hell of a shock. In public as well. He'd played to an audience that day. Sadly, her meteorological obsession remained unchanged, hence his preference for a little quiet post-humping reflection up on the bedroom window ledge.

Now alert, Bertie was about to hop down and scamper off to investigate when he heard another squawk. Distance dulled the call, but that one definitely sounded like a cry for help. He became aware of the distinctive rattle of Milly's cage as it trundled over gravel outside and peered back through the window. To his amazement, he saw a strange man sliding Milly's cage into the back of a van. She looked up and caught Bertie's eye even as the doors slammed shut. Moments later, the van made off down the lane.

A wave of agitation swept over Bertie. That shouldn't have happened. Mummy and Sparrow Man from the zoo had promised Milly would be staying for some days. His concern grew swiftly. He half-hopped, half-fluttered down the stairs and scampered into the lounge, but there was something very wrong with Wilf. He knew how people were supposed to sleep. They lay down flat and made funny rasping noises with their mouths open. Daddy was especially good at this. However, Wilf was propped against the sofa, his rear end skywards, his face squashed flat against the rug. Now, that didn't look comfortable at all. Something was very wrong here. Bertie chirruped in an attempt to wake him, but there was no response. He tickled an ear with the tip of his bill. Again, nothing. Perhaps this needed something a little more vigorous, so he tugged hard on a wisp of hair and squawked in surprise when it came loose in his beak. He felt an intense pang of guilt. Wilf's plumage was exceedingly sparse at the best of times and now he'd pulled out a large percentage of what little remained.

Obviously, Wilf was dead. That was an unsettling thought. Maybe that's why he hadn't helped Milly. Bertie knew Wilf would have stopped the strange man if he could, but he hadn't. Because he was dead. And now even balder. Pity. Bertie had really liked Wilf, but he had no time to mourn. Milly had called for help. She was his mate. He had to do something. With Celeste nowhere to be seen and Wilf now dead, the moment for action had arrived – and Bertie was the sort of macaw who understood the need for action. Time was of the essence and he needed to get after Milly, so he stuffed the plucked strands of hair under the sofa cushion – just in case there was a slim chance Wilf was still alive and he needed to hide the evidence – then scuttled into the kitchen and, heading for the back door, nosed open Sebastian's cat flap. Finally, that damned animal had proved useful. He squeezed his bulk through and, once outside, immediately took to the air. Like a huge blue bomber, Bertie banked around the side of the house in a flash of azure, gained height and set off in hot pursuit of the van.

CHAPTER THIRTEEN

Bertie could be a determined flyer when occasion called and swiftly made up the distance, closing in steadily on the back of the van. He tucked himself in close, slipstreaming in its wake, coasting along, conserving his energy. He had no idea where he was, but he knew he had to stay with Milly. Fortunately, the van avoided the big roads and soon turned on to a smaller lane, slowing significantly as it negotiated its way between tall hedgerows.

Miller drove casually, neither speeding nor dawdling. As an accomplished field operative, he knew what he had to do to blend in, to pass invisibly amongst people, to avoid arousing the interest of the police. Especially to avoid arousing the police. The secret was simple. Act normally. Drive normally. Why so many criminals were unable to understand this was quite beyond him, but then again most of them were not very bright. British prisons were full of not very bright people. He had no plans to join them.

A careful man, was Miller.

He was pleased that the macaw behind him remained docile and silent. The lane ahead narrowed even further. Grass made an appearance, a green stripe down the middle of the worn tarmac. You certainly don't see that in London. He glanced in the mirrors to check he was not being followed and immediately stamped on the brake.

'What the hell!' he muttered. The merest flash of blue had caught his eye. Twisting around, he checked the cage. It was still occupied. The macaw glared at him. Without hesitating, he leapt from the van. He knew what he'd seen, but it was impossible – the cage was still firmly locked. Miller walked to the back of the van and peered around the corner, a hand on the haft of his knife. Nothing. He circumvented the vehicle completely. Still nothing. Then he did so again in the opposite direction. He even climbed up to have a look on the roof and got down on his hands and knees to peer underneath. Again, he drew a complete blank. He examined the hedges on either side of the lane and then stood for a full minute listening, but heard only the tick of cooling metal and the usual rural symphony of insects, husbandry, birds and wind. Still not entirely satisfied, he finally got back in and drove away. He could have sworn on his mother's grave he'd seen another blue bird following close behind, but he was very definitely on his own. Warily, and looking in his mirrors frequently, he started off again.

Had he been bothered to climb to the topmost branches of the nearest tree, he'd have come face to face with an angry macaw.

Presently, Miller turned down a rough track which ended in a small collection of dilapidated, lichen-stained farm buildings arranged around a small yard. Rusty agricultural machinery cluttered one corner. He parked the van and reconnoitred, still disturbed by the inexplicable appearance of another blue bird. The buildings were deserted. There shouldn't be anyone around. He'd arranged with the farmer to rent the yard, paying handsomely in cash to keep the man away. No questions were asked, none were answered. They both understood each other perfectly. The farmer didn't give a toss once he had his money. Miller was entirely confident he had the place to himself, but he was still a cautious man and spent ten minutes or so walking from building to building before unloading Milly and wheeling the cage into an old barn.

Bertie watched from a nearby tree, well hidden behind the trunk. A pair of elderly thrushes hopped up to say hello and generally fuss over their guest. It wasn't often something huge and blue dropped by for a chat. Did he want to stop for tea? They were most insistent. Bertie declined politely, having never really developed a taste for snails and earthworms. He had a much more refined, sophisticated palate. Pears in particular, but his mum only allowed those on special occasions. Unsurprising considering the way they accelerated his digestive transit.

The thrushes fluttered off, allowing him to return to the task in hand. There was no movement for a long time so he dropped from the tree and glided across the field, scant inches from the soil, homing in on the cluster of buildings. He found a quiet corner and peered in through a dirty window. No one was in sight. He tried another barn. Again it was deserted, but the third came up trumps. A tile had slipped near the ridge of the roof. Bertie stuck his head in and peered around. Down below, he saw Milly in her cage. The man was there as well. He showed no sign of departing and sat on a bale of hay peering intently at his phone.

Bertie was not stupid. He knew it would be impossible to release Milly from her cage while the man was sitting beside her, so slipped inside the roof, glided silently to a distant rafter and, receding into the darkest corner, settled himself down to wait. He hoped something would happen soon. He was already feeling peckish. Suddenly, snails and earthworms seemed almost appetising.

Almost.

'Well that was a complete waste of time,' muttered Celeste angrily, stilettos clattering through the front door. 'There was no such doctor at the hospital. Wilf? You there? Fallen asleep again, have you?' She walked into the lounge to find Wilf as Miller had left him: face buried in the rug, knees drawn up, bottom pointing to the ceiling. 'You really should try dozing off in a more traditional position. Wilf? Are you all right?' She knelt and shook him gently. His precarious point of balance disturbed, he collapsed like an unwanted 1960s tower block. Celeste saw the ugly swelling below one ear and caught her breath. 'Wilf!' she cried, shaking him urgently. 'Wake up!' To her profound relief, he groaned, the sound distant and vague. His eyes fluttered open. 'Come on, Wilf, speak to me.'

'Wh – what?'

'Lie still. Don't try to get up. I'll get some water.'

Wilf's head throbbed so hard he thought he was going to pass out again. He rarely suffered headaches, even after sinking enough beers to mellow an entire rugby team, but this one was a corker. What the hell had happened? He remembered checking his stars in the paper, then – nothing. He touched the base of his skull and hissed with pain on finding the tender lump so obligingly left there by Miller. Now he knew what had happened. He levered himself into a sitting position and accepted the glass from Celeste, washing away the dusty taste of Axminster. He felt better immediately. The scrambled cogs of his mind began to spin again. 'I'm OK. Honest,' he said in answer to her concerned look.

'You don't sound OK. I'm calling the doctor.'

'For this? No.'

'Don't play the hard man with me, Detective Sergeant.' Celeste was not in the mood for heroics. 'You've been knocked unconscious. That's dangerous at any age, let alone yours.'

'Thanks, but I'm not that old – nor thin-skinned.'

'Well, I'm still worried.'

'It's not me you should be worried about.'

'What do you mean?'

'Did you find that doctor? No, of course you didn't. With you off to Cheltenham on a wild goose chase, that just left me to deal with,' said Wilf quietly. He stood, swaying unsteadily, holding on to the sofa for support and rubbing his neck gingerly. 'Someone wanted us out of the way.' He glanced around. 'Where's Milly?'

'What do you mean?'

'Where's the cage?'

Celeste spun and stared at the empty spot where Milly's cage had stood. 'Oh, no,' she whispered.

'What about Bertie?'

If Wilf thought Celeste was upset before, he really knew she was now. The blood drained from her face, her eyes widened.

'Bertie!' she called urgently. 'Are you here? Come to me, my darling.'

An ominous silence filled the cottage. Wilf staggered into the hall and headed for the front door. 'Search every room,' he ordered over his shoulder. 'I'll check outside.'

The cottage wasn't exactly Blenheim Palace. It didn't take them long to confirm both macaws were missing. Celeste, ashen-faced and visibly trembling, pointed at the kitchen table. Wilf followed her finger to the impaled note and feather. The blade was driven deep into the soft pine. Whoever did this was strong.

The note was short and explicit. *The parrot is mine. Call the police and you'll never see him again. You will be contacted.*

'Printed, not hand-written,' muttered Wilf, his long expertise coming into play automatically, shouldering aside the last vestiges of grogginess. 'This is virtually untraceable unless the actual ink-jet cartridge can be found. If these people are in any way professional – and it looks like they are – then the cartridge has already been destroyed. The paper is standard photocopy quality, probably pulled at random from a new ream. There won't be any fingerprints.'

Celeste examined the blue feather carefully and saw a speck of blood staining the quill tip. 'It's not Bertie's,' she finally said, unsure whether to be happy or sad. 'This is a body feather and the colour's too pale. Bertie's feathers are darker, more violet. This comes from Milly.'

'And the blood?'

'Definitely pulled out, either in a struggle or simply plucked. No doubt about it. A feather that drops naturally does not have blood on it.'

'I would imagine that's painful.'

'How would you feel if someone grabbed a handful of your hair and ripped it out?'

Wilf explored the sparse fringe still clinging to the back of his head and found a raw patch. 'Actually, come to think of it…'

But Celeste wasn't listening. She recovered fast. Doreen would have heartily approved. 'Ruined my bloody knife, as well,' she muttered. Her mind focused, she looked around the room, examining it with detective eyes. Well, she was standing next to Wilf, after all. 'Then that call was designed to get me out of the house.'

'No doubt about it.'

'How did they get our number? We're ex-directory.'

'Someone has done their research. They also knew Mrs Badham worked here and that she doesn't have a mobile phone.' Glynis's suspicion of technology was common knowledge around the village. Except for vacuum cleaners. She loved vacuum cleaners.

'Can you trace the number?'

'I won't even bother trying. Anyone smart enough to lure you away so easily would have used a pay-as-you-go disposable mobile. That'll be a dead end, believe me. The phone will already be in some ditch or the river.'

'Whoever sent me to Cheltenham must also have been watching the house. They waited for Colin to leave.'

'Undoubtedly. It must have come as a disappointment to discover I'd stayed behind. Forced their hand. Whoever did this also knew how to knock me out. Never happened before in all my years as a policeman in London, then I come down here to the so-called peaceful countryside and get my brains bludgeoned out. I'm telling you straight, woman, it's not safe being around you.'

'Why won't people just leave me alone,' she sighed

sadly. 'All I want is some peace and quiet.'

'You'll get none of that while you're married to James. He's obviously upset some powerful and ruthless people. This is their response to his dumping their cash on a bag lady.'

Celeste had already come to the same conclusion. She had no doubt this was a political manoeuvre, a measure designed to bring pressure on James via herself, but she now knew this also affected Doreen and the Sisterhood. They understood the ramifications and were deeply concerned their moderating influence would be undermined by these conspirators, so concerned they'd revealed their existence to Celeste before calmly announcing she would be their next leader. She felt overwhelmed. She'd started off that morning with just a hairdressing appointment to look forward to and by tea time had been inducted into an ancient organisation of global influence and thrust into a struggle against an unseen enemy of deadly intent.

The family Timbrill had led gloriously uneventful lives for two years, then crises came at them in squadrons.

Great, just what she needed. As if her life wasn't complicated enough already, she now had another major problem on her hands and, unfortunately for Doreen, the safety of Bertie was far more important to Celeste than the welfare and stability of the rest of the planet. 'What's puzzling me is why the cage has gone as well as both macaws. One bird in one cage I can understand, but not two.'

'Do you think it's possible to put both birds in the one cage?' he asked.

'You won't get Bertie in a cage without incurring severe physical harm or possible loss of limb.'

Wilf reviewed his extensive knowledge of the macaw and came to the same conclusion. 'I haven't seen any severed ears scattered about the place, so I think we can discount that.' He pursed his lips in thought, staring at the

193

note and looking around the lounge again. 'Here's what I think. Milly's been taken, which explains the feather, the note and the missing cage, but whoever did this must have thought they had Bertie. Now, here's the interesting part. I think Bertie's followed them. It's the sort of daft, heroic thing he'd do. Remember how he chased off Pritchard and Coberley?'

'All too well, and then got himself hopelessly lost in the process.'

'I don't think he's lost. That cage is bulky, much too big for a car, so whoever's done this must have had a van like Colin's at the very least, and a van's big and easy enough to follow on the wing. One thing puzzles me, though.'

'The cat flap,' replied Celeste, reading Wilf's mind. 'He uses it all the time.'

'Ah, I did wonder.'

'Oh, crap,' she said suddenly. 'We have to tell Colin. Hell, how do we tell Colin?'

'We tell him the truth,' said Wilf firmly. 'The sooner the better,' he added pointedly, holding out his hand. Celeste handed over her mobile. Wilf scrolled through the contacts.

'Hello, Colin?'

'Celeste? You got a cold?'

'No, obviously it's not Celeste. It's Wilf. Why, do you think she sounds like me?' he said sarcastically, his sour nature never far below the surface.

'Hardly. What's up? How are the lovebirds getting on?' Colin was using a hands-free set as he drove back down the M4 heading towards London.

'There's no easy way to say this, Colin, so I'll just come out with it. Milly's gone.'

There was an ominous silence. 'What?' Colin's tone was truly glacial. Inhabitants of the toasty part of hell started reaching for their anoraks. 'What?' he said again, his voice rising an octave. Or two! 'What the f –'

194

'I think we need to look at the positive, here,' interrupted Wilf, keen to move the conversation forward – and equally as anxious to prevent a serious road traffic accident – but Colin wasn't having any of it. The conversation was remaining exactly where it was.

'What's positive?' he screamed. 'Exactly what part of this can be described as positive? Jesus H. Christ, Wilf, what the bloody hell have you done?'

'I've done nothing,' protested Wilf. 'Celeste's house has been burgled. Both Milly and Bertie are gone.'

'Bertie! Gone!' howled Colin. 'Two of the most biologically robust and prolific members of our breeding programme! Gone! Have you any idea of the consequences if both birds are lost? We could be looking at eventual species extinction.'

'He's not calming down, is he?' whispered Celeste. Wilf held the phone away from his ear to prevent his cochlea from vaporizing. He'd been here before. Experience had taught him that Colin liked to vent himself. Spectacularly. Small man, big temper. Any copper will tell you it's always the small men who cause the biggest problems.

'He does seem a trifle upset,' agreed Wilf. 'I'll give him another thirty seconds, see if there's any improvement.'

'No,' replied Celeste. 'Give me the phone. Colin, I need you to stop shouting,' she said firmly. 'It's not helping. No one is more upset than I am at the loss of Milly and Bertie.'

'I doubt it,' hissed Keynes. Wilf winced. Even without speakerphone he could still hear the aviarist clearly – and that was the wrong thing to say.

'Colin – that's hurtful and unjustified.' Celeste's voice wavered. 'I expect better from you.'

There was a significant pause. 'You're right, Celeste. I'm sorry, that was an uncalled-for remark.'

'Thank you, apology accepted. Now, what measures do

you take to protect such valuable birds?'

'She's ringed, of course, but without the cage, we're in the dark.'

'Hold on, what do you mean, without the cage?'

'Well, when you said the birds are gone I assumed the cage is still parked in your lounge.'

'No, we think Milly's in her cage and Bertie's gone after her.'

There was a silence, eventually broken by an odd strangling sound. 'Are you having a heart attack?' asked Celeste. She glanced at Wilf. 'It sounds like he's having a coronary.' Like Wilf, she was fearful for those sharing the same part of the motorway as Colin's van.

'Hallelujah!' he shouted finally. 'Celeste, that's the best news you could have given me.'

'Best news! Are you kidding? Why?'

'Because Milly's cage has a GPS chip hidden inside the mirror ball.'

'You're joking!'

'I never joke about my birds,' replied Colin flatly. 'You should know that by now. She's a very valuable specimen and the zoo wanted to ensure her safety. Being the most travelled of all our residents, we felt it prudent to take special measures. If she's in her cage, then she can be tracked easily. You can tell the police when they arrive.'

Wilf was gesticulating urgently like a semaphore operator who'd inadvertently stabbed one of his flags into a live electrical socket, so Celeste handed the phone to him. 'The police are not going to get involved. Not yet, anyway.'

'And why not?' asked Colin carefully. 'No, don't answer that. Just promise me one thing.'

'Yes?'

'Don't do anything until I get back to you. I have to be there. Milly's my responsibility. It's my job. You must wait for me before going on a rescue mission.'

'Sorry, Colin. It could be dangerous. I don't want you

involved.'

'Then you don't get the chip ID.'

'That's obstruction,' spluttered Wilf. 'And blackmail.'

'Yes, it is. I'll be back with you inside an hour.'

'Listen, Colin, there may be a lot more to this than meets the eye.'

'Meaning?'

'I can't tell you just yet, but if what I think proves true, there are much deeper plots here than mere burglary. Milly's not been stolen, she's been kidnapped.'

'Kidnapped! This wouldn't have anything to do with James, would it?' Nobody could accuse Keynes of stupidity.

'I couldn't possibly comment. That's a clue, by the way. It means yes.'

'You're playing out of my league, Wilf. I just want our macaw back safe and sound.'

'And I promise I'll get her back, but this is the best chance I'll ever have to get to the bottom of this conspiracy. I'm on the case, Colin, but you need to trust me.'

There was a long pause. Wilf was relieved to hear the normal sounds of motorway traffic in the background as opposed to screeching tyres, crunching metal and approaching sirens. Despite his outburst, Colin was still in control of his vehicle. 'All right, what do you want me to do?' he sighed in resignation.

'Send the mapping app and chip ID to my mobile.'

'There's a service area coming up in a few miles. I'll pull in and text you the moment we finish this call. Anything else?'

'Yes, and this is the hardest part. I want you to carry on as if nothing's happened. Go back to Regent's Park and act as if everything's fine. Milly won't be missed for a week and I need that time to find out who's behind all this. I have a very strong conviction that whoever's taken Milly thinks they've got Bertie. We can tell them apart, but few other people can unless they're sitting side by side. To a layman's eyes, one hyacinth macaw looks very much like another. Someone's been instructed to pinch a large blue bird and that's exactly what they've done. It was sheer coincidence that Milly was at the cottage. She's been taken by mistake, but no harm should come to her if we keep it quiet. If you go to the police, then experience tells me the kidnappers will know pretty quickly, at which point Milly becomes surplus to requirements and will be disposed of, quietly and in a place we will never discover. Then they'll come back for Bertie, only this time we won't have a GPS fix on him and he'll never be recovered.'

'So what you're saying is that so long as they think she's Bertie, she's safe.'

'Exactly. You need to trust me on this one, Colin.' Wilf was a persuasive man. As plod, it had been one of his core skills and he knew exactly what psychology and tone of voice to use on Keynes. Celeste shook her head in admiration.

'That's a hell of a thing to ask, Wilf,' muttered Colin dubiously. Almost there.

'It's nothing more than I know you can give.' Wilf played his ace.

'A week, you say?' Got him!

'Can you stretch to ten days?' Might as well push your luck.

'Go on then, but let me make one thing very clear. If Milly has not been recovered in ten days, then I'll be mounting a rescue mission myself with as many policemen as I can get. Remember, I also know where she is. I'll be monitoring her every movement on my computer. If she is lost, there will be consequences. There'll be no hiding place from me. I'll stick a bloody GPS chip up your arse and follow you to hell and back. I'll have your guts for garters, Thompson.'

'Then you'll be second in line behind Celeste.'

'That's it – over there by those trees!' Wilf and Celeste stood beside the car and examined his smart phone. A map spread its complex veins across the screen. Roads laced together like varicose veins on the back of a pensioner's calf. Two dots glowed, pulsing every few seconds. The first, bright green, indicated their position. The second, stark red, indicated the location of Milly's cage. They had not driven far. Once the map application had been downloaded and the chip identification keyed in, the screen sprang into life, revealing a surprisingly familiar location. A fifteen-minute journey had brought them to just beyond the sleepy village of Deerhurst. Across the fields, not even a quarter mile away, they could see a cluster of low-roofed agricultural buildings partially hidden by a sparse belt of hawthorn trees. Celeste had pulled into a lay-by under a sycamore and they peeped over the hedge. Cows paused from grazing to peer at them, heavy-uddered, strings of drool and half-masticated grass hanging from their loose-lipped mouths. The only sound was cud being chewed, the swish of tail and occasional bubbling release of intestinal gas.

Classy.

'It's the perfect place to hole up,' murmured Wilf, staring intently through Celeste's binoculars. 'Remote, quiet, enclosed.'

'See anything familiar?'

'Like what?'

'Well, how about a blue macaw?'

'No. All's quiet over there. No sign of movement at all.' He scanned back and forth with the glasses. 'The track leading to it comes in from the right. Looks like a square of buildings, probably surrounding a yard. There's no farmhouse or cottage so it's very private. Again, someone's done their homework. To find and rent such a place takes time and money. This has been some months in the planning.'

'Worrying, isn't it.'

'Yes. Very much.'

'I still think I should phone James.'

'Let's not go over that again.' Wilf had persuaded Celeste, very much against her better judgement, not to call her husband, using the same argument as he had done with Colin. 'Calling him might not be such a good idea. Naturally, he'll want to return here immediately and that will be noticed. Especially by the press. Tactically, that could be a bad move. I'll have a nose around first. See what I can see.'

'What are you going to do?'

'I'll follow that hedgerow. It'll take me almost all the way there. I can see a blind spot on this side.' He handed the binoculars to Celeste.

'No windows.'

'That's right.'

'Do you think they'll be patrolling?'

'Celeste, this isn't Stalag Luft Three!'

'Well there's no need to get snippy.'

'Sorry. I usually work alone.'

'I can see why.'

'Do you want me to go and rescue your sodding macaw or not?'

'Language,' she retorted primly. 'Whatever we do, we do together. Besides, what makes you think you'll be able to communicate with Bertie if you come across him over there. You'll need me to persuade him to leave Milly.'

'No, Celeste. What I said to Colin still rings true for you. This could be dangerous. We have no idea who's over there or how many of them there are. I'll go and have a look. There's no reason to suppose Milly's not in her cage, and there she can stay, but if I find Bertie I'll bring him back one way or another. If he won't listen to me then I'll wave you over.'

'Sure,' she said in a manner Wilf had come to regard with deep suspicion. Her apparent acquiescence was most perturbing. This was too easy.

200

'Are you armed?' she asked.

'For God's sake, woman, I'm a police officer, not bloody Robocop! This is England. If you get caught carrying a gun here it's a minimum five years.'

'Just asking.'

'Why? Are you?'

'Oh, yes,' replied Celeste airily.

Wilf's shoulders sagged. 'What have you brought?' he asked with weary resignation. This was much more like the Celeste he knew so well.

'Only my whip, of course. It's all I need.' She produced a wicked-looking bullwhip from the boot of the car.

'Put that back,' he ordered.

'Not a chance,' she smirked. 'Come on, let's go and see what trouble we can get into.'

Before Wilf could protest any more, Celeste climbed over a stile in the hedge and set off for the buildings. 'Are you coming or what?' she called back to him over her shoulder. Wilf couldn't fail to be impressed. She showed no sign of fear. Caution, yes, but no fear. He shook his head and followed. This was a woman who'd defended her home against two of the best trained Black Ops agents on the planet with passion and a generous dollop of savagery. Fear did not appear to be in her lexicon. He caught up and together they headed towards the distant buildings.

This could get very interesting indeed.

CHAPTER FOURTEEN

Wilf and Celeste stood close to the corner of the farm buildings. Partially concealed by the hedge, it had taken them less than five minutes to traverse the field, watched with bored indifference by the herd of ruminating cows. Wilf was relieved to discover Gloucestershire cows appeared to be the laziest in England by a country mile. The odd irritated flick of a tail was the only indication of their excitement at having two people drop by for a visit.

He scanned the buildings carefully. Dirty walls of lichen-stained concrete blocks and battered corrugated tin gave the place a dismal, neglected air. Some aromatic by-product of dairy production was piled up nearby, steaming gently, and as if that wasn't enough to deter souls of a sensitive disposition, the walls were peppered with warnings of asbestos. The signs looked tatty and weathered, but when Wilf peeled one back, the adhesive was fresh.

'Made to look old,' he breathed. 'No asbestos here, but someone wants to keep nosy parkers away.' He edged along one wall and looked around the next corner, beckoning Celeste to follow. They stopped at a grimy window and peered inside. Agricultural detritus cluttered the place, rusty, dusty and laced with impressively large cobwebs. Light dribbled in through several ragged holes in the roof, broken tiles littering the floor. 'No one here. The entrance to the yard must be around the next corner. I'll go and have a look. Stay here. No, here. Don't move, I'll be right back. Wait, where are you going?'

As usual, Celeste completely ignored his instructions

and crept off. He shook his head sadly. So much for the authority of a police officer. Now advancing with greater caution, they carefully stole up to the gateway and peeped into the courtyard. A white van was parked in front of the largest building in the complex, the only one that appeared to be weatherproof and in reasonable condition. If the density of the signs were anything to go by, this building appeared to be constructed entirely from asbestos. Including the windows. To approach courted immediate death by mesothelioma. They spent a few seconds registering what they'd seen and, unwilling to cross the open entrance for fear of being spotted, retired back to the hedge.

'That's where she is, in that building by the van,' said Wilf

'Really? You think?'

He shot her an irritated look. Celeste shrugged. 'Now you know what it's like working with you. What next?'

'I want to have a look in that barn.'

'So do I. What about the van?'

'Someone's definitely at home. A plan so carefully thought out would not allow for such an exotic and valuable asset to remain unguarded. Milly will have a minder in there. The van will also be needed in case they have to move her quickly.'

'Did you get the registration number?'

'Of course. Sending it to Sergeant Drewing right now, but I can tell you for certain it'll be a rental hired by a Mr John Smith. Or stolen. Guaranteed.' Wilf tapped away, sent the text and pocketed his phone. 'Right, let's go. I'm afraid we have to navigate our way around the poo pile this time.'

They set off in the opposite direction, hugging the outer walls, giving the manure mountain a wide berth and searching for windows, but there were none on that side of the complex. Then Wilf touched Celeste's arm and pointed upwards. A block had been removed, a vent of some kind high up in the wall of the barn, through which they could just hear faint music, scratchy, as if from an emphysemic radio.

'I don't think you could reach that even on my shoulders,' he breathed.

Celeste produced her smartphone. 'Then I'll take a video,' she said softly.

'Good idea.' Wilf stood with his back to the wall, cupped his hands and boosted Celeste upwards. She was surprised how strong he was. There was much undignified scrambling and wrapping of legs around his neck, accompanied by frantic middle-aged person's waving of arms before she found a point of balance and slowly stood up on his shoulders. Her heels dug in, making him wince. She reached up as high as she could with the phone and, pointing it into the vent, panned in every direction before lowering herself, again with legs scissored around his neck. Wilf got a noseful of knee and nearly choked when she yanked hard on the collar of his mac, his eyes bulging. 'Sorry,' she murmured in a tone of voice that indicated she was not sorry at all.

They huddled. Celeste called up the video and they both peered at the phone. Unsurprisingly, the image was anything but steady, but it was clear enough for them to see what they needed to see. The interior of the barn was surprisingly spacious. Light poured in through poster-dotted windows overlooking the courtyard, illuminating a few much more modern farming implements scattered around in careless abandon. Then they spotted Milly in her cage – it was just too big to miss – and nearby, bivouacked beside a small olive green tent, a man sat in a folding director's chair, sharpening a knife on a whetstone, his back to the camera and a radio at his elbow, the source of the music. Supplies and a camping stove indicated there were no immediate plans to move on.

'That must be the man who knocked you out,' she whispered. Wilf nodded.

As they watched, he turned the radio off and made a call on his mobile, his voice echoing faintly in the empty barn. 'I have the package and it's stored at the agreed location. No, the operation was simple enough. I was not seen. The message has been left as you ordered. No, the target is not under observation at this moment. I'm waiting for my team to arrive to guard the package, then I'll return to the prime location and resume surveillance. In the garden, of course. They'll be here within the hour. Certainly, sir, I'll not let her out of my sight again. I'll make the first call this evening. Just a preparatory conversation to stoke her fear. Thank you, I know I'm good. There won't be any mistakes. Then we can move on to the actual demonstration of our intent. Yes, I think a ritual plucking should suffice. I'm looking forward to that, too. Not a bloody chance, the countryside is a dreadful place. It stinks. I understand my fee amply compensates, but you want to try coming down here sometime. It's beyond medieval.'

The man snickered nastily at some comment, ended the call and turned on the radio again. He settled back and resumed sharpening his knife. Wilf looked at Celeste as the video continued. She gnawed at her lower lip anxiously. Wilf knew she was searching for any sign of Bertie, but the video drew a blank.

Except right at the last moment.

Half a second before the end, the image of the barn was suddenly obscured by something so close the camera was unable to focus properly. Celeste jumped. Wilf frowned. 'What the hell was that?' She paused the video. He stared for a few moments, then turned the phone upside down and pointed. A big brown eye glared at them, blurred almost out of recognition, but both instantly identified that unique expression: curious, questioning, alert. The head was cocked so far to one side that it was almost inverted, confusing them for a moment, but a faint haze of unfocused violet confirmed it was Bertie.

206

Celeste trembled with relief, squeezing Wilf's hand. 'Thank God,' she breathed. They heard a faint scratching above them and, looking up, saw Bertie's head poking out of the vent. Obviously curious about the phone, he'd decided to investigate, but it was a very tight fit for the burly macaw. He pushed and heaved before finally squeezing his way out through the vent, his immaculate plumage dusty and draped in cobwebs. Normally, Bertie would be chuckling away happily on seeing his mum again, but she held a finger to her lips and he knew she wanted him to keep quiet. Celeste pointed back towards the car hidden behind the hedge and flicked a hand signal. Bertie responded, launching himself silently and gliding low across the field like a scrap of blue paper blown in the wind. They followed, using the hedge as cover again until they reached the lay-by. Bertie sat on the door mirror preening himself. Wilf could have sworn there was a look of irritation on his face as he flicked away the dirt and dust.

'Hello, Mummy, hello, Wilf,' he said, looking up, his head bobbing in pleasure. So Wilf was alive after all. Probably best not to tell him about the hair-plucking.

'You brave boy.' Celeste fussed over him, pulling a cobweb from the top of his head and kissing him affectionately. 'I'm so proud of you.' Bertie swelled with the praise, puffing out his chest.

'I'm hungry. Have you any nuts?' he asked optimistically.

'Time to go home,' replied Celeste. 'Then you can have nuts.'

Bertie looked back towards the distant buildings. 'Milly?'

'Milly is safe for now. We will get her back soon.'

Bertie thought about this. Now that Mummy and Wilf were here to help, he felt more inclined to action, to swoop into the barn and eviscerate the man before rescuing Milly. Even Bertie knew he'd get guaranteed sex in return!

However, Mummy was always right – and he was *very* hungry. So hungry, in fact, he'd actually been considering rejoining the thrushes for a snack of snails and earthworms. Milly was a lovely mate, but her conversation still remained limited to describing conditions normally only to be experienced during November in the North Sea. She seemed safe enough with the bald man for the moment. Perhaps he should wait. 'Promise?'

Celeste had never lied to Bertie. 'Promise,' she said firmly. 'Now, let's get you into the car.'

The drive back to Prior's Norton took no time. Bertie scampered in, claws scratching on the floorboards, and immediately fluttered to his perch, settling himself down to demolish a handful of fat walnuts heaped in his bowl, his attention solely on his food.

'Any news from Ian?'

Wilf examined his phone. 'As I suspected, the van's on false plates. That'll be a dead end. Still, we've learnt a lot.'

'At least we know Milly's safe.'

'I'll text Colin. Hopefully, he won't have another heart attack.'

'Cup of tea?'

'So long as I actually get to drink it this time rather than have it scald my privates.' Taking tea with Celeste and Bertie had its own unique hazards.

'No lasting damage?'

'Don't know. I haven't yet had the chance to test my bits since that little incident.'

'That was two years ago! Wilf, you're just not trying hard enough.'

'I'm doing my best,' he protested. 'Honest!'

'Well I hope you have more effective plans for rescuing Milly.'

'We could take her back at any time, but that grunt over in the barn is not our main target. I think we can use him to draw out the big boys.'

'The man at the other end of the phone. How?'

'Let's have another look at the video and see if we can come up with a plan.'

'They're in the garden,' she hissed in outrage when the recording had finished. 'They're in the bloody garden!'

'We know that now, but they don't know we know. We can use that.' Wilf pondered. 'We've been lucky. There's been a gap in their surveillance. At any other time they would have known we were on to them straight away, but without someone maintaining their watch here we've been able to get Bertie back unseen. It's critical to keep Bertie out of sight at all times so we can continue the ruse. If they discover they've got the wrong macaw, then I wouldn't bet much on Milly's life.'

Wilf peered at Celeste. 'That camp is certainly not permanent. They're probably planning to use the barn as the venue for Milly's abuse. It's nicely remote. You realise that immediately after this ritual plucking, they'll almost certainly kill Milly. All her feathers will be removed and stored in a handy plastic bag. These will be sent to you on a regular basis to fool you into thinking she's still alive. To keep you on the straight and narrow. No use-by date on a feather, is there. That way they won't have the inconvenience of actually caring for their captive. If these men are commercially astute enough to build their own empires, then they'll certainly recognise a bargain when they see one. Comes to something when a bag of feathers can effectively give you political control of a country.'

'Then we have to act fast. I agree we need to keep them thinking they have Bertie, but it'll be difficult keeping him hidden for long. He's got wings, you know. And access to a cat flap.'

'So I've noticed. We need to get him into hiding, and fast. We know this window of opportunity will close very soon. Enemy reinforcements will be arriving shortly, allowing Barn Boy to return to his lodgings in your shrubbery. I don't think we'll be able to keep Bertie's presence here a secret for very long once the spies are watching.'

'We need somewhere private, somewhere really quiet.'

Bertie, having wolfed down his entrée of nuts, paused before commencing on the main course of more nuts. He hadn't contributed much to the conversation – he never did when he was really hungry – but he knew the meaning of quiet. He liked quiet. Quiet was a good word, easy to learn, easy to remember. Monosyllabic. Bertie pondered on this. Funny how the word used to describe simple words is so complex. He could tackle any monosyllabic word with an excellent chance of success, but not the word employed to describe those words. Still, humans had no inkling of the complexity of his own language. His trills and squawks appeared to be just a discordant noise, but in fact contained subtle multi-harmonics that conveyed huge amounts of information.

However, his mum was now looking for somewhere quiet. Their home was quiet, but apparently not quiet enough. He had a good think – and only one place came to mind. 'Temple, go to Temple!' he chipped in brightly. He thought of the vast underground space, just the best place ever for flying indoors – and very quiet, too.

'Temple?' asked Wilf cautiously. 'What's that?'

'Of course,' Celeste exclaimed softly. In a flash of intuition, she realised Bertie's part in this complex affair was, in fact, ludicrously simple. All he had to do was tell her what to do in these critical moments. His choices were not made through reasoning or any other logical process, but merely came from a mind uncluttered by doubt or indecision. Celeste knew he was right. 'Good old Bertie!' Better the suggestion come from him. Less suspicious. 'He's done it again. Somehow, and I have no idea how, he always manages to say the right thing at the right time. He's such a clever boy.'

'Do you mind explaining,' asked Wilf.

'Yes. I'll call my old friend Doreen. She's got this place up on the Cotswolds called Temple Hall. It's the perfect location and she'll help, no questions asked.'

'Why is it the perfect location?'

'The place is huge. There's plenty of places to hide Bertie.'

'And how will we get him there without Barn Boy noticing?'

'Instead of trying to conceal Bertie here – something we both accept will be an almost impossible task since I will not have him caged in any way – you take him over to Gav's cowshed in the next field. That eliminates all chance Barn Boy might have of catching a glimpse of him through any of the windows. Then we just wait for him to resume his surveillance, at which point I'll very publicly decamp to the Hall and stay there, forcing our enemies to follow. I am their primary target after all. How else will they be able to keep tabs on me except by following? With him chasing me, you and Bertie can then tail the tailer, so to speak. That way you can keep him under surveillance while he watches me. You can also see who else arrives, and at the last resort, can call in the police if things get ugly.'

'In what way would that help? We're merely replacing one location with another.'

'True, but there's safety in numbers, especially if there's a gang involved. You said yourself these people are at their most effective when their target is isolated. I won't be isolated at Temple Hall. She has a staff of half a dozen or so women who keep the place going. You'll love it. All those damsels to protect. And the sheep, of course.' She hated manipulating Wilf. He was a tenacious and intuitive detective, excellent in a crisis and exceptionally difficult to deceive, but she could not betray her promise of secrecy to the Sisterhood. Now Bertie had offered a plausible way of persuading Wilf they needed to go to Temple Hall, where the entire resources of the Sisterhood could be brought to bear. As Doreen had sensibly pointed out, they needed all the help they could get if they stood any chance of defeating this subtle and pernicious enemy.

'I don't know,' said Wilf pensively. 'We're up against some violent people. A clout around the head and giving your husband's knackers a good squeeze is probably the least harmful thing they could do, especially if women are around.'

'As I've told you on plenty of occasions before, I can look after myself. Why don't you believe me?'

'It's still too risky.'

'I've been learning self-defence.'

'What?'

'Norton Village Hall, Protect Yourself Combat Course for Women, Intermediate Class, Grade Two. I can kick your arse anytime!' she added flatly.

'Celeste, what has country life done to you?'

'Thought I'd better take precautions after what happened in London.'

'I seem to recall you had no trouble kicking arse on that occasion.'

'True, but now I know how to do it with my bare hands. You wouldn't believe the damage I can do with a soup spoon.'

'I still don't like it,' he grumbled, like a father who's just discovered a condom in his teenage daughter's handbag. 'And what about James? We need to make sure he's safely out of harm's way, especially after he gave all that money away.'

'I love my husband very much, but, unlike you, he's not got a reputation as a man of action. He's also an MP. There's a certain stature and gravitas that goes with the territory. Of course he'd help if he could, but he has dodgy knees and a bruised happy sack. He's already walking wounded. We also need to consider what the consequences for his career might be should any of this come to court at a later date.'

Celeste knew she had to protect James at all costs. If he was as important as Doreen said he was, then keeping him safe was as much a priority as rescuing Milly and defeating their adversaries. However, she was uncomfortable sidelining him. Their marriage was based on mutual trust, honesty and very large amounts of rope, yet she now had responsibilities to Doreen and the Sisterhood as well as to her husband. Their fate was already bound up with hers. And Bertie's.

If Doreen's hippy-dippy psychic was right, the only chance they had of prevailing against this shadowy organization was with Bertie's help, and he'd told them to go to Temple Hall. Loath as she was to place Britain's future political stability on the nut-fuelled suggestion of a hyacinth macaw, she had to admit it made a lot of sense.

'Listen, Wilf. I know this doesn't exactly inspire you with confidence, but Bertie's proposed we go to Temple Hall and that's good enough for me. He's got this strange habit of saying the right thing at just the right time. He brought down the last government, for heaven's sake, and the consequence of that has been this sudden resurgence of democracy at Westminster. And now that is under threat. Some seriously unpleasant people have attacked my husband and my favourite policeman. They've kidnapped my darling's girlfriend and will be phoning me in a very short time to begin the process of corruption which will undoubtedly involve her abuse. This is simply not acceptable. We need to have a strategy to counter this. We need to take the initiative. We need to unbalance our enemies. We need to do something unexpected, to force them into reacting to us. We know they'll be calling very soon, but if I'm not at home and have turned off my mobile then they'll have to physically come after me to deliver their message in person – and moving to Temple Hall will achieve all that.'

Wilf had to admit she put forward a powerful argument, but still couldn't help but feel he was being manipulated in some way. His finely honed instincts told him there was definitely something going on that she was not prepared to tell. He glared at her with his best disbelieving criminal interrogation face, but her only response was a cool, steady stare.

Wilf sighed unhappily. 'There's already enough evidence to involve the police, but I'm not quite ready to bring in uniform unless it's absolutely necessary. I want to get my hands on Barn Boy's phone. I've no doubt there's enough information on it to identify and implicate his bosses. I've had many successful convictions based solely on evidence taken from a smartphone, but I have to warn you that doesn't always happen. Powerful people have a habit of slipping through the net. They can afford to buy their way out of trouble. That man holding Milly is just a foot soldier, we need to bag the generals, otherwise the threat will just return, next time in a more potent form. This will be the only realistic opportunity we'll have to beat them.'

'I understand. That's why I'm going to Temple Hall.'

'Hmm,' he muttered, obviously still unconvinced. 'I've got a bad feeling about all this.'

'Wilf, you have a bad feeling about everything.'

'True,' he admitted. 'I am a grumpy old bugger, aren't I?'

'It's part of your lovable charm, but you're just going to have to trust me on this one,' said Celeste. 'I need a leap of faith. If Bertie says Temple Hall, then Temple Hall it is. I'll go on my own if I have to, but I'd prefer my muscle to be there watching my back.'

'Temple Hall,' said Bertie around a mouthful of nut. 'Very nice place.'

Wilf looked shrewdly at the macaw. His mind was so alien it was impossible to tell what thought processes motivated him, but he had to agree the bird had a knack, every so often, of uttering just the right phrase at just the right time. As the previous Prime Minister had discovered to his cost. 'Goddammit,' he muttered unhappily. 'All right, I give in – but under protest. I still don't like the idea of involving civilians, especially against a gang, but I suppose we need as many troops on our side as we can get.' Wilf thought for a moment. 'OK, I'll take Bertie over to Gav's cowshed and keep him there until you're gone. Once Barn Boy follows, we'll follow him. I presume you do have another vehicle apart from your own car.'

'Er, yes, sort of…'

Once Wilf and Bertie were safely out of the way, Celeste packed a small overnight bag. She thought of phoning James, but knew he'd be in the House. The Speaker took a dim view of any interruption – especially if the ringtone was *Calamity Jane*'s 'Whip-Crack-Away!'

She was about to leave a text when she heard gravel crunching outside. Cautiously, Celeste twitched a net curtain. A taxi pulled up by the front door. 'Now what?' she muttered irritably. 'It's like bloody Piccadilly Circus around here.' The passenger paid and got out. Her heart sank. 'Oh, no! Just what I don't need.'

An hour later, having given Miller ample time to resume his surveillance, Celeste clattered out of the cottage carrying her overnight bag. She made a show of checking all the windows and doors were shut, then jumped in her car and made off with some urgency.

Wilf discreetly observed from across the field. He scanned the garden. There was a particularly unkempt corner that interested him. Tangled and leafy beneath several trees, their branches drooping, it was the perfect spot for a little covert spying. He'd already noticed the birds gave that part of the garden a wide berth and had his suspicions. Within a minute of Celeste's departure, he saw furtive movement amongst the undergrowth, then the sound of a vehicle starting up and receding into the distance. Celeste's tail was on the move.

Time to go!

'Come on, Bertie, let's get on the road.' Wilf sprinted across the field, the macaw flying at his side. He headed for James's rusty corrugated tin garage, opened the door and peered into the gloom. An old Sunbeam sports car sat on blocks, its wheels and seats missing, its bonnet up to reveal an engine short of a cylinder head. As a mode of transport, even Wilf could see it required some work to make roadworthy, but he dismissed the convertible immediately and focused his attention instead on a tented shape. Wilf swept the dust sheet to one side and grinned. 'Oh, yeah,' he murmured, 'this'll do nicely.'

Bertie waited outside. The garage was too dusty for him. Having only just restored his plumage to its usual immaculate state, he had no intention of getting filthy again. Best let Wilf go in – cobwebs would probably make him more attractive.

Moments later, the peace was shattered by the thud of a powerful engine. The garage doors burst open and Wilf powered out on the only other available vehicle – James's motorcycle combination. The vintage Royal Enfield rattled and roared like an irate dragon. Bertie didn't like the noise too much, but remembered his mum's instructions.

Follow Wilf.

Stay with Wilf.

Obey Wilf.

Help Wilf.

'Jump in!' shouted Wilf over the noise. Unable to find James's helmet, he had to settle for Celeste's. He knew it was hers because it was a shocking candy pink and studded with sparkling crystals. And then there were the novelty antlers, pointing up and outwards on either side like perky coral branches. Wilf would have preferred to lose the antlers, not that he bothered much with his image at the best of times, but had no time to figure out how to remove them without dismantling the visor. The antlers would have to stay. He looked like a disturbingly effeminate Viking warrior.

Bertie hopped into the sidecar and peered around with lively interest. He'd been in this moving bathtub before, but only on his mum's lap while The Kneeling Man drove. The cockpit seemed awfully empty without her, but he took a firm grip both on his courage and the leather seat and squawked in surprise when Wilf gunned the engine and dropped the clutch.

Wilf hadn't been on a bike for almost forty years, but the instinct to ride had never entirely disappeared. Hot, oily smells wafting up from the engine invoked a fond wash of memories, of misspent youth and racing around the South Circular in days long before speed cameras. Skills long dormant stirred into life. You never forget.

Like swimming.

The motorcycle leapt forward. Bertie hunkered down behind the windscreen, scrabbling to maintain his balance. Buoyed more by enthusiasm than ability, Wilf careered around the bend at the bottom of the drive with the sidecar wheel high in the air and pounded away in pursuit of Celeste and her tail, a grin on his face, mac belted tight and pink antlers flapping in the wind.

CHAPTER FIFTEEN

Miller parked his van just beside a small copse on the ridge across the valley from Temple Hall. He examined the old building with field glasses. An early evening sun bathed it in glowing orange. Normally not one to be moved by beauty, let alone architecture, he had to admit it was a very lovely building. He scanned it thoroughly. Nothing moved. Timbrill's car sat on the drive, the only visible vehicle on the premises. Timbrill's wife had been met at the door and hurried inside, dragging her case. Miller recognised the signs. He'd seen worried women before. He enjoyed worrying women. The sense of power was addictive – and soon he'd be honing his skills once again. He looked forward to their meeting. The bitch had brought it upon herself by fleeing here. He could easily intimidate his victims over the phone, but that was no longer possible. Miller considered this an added bonus. To truly terrify a victim required a face-to-face encounter. Shame he'd only been instructed to violate the bird. He rather fancied bringing the snooty cow down a notch or two. Slap her around, loosen a few teeth, perhaps, or maybe worse. He smiled at the thought of her pubes. Never seen ginger curlies before.

Tailing her had been easy. Skilled as he was in covert surveillance, he'd hung back, tucking in behind a lorry for part of the way, always keeping several cars between him and his target, varying his distance, even overtaking her on one occasion and observing her through his mirrors. Piece of cake.

A careful man, was Miller.

Pity, then, he'd completely failed to notice a motorcycle and sidecar drifting along far behind, often hidden by the bends in the road – but always there. The tailer was being tailed.

'She needs to understand just how serious we are. It was a big mistake for Timbrill to dispose of that cash. She has to pay for his stupidity,' said a tinny voice. Miller's tablet lay propped on the dashboard. A video link connected him to his employer, safe in his distant Fortress of Fulsome Fortune. Netheridge sat at ease around the table with the others. Still one short, Miller noticed. Damn, that was a consummate piece of poisoning. He swelled with pride at his achievement.

'I agree,' he replied, 'but I think it might be wise to avoid executing the next stage of our plan at Timbrill's home.' He considered the lanky old codger he'd coshed at the cottage. 'It's far too public. Damned neighbours are always dropping in unannounced to borrow a cup of sugar. Why's it always sugar? Is there an unspoken rural convention stating you must never buy sufficient sugar to cover your own requirements?'

'Not now, Miller, if you please,' said Netheridge. 'Would it be unreasonable to ask that you at least attempt to keep your mind on the job?'

'Of course, sir.'

'So why has she changed location?' asked Woolley.

'Women are irrational and unpredictable creatures. That's why men are leaders in almost every country in the world,' observed Brasenose with airy condescension. 'In addition, they do not have the intelligence nor the logical pragmatism to make any significant contribution to human society – but they are very good at having babies,' he added. The others chuckled indulgently.

Miller had to bite his lip. The most dangerous and accomplished agent he'd ever encountered had been a woman. He wondered just how well the men on the other end of the link would fare had they been locked in a room with her. 'Since she's no longer at home we are unable to threaten her over the phone. I was only able to obtain her landline number since her mobile is on the restricted list because of her husband's position. She has inadvertently forced our hand by fleeing to this place, but I don't see any reason why we can't take advantage of this unexpected situation. As you know, our surveillance has indicated she's been here before. The visit she made was the only significant departure from her normal domestic routine during the entire period we've had her under observation. Surprisingly, she took the macaw.'

'Is that relevant?' asked Brasenose.

'As anyone with military training will tell you, any deviation from a set routine is relevant. The need to take the macaw outweighed the disruption of doing so. I find that interesting. The question you should be asking is what's down there at that particular location which required the attendance of the bird?' God, they were thick sometimes.

'Maybe it's no more than just a pleasant place to visit,' suggested Woolley. 'You do have a habit of overthinking these things, Mr Miller.'

'Perhaps,' he muttered. Jeez, they were in a right snotty mood today. Probably made a couple of million pounds less profit than usual. 'However, now the panic's set in, she thinks she's safe here. Unreachable. Out of the way, but it works for us as well. This location is much more isolated than her home. It's here we can advance our plans and abuse the bird without fear of interruption.'

'What do we know of this Temple Hall?' asked Woolley.

Miller opened his laptop and searched for Temple Guiting Hall. Pages scrolled quickly. He absorbed information and conveyed what he saw in terse sentences to the MIGS.

'Sixteenth century, Grade One listed. Several hundred acres. Appears to be home to some kind of women's commune.'

'Women?'

'With luck, lesbians,' he added speculatively, grinning.

'We're not interested in that.'

'No, of course you're not.' Christ, they had no balls. Literally.

'Can you possibly limit your observations to something useful?' muttered Brasenose peevishly.

Hello! Miller recognised that tone of voice. Time for some fun. 'The Hall and its residents are pillars of the local community and winners of the Best Cauliflower In Show at the village fete for the last twelve consecutive years. Impressive.'

'But not relevant,' snapped Woolley. Miller snickered at his impatience. He liked to tease them all, especially Woolley, who'd had his sense of humour surgically removed at about the same time he'd parted company with his umbilical cord. Lighten up, you depressing old fool.

Miller examined photos and plans of the Hall while the others fumed in silence at the delay. Netheridge smirked behind his hand. Miller was brilliant at annoying them, pay-off for the dismissive arrogance in the way they treated his man. Miller's military training had included psychology and he knew how to goad an enemy.

However, examining a target vicariously was certainly no substitution for visiting in person, especially when planning a raid. 'Luckily for us, the occupants appear to have always been exclusively women, as noted in several historical sources, and apparently it still is, according to the current Electoral Roll. This makes penetration much easier,' he quipped darkly. No one laughed at his joke. Miserable buggers. 'Unfortunately, the Hall has always been privately owned and is never open to the public. This makes reconnaissance tricky. I need to have a nose around before finalizing my assault planning in case of unexpected obstacles, however ...' Something caught his eye and he leaned back with a smile. 'Excellent. I know how to get in there,' he said. 'Leave it to me. All I need is a bobble hat and an unnatural addiction to rambling!'

Jenny had just cleared away her dinner debris when she heard the heavy Trojan Horse knocker thump against the front door and, wiping her hands on her apron, went to investigate. A man stood there, dressed in an entirely familiar manner. She guessed immediately the reason for his visit.

'Can I help?' she asked.

'Good evening. I've been walking in the neighbourhood and decided I really could not pass up the chance of visiting your Roman Baptistry. I hope it's not too late, but would it be possible to see it?'

'Certainly, Mister –?'

'Johnstone. Humphrey Johnstone.'

Jenny was no psychic, but even she could see the man wasn't a Humphrey. He looked more like a Logan. Or a Dirk, maybe. Perhaps a Ryan. There was the air of a military man about him. He was about average height, but very compact. There was not an ounce of fat on his muscular frame. Jenny guessed he worked out regularly. No one she'd ever met looked so fit. Bet he didn't tell the boys down the gym his name was Humphrey.

Miller smiled winningly, pulling off his woollen beanie to reveal a shaven head. She was rather attractive, despite the wellies. Keep your mind on the job, man. He followed her through the old house, eyes missing nothing, even her sexy little rump. They went down some stone stairs and into the baptistry. Miller enthused appropriately. He was a good actor.

'Well, isn't this just delightful. What a little gem of a place. May I take some photos?' The smartphone came out. 'Oh, no signal,' he frowned.

'No. Mobiles don't work down here,' commented Jenny. 'It's the perfect dungeon when you think about it. Just the place to lock someone up, but your camera should still work.' Miller snapped his way around the structure making all manner of complimentary remarks – Jenny thought he seemed unusually excited about the stout oak door and its heavy bolt – then they made their way back up to the entrance hall. He thanked her profusely and turned to go, when his attention was caught by some of the paintings hanging on the walls. The phone reappeared and he took a snap of every canvas, including the striking portrait of Helen of Troy by Sir Frederick Sandys hanging over the ornate fireplace. He stared at it long and hard, thanked Jenny again and departed. His mobile stayed out as he strode down the gravelled drive.

'Yes, Mr Netheridge, I've just been given the tour. No, I can't see any problem. Please inform the others we can take the place any time you like. There's even the perfect spot to hold the women. Tomorrow morning suits me as well. I'll get that implemented immediately. However, I'll need all of my team here to ensure a clean strike. Yes, even the guard on the bird. Well, I suppose I could bring the cage with me, but I won't risk exposing our primary asset until we've secured the location. Listen, why don't you come down and help out? You're always grumbling you want a bit more action. Here's your chance. You mind the bird while we move in, then you can bring it here and watch me get the results you want so badly. You'll have a great time. It'll be an education. Good, see you tomorrow, then.'

He finished the call, then immediately made another. 'Your friend has given the go-ahead. The operation will start tomorrow morning. He's taken the bait. Eager? Yes, I'd say so. A brilliant idea of yours, implicating him at this advanced stage.' Miller was a man with many irons in numerous fires. He liked to keep his income streams varied. A complex character. Multiple layers. Onion Man. In other words, a disloyal, snide, repellent, untrustworthy, two-faced low-life. 'Sir, there's also a few paintings here I know you'll be happy to add to your collection. Sending the pictures now. Several Pre-Raphaelites, a Reynolds and a Gainsborough.' He listened, trudging stolidly down the gravelled drive while his contact pored over the photos. 'I know, who would have believed it. Definitely a Sandys. My usual commission? Thank you very much.' Miller smiled broadly. He knew many thousands of pounds were now coming his way. 'There's no security here at all so it's quite safe to come down yourself. I know you like to make a collection personally whenever you can. I'll text to tell you exactly when you'll have private access. It'll be a narrow window of opportunity, but easily enough to get the job done. All you'll need is a small stepladder. No, the women won't give us any trouble and I have the perfect prison. I'll use the usual team. We can melt away once you've made the collection, leaving your friend exposed. Yes, I'll make sure I call the police. No doubt we can ensure the poisoning comes to light as well. Oh, I don't know, maybe fifteen years. Bars, buggery and bananas. A fitting end, don't you think,' he chuckled grimly. 'One last question – how much of a clean-up afterwards? Sure, we can do that, but it seems a shame to torch such a lovely house. Yes, I realise you need to eliminate all traces of a collection. No, I'm not going soft. I can assure you of my complete loyalty, but there's no –'

Miller glared at his phone. He didn't like being cut off so imperiously. His boss knew that as well. 'Distrusting bastard!' he snarled.

'You!' exclaimed Jenny.

'Yes, me,' replied Miller smugly.

'Humphrey Johnstone.'

'The very same.'

'I'll bet that's not your real name.'

'No takers.'

'This man came here yesterday evening to see the baptistery,' explained Jenny to Doreen. 'He took lots of photos.'

225

'Reconnaissance,' said Sandra.

'Precisely.'

'And now burglary?'

'Amongst other things.' Celeste went cold at Miller's tone. The implications were disturbing. Wilf had been right. Maybe it had been a bad move to involve Doreen, despite her insistence. They were following a risky strategy. Still, at least they'd had a little time to prepare. If all went to plan, these men were in for a hell of a shock.

Miller stood in front of his gang, a hand-picked group of four mercenaries, all in black. Three were flinty-eyed hard men, well-muscled, silent and menacing, the fourth a larger gentleman of generous girth with an acne-scarred face and the empty eyes of an assassin. They'd swarmed in without warning during breakfast and moved swiftly through the Hall, sweeping the women into the kitchen.

Martha stepped forward, placing herself in front of Doreen. 'You leave them alone, or else.'

'Or else what, old woman? You'll give me a particularly harsh blue rinse?' sniggered Miller.

'You're a very rude man,' retorted Martha indignantly.

'I am,' he agreed genially. 'I'm delighted to say I have a deeply unpleasant character. In fact, I'm going to show you just how unpleasant I can be.' He flicked a hand and the corpulent gentleman stepped forward and prodded Martha with a stun gun. There was a *phutz* and Martha collapsed with a scream, twitching convulsively. Cutie cried out, lunging forward, but was held back by Doreen. Her face was set like stone, her eyes glittered pure hatred. 'That was unnecessary,' she ground out, her voice low and dripping with venom.

'True, but as I said, I'm a deeply unpleasant person. As a man unconstrained by conscience, I felt you needed a demonstration. Besides, I do like to see old biddies twitching at my feet.'

Celeste bent to Martha, cradling her head. She jerked convulsively, her cheek ticking. 'I'm so sorry,' she whispered, 'but I've wet myself.'

'That's OK, Martha. I'll make them suffer for this.'

'Don't count on it, Tinkerbell,' said Miller. 'Ladies, mobile phones on the table, please. Thank you. Now, put these on everyone, then yourself. Try not to get too excited.' He tossed a chain onto the floor, half a dozen pairs of handcuffs padlocked through its links. 'Chop, chop, or Granny gets another shock.'

Celeste gave Miller a long, hard and definitely unfriendly look. This was the man who'd knocked out Wilf and held Milly captive at the barn. From James's description, she realised he was also the man who'd bruised her husband's joy compartment. When the reckoning came, he would suffer. She bent to Martha. 'Have faith,' she whispered, kissing her forehead. 'Your hair will save us.' Martha's brow furrowed as the cuffs clicked around her wrists. Cutie followed, then Jenny, Sandra and Doreen. Lastly, Celeste snapped the bracelets around her own wrists. All six were now cuffed together. They helped Martha to her feet and all stood in a little group.

Miller smiled nastily. 'Now then, along to the baptistery. With its nice strong door.'

Jenny led the way down to the Oracle, chain clinking. They all ducked their heads to get under the low lintel. The chamber was dark and musty, its rough stone roof soot-stained and black. Celeste peered around in the gloom, the only illumination a pale shaft of light filtering down the chimney high in the roof. 'Charming,' she murmured.

'Don't get comfy, we'll be coming for you very soon,' said Miller, pointing at her. 'Then you'll see the real reason we're here.' The heavy door slammed and the bolt was thrown. They heard melodramatically villainous Sir Jasper-style laughter through the thick oak, then receding footsteps.

Doreen turned to Jenny and patted her arm. 'Well done, Jen. You can add acting to your many talents.'

'Thank you, Gaia. I was still scared, even though I knew they were coming.'

'So was I, but it was essential to lure them here. We plan to catch the generals through their soldiers.'

'What did you mean, my hair will save us?' asked Martha.

'Ah, yes,' said Celeste. 'Your bun. So stylish, so useful, so obsessively controlled. May I borrow a hair grip?'

Martha obliged. Celeste bent and twisted it into a particular shape before inserting the end into the lock on Doreen's handcuff. A dextrous wiggle produced a click and the cuff fell open. Celeste received an extremely old-fashioned look and shrugged. 'An essential life skill. Well, it is for a woman with my particular tastes.' They were all free inside a minute. Celeste separated each pair of handcuffs from the chain. 'Keep your own cuffs,' she said. 'You may need them.' The heavy chain went into her pocket.

Doreen gave Martha a comforting hug. 'That was an Oscar-winning performance.'

'I wasn't acting. I really did pee myself.'

'Oh. Sorry, I thought you were joking. Perhaps you should work on your pelvic floor exercises,' she suggested. 'Cutie, what have you got?'

'Just here, Gaia.' Cutie stood facing the far wall of the Oracle. The stonework was smooth, the blocks well laid. 'See – the lime mortar is still a different colour, even after five hundred years.'

'Of course, the original tunnel to the Temple.' said Celeste.

'That's right. We needed to entice them into imprisoning us in a place they thought was secure but we knew had a way out. Thanks to Jenny, they took the bait.'

'I'm still uneasy about involving you all.'

'Don't be ridiculous, Celeste. We've drawn together every element of this conspiracy neatly and without suspicion. They are here now specifically because of you, and you are here because of Bertie's suggestion. That was his part. I've told you before, Maggie knows what she's talking about. She told me to gather you both in and I've done so. The confrontation was always meant to be here, at Temple Hall. Only now will it be possible to defeat them and prevent their corruption from spreading.'

'So you're still allowing yourself to be led by a weirdy-beardy punk priestess.' Some of Celeste's scepticism resurfaced. 'Endangering us all and subjecting Martha to a nasty attack.'

'Running the world's not always easy, Celeste,' replied Doreen firmly. 'Subtle visions require subtle planning. You'll soon get the hang of it. Don't forget – Helen of Troy's blood runs in your veins so you've got a head start.' She turned back to Cutie. 'We need to loosen this stone and the rest will come out easily. Pass that poker, Jen.'

Normally used to stir the oracular flames, the steel poker admirably doubled up as a scraper. The soft lime mortar crumbled easily and the block was loose within minutes. A good push and it fell through, revealing a narrow tunnel beyond. The remaining wall was soon dismantled. They filed along the passageway led by Doreen's pencil torch, fingers trailing against the smooth masonry. Again using the poker, Cutie forced a breach in the matching wall at the far end and they emerged on to the hexagonal landing in the Temple passageway. Creeping back up the stairs, they carefully opened the secret panel and stepped into the library beside the great stone fireplace.

All was quiet, but distant voices drifted out of the kitchen. Male voices. Laughing, complacent, arrogant. Such a thing had not been heard in the Hall for many centuries.

'What's next?' asked Jenny.

'Much as I'd like to, we can't sneak away. We must protect the Temple at all costs, even if it means putting ourselves in danger. That's what we signed up for.' Doreen was adamant. Her tone brooked no argument. 'We can't leave them to roam at will through the Hall, but we don't have much time. They'll be coming for Celeste at any moment.'

'We should use that tippy-trappy thing in front of the library door,' said Cutie. 'That's what it was designed for.'

'You mean the oubliette.'

'Technically, it's not an oubliette. It's a tippy-trappy thing,' she insisted.

'Is it still working?' asked Sandra.

'Should be. We greased the mechanism not a few months ago.'

'The timing's got to be spot on. We need all five of them together at the right time. Who's going to be the lure?'

'I'm Gaia. The responsibility is mine.'

'No,' said Sandra firmly. 'I'll do it. You and Celeste are far too important, Martha's got soggy knickers, Jenny can't run for toffee in those wellies and I'll need Cutie to operate the trap.' Doreen looked doubtful, but eventually nodded.

'We also have to consider the possibility that they might not all follow Sandra,' added Celeste. 'These are professionals. If they see she's out, they will almost certainly split up to search for the rest of us. That's what I'd do. Did Maggie say if there was going to be an actual physical fight?'

'Not specifically, but it looks like we're heading in that direction.'

'In which case things could get close up and personal. We already know they're armed – I saw knives tucked into belts and there's that stunner to contend with – so we'll have to defend ourselves. I know we've had very little time to make preparations, but do you have any actual weapons? An old place like this surely has a few swords hanging on the wall. Pikes, perhaps? The odd crossbow –

230

anything at all?'

Doreen turned to Jenny. Jenny shrugged and glanced at Sandra. Sandra peered at Cutie, and Cutie stared long and hard at Martha. Martha, despite her distress, expressed indignation. 'Now why are you all looking at me like that?' she protested tartly. Cutie folded her arms, fingers tapping elbows, and continued to stare. Martha caved in completely. 'Oh, all right. Yes. I've got a whip. It was going to be a welcome present for you, Celeste. I heard you're pretty good.'

'I've had some experience,' replied Celeste dryly.

They conversed quickly in hushed tones, finalising their plan. With tasks allocated, each crept off through the house, using the servants' passageway to keep out of sight. Sandra gave them five minutes to get into position, then composed herself and marched boldly into the kitchen.

'Hello, boys,' she said primly. 'Listen, I've not had sex for more years than I care to remember and I'm absolutely gagging for a bit of cock. Actually, quite a lot of cock. I'd happily take on the lot of you, but frankly, I don't think you're up to it, especially Lardy-Arse over there!' She nodded contemptuously at the portly thug who'd zapped Martha, his face buried in one of Jenny's lemon drizzle cakes. 'Then again, you did Taser an old lady and lock us up in a smelly cellar, you ugly, festering, soft-knobbed, useless sacks of badger crap, so I guess your luck's out.'

Miller looked up from his smartphone, dark-eyed and shaven-headed, tossed the mobile onto the table and stood up very slowly, a knife suddenly in his hand. 'So you think we're not up for it, eh,' he snorted, leering nastily and clutching his groin like a randy pop star.

'Oh, bugger!' Sandra exclaimed as the others jumped to their feet. She didn't wait around any more and took off like a whippet with a habanero stuffed up its fundament. No man liked his virility scorned, and her carefully aimed insult almost blinded them to the obvious fact that the women had escaped.

Almost.

'Split up,' hissed Miller. 'You two, go after this bitch. Leach, Skinner, search for the rest. Don't be nice. Maximum persuasion. Call out if you find that ginger cow.'

'Which one? They're all bloody ginger!'

'The primary target, numbnuts. Go!'

The men leapt into action, scattering chairs. Sandra's chosen pair were the same two thugs who'd destroyed the toilet at *Choccy, Toffee & Coffee*. Having successfully gained their full attention, she heard the two men crash after her, howling like wolves, but she had the home advantage – she knew the Hall inside out and slowed her pace, allowing her pair of ardent suitors to gain a little. Another howl. She flew around a corner and pelted down the panelled corridor leading to the library. A Turkish carpet lay tacked to the oak floor ahead. The trap!

Cutie peeped out of the library door, a cheeky grin on her face. 'Got company?' she called.

'I wouldn't be running otherwise,' panted Sandra, scampering over the carpet and skidding to a halt. 'Come on, I'm all yours,' she called lasciviously, twerking at them, her denim-clad rump wobbling from side to side like a pair of silicone-filled hooters startled into motion by speedy passage over a cattle grid. Obliquely, she heard a muted clunk. Cutie had withdrawn the lock, freeing the trap.

'You're gonna love this, sister,' sneered Toilet Thug One. Both stepped onto the carpet – and the trap was sprung. The balanced floor tilted downward as their weight passed over the tipping point. With a cry, Toilet Thug Two fell into the yawning blackness opening up at his feet. Down he went, disappearing into the dark, sliding into the oubliette beneath, a deep windowless pit with smooth stone walls. Toilet Thug One managed to jump back, arms windmilling as he teetered on the very edge of the trap.

Celeste stepped out of a doorway behind him, uncoiling

the whip. 'Hey, moron,' she whispered. He turned, saw her standing with braced feet, a peculiar gleam in her eyes. Confident in his superior strength, he squared up to her, flexing his arms. Muscles, honed by weights and steroids, bunched impressively. 'Big mistake,' he growled.

'I beg to differ,' retorted Celeste. The whip hissed through the air. She judged its trajectory with effortless skill. The tip flicked an inch from his nose, cracking like a pistol shot. His reaction was instinctive – and disastrous. He jumped backwards with a squeak, boots scrabbling on the very edge of the oubliette. Celeste lashed out again on the return stroke, but this time the whip found its mark, slashing viciously across his neck, drawing a thin line of blood. He jerked spasmodically – and down he went as well, tumbling into the pit. A cry and curse from far below indicated his fall had been thoughtfully broken by his colleague. With them both safely trapped, the floor rose up, its balance restored. Once level again, Cutie threw the bolt to lock it in place. Celeste coiled the whip. 'Nicely done, Sandra,' she said. 'Has it really been that long?'

'I'm not at liberty to say,' Sandra replied tartly. 'But it has been a while,' she added with a sigh.

'Then we'll have to do something about that, won't we.' Celeste eyed the floor. No sound emanated through the oak boards. 'When was that little beauty put in?'

'When the Hall was built,' said Cutie. 'A last line of defence for the Temple.'

'Handy. Right, two down, three still at large. Let's go find Humph and the rest of his gang.'

'Careful, Celeste, he's got a knife,' warned Sandra.

'It won't make a ha'porth of difference.'

Cutie and Sandra glanced at each other, then stepped in behind Celeste, both buoyed by her supreme confidence. This woman had no concept of fear.

CHAPTER SIXTEEN

Jenny was being pursued. She'd been spotted by Lardy-Arse and dashed through the kitchen, a place bristling with cleavers and whisks and all manner of handy weapons, but with Leach bearing down on her she barely had time to snatch up the only object even conceivably suited for defence – her favourite frying pan. Thus armed, she scampered away. She could have outrun him, of course, even in wellies. To be honest, so could've Long John Silver with his Sunday afternoon leg fitted, but where was the fun in that. Stick to the plan, girl. Instead, she cantered towards the vegetable garden at an easy pace, one ear on the frantic huff-puffing behind. The man was seriously out of condition. A sadist, certainly, but a desperately unfit one.

Jen slipped through a gate into the walled garden. Now she was on home territory and headed for the far corner where a traditional Victorian timber glasshouse leaned against one wall as if thankful for the support. The slanting roof comprised rows of glass panes, green-edged with moss and streaked with lichen. The humid air inside was filled with the unique scent of geraniums and moist soil. Jenny skipped over the highly patterned floor, loose tiles rattling beneath her feet. They must have once been bright and colourful, but were faded now after more than a century of exposure to the sun. Plants encouraged into enthusiastic luxuriance bushed out on either side, fragrant and lush, every square inch filled with exotic species.

The place was awash with weaponry.

Leach smirked. He'd found the prettiest of the lot, now

235

she was trapped in that greenhouse. Probably thought he hadn't seen her slip inside. Fool! Holding his stun gun in one hand and the last remnants of lemon drizzle cake in the other, he stood in the doorway. She was his, there was no escape – and she knew it. She stood at the far end staring at him. He wanted to think she was cowering – frightened women were so much more pliant – but she seemed far less cowed than he'd hoped. Actually, she looked fairly pumped-up. Hmm, a few zaps from Stewie the Stunner should sort her out. Then he'd have some fun. He stuffed the last of the cake in his mouth, wiped his lemony fingers on his chest, and advanced down the greenhouse, a crumb-covered smile playing on piggy lips. 'No escape,' he announced confidently.

A tomato splattered against his shoulder. More shocked than hurt, he saw she'd fired it from a catapult. The impact was barely noticeable. He sniggered. 'Try harder, sugar tits. You'll need something more substantial than a vegetable to stop me.'

'Tomatoes are fruit, you cretin.'

'Don't care, I'm still coming for you. Nice quiet place, this. You and me all alone. Quite romantic, don't you think.' He unzipped himself and fished out Mr Sausage. Might as well let her know what was going to happen.

Jenny grinned. Excellent – he was circumcised! Now she had another potential target. She brought the catapult up again, pulled it back to her cheek, the strong elastic creaking under the tension. She was a good shot, having used the catapult regularly to scare pigeons off her cabbages, but knew stones would not stop this man. She needed heavier artillery.

The tomatoes possessed a deadly payload of chilli pepper.

And not just any pepper. Jen's pride and joy was her Dorset Naga, a prince among peppers. Nagas made a Scotch Bonnet look about as punchy as a week-old watercress sandwich. In India, peppers from the same family were smeared on fence posts to see off wild elephants! She'd prepared a bowlful, each plump tomato stuffed full of crushed pepper flesh.

Now she aimed for his eyes.

The tomato hit him in the face like a missile, exploding spectacularly.

The screaming started pretty quickly after that.

Flesh reddened as she watched, swelling obscenely until his features became a horribly distorted mask. The stun gun clattered to the floor, forgotten, abandoned as he sank to his knees, fingers clawing at his eyes. She knew the peppers were volcanic – they'd come with more warnings on the packet than weapons-grade plutonium – but this was beyond anything she could have imagined. Jenny almost felt sorry for him, then remembered this was the man who had made Martha pee her pants and followed up her first salvo with a direct hit on his foolishly exposed manhood.

This elicited a further shriek of agony as the Naga went to work, burning his bellend hideously. He writhed, arms waving as if he couldn't decide which part of his anatomy to comfort first.

Jenny was impressed. Damn, she'd have to grow some more of these little beauties.

She thought the fight had gone from him, but Leach lunged forward to grab her ankle. Jenny squeaked, kicking and stamping until he lost his grip. He staggered to his feet, eyes slitted and burning like coals, his dangler raw and crimson, and reached for her with clawed fingers.

Jenny didn't mess about. She grabbed the frying pan and swung it with every ounce of strength she possessed. It was a sweeping, full-on, two-handed strike, the impact actually lifting her feet from the floor. An impressively loud metallic clang echoed around the greenhouse as the base of the pan smacked him square in the face. Startled birds took to the air from nearby trees.

It really was a hell of a wallop. Wronged wives the

237

world over would have heartily approved.

Poleaxed by the blow, Leach sank to his knees and toppled forward like a felled spruce, straight-backed, arms by his side, his mangled face smashing against the tiles.

Jenny was genuinely astonished. So it wasn't an urban myth – you really could flatten someone with a frying pan. She examined her weapon. Its handle was badly bent and a nose-shaped bulge humped the centre of its base. 'Bastard!' she exclaimed softly. 'That was my best pan.' She pulled out the handcuffs and secured one inert wrist to a metal stanchion. The stun gun went into her pocket. 'Shouldn't have pissed off the cook!' she muttered at him, then fled the greenhouse, slamming the door on his prone body.

'Come out, come out wherever you are,' growled Skinner. He'd just seen the kid and the incontinent old woman slip through the study door into the flower garden beyond and had set off, padding silently like a hunting leopard, but his confidence was shaken by a distant scream, shivering, shrill and shot through with agony. He stopped dead in his tracks, listening. Another dreadful cry drifted down the wind. That was no woman. Leach? He paused, listening intently, but the cries were not repeated.

'Goddammit,' he muttered, now a little unnerved. He'd fought in nasty little wars all over Africa, hawking his expertise to the highest bidder, and was ruthless to his enemies, yet there was something unnerving about the tranquil house. Where the hell had they gone? Now more careful after the screams, he pulled his knife and darted into the garden, crouching, ready for anything. He already knew the only other gate in the wall beyond the flowers was secured. He and his colleagues had entered through this gate and locked it behind them to ensure privacy. The two women would be trapped and at his mercy. Perhaps he'd cut them a little. Teach them a lesson. He grinned at the thought. Miller always came up with some great jobs.

Something gloopy splattered against his chest.

Startled, Skinner peered down and pawed at the mess. It was very sticky. He smelt his fingers. An overwhelming sweetness filled his nostrils. A lick confirmed his suspicions. 'Honey,' he guffawed. 'Is that the best you can do? Hoping I'll eventually pass out in hypoglycaemic shock?'

Two figures emerged from a honeysuckle-covered trellis, both swaddled in protective suits and meshed hats, their hands held behind their backs. 'Dumbarse! Hypoglycaemia is caused by a lack of sugar,' sneered Cutie. 'You should be more worried about what comes with the honey.' She and her companion held out their hands. Skinner frowned. They appeared to be wearing boxing gloves – but those gloves seethed and shimmered.

And hummed.

Cutie knew they were ill suited to a physical confrontation. Neither possessed the bulk, muscle or psychological propensity to violence. This is a common failing amongst librarians. However, they had one priceless advantage – they were both very smart women indeed. They also knew how to arouse a host of small but surprisingly aggressive winged helpers.

She and Martha flung themselves at Skinner, flicking great gobbets of bee-coated honeycomb over his torso and face. Surprised, he jumped back. Nothing happened for a few moments. The bees just flew away, some dropping to the ground around his feet and twitching forlornly. Skinner looked at the golden mess stuck to his shirt and chuckled. 'Nice try, ladies, but – ouch!' The first sting caught him in the neck. He slapped the insect away, leaving the barbed stinger behind, its venom sac pulsing.

'Shouldn't have done that,' said Cutie. 'I'd start running for shelter if I were you. Try the potting shed over there.'

Skinner hissed. Another sting, this time on the chin and bloody painful. Then another. And another. A dawning

239

horror gripped him when four came in quick succession, like machine gun bullets. Suddenly, a boiling cloud erupted from the hive nestling behind the honeysuckle. Compelled by pheromones leaking from the broken stingers, the bees smothered Skinner in an instant. He waved his arms frantically, but that had never really worked as a defence at any time in the past and so it proved on this occasion as well. The insects attacked with mindless determination, sacrificing themselves without hesitation. Skinner caught an excruciating sting on the eyeball and almost puked at the pain. A desperate need to find sanctuary replaced all thought of attacking the women. He sprinted for the brick potting shed with admirable vigour, the swarm trailing in his wake like smoke from a steam locomotive, launched himself through the heavy plank door and kicked it shut.

Cutie scampered after him and turned the key in the lock. 'And that's how we do it around here,' she crowed triumphantly. Bees swarmed all over the shed, buzzing angrily. Some crawled under the door to continue their attack. Sounds of frantic stamping and whacking emanated from within. 'Seems he'll be busy for some time,' said Martha. 'Shall we get back to the others?'

Celeste knew Miller would be the most dangerous combatant of them all. He was the ringmaster, the lynchpin between the troops on the ground and their distant and as yet unidentified commanders. This needed to be handled delicately. Difficult, seeing as he appeared particularly intent on doing her some damage, but she remained hopeful she might be able to extract some information from him if at all possible.

He had a knife. Men who carried knives were readily disposed to using them. The knife worried her, but she was armed herself and had complete confidence in her own skills. Martha had chosen well – the whip was a little beauty. Braided rawhide with a short stock, ideal for close

240

quarter encounters, and she'd added some extra zing by knotting the last four inches. She wanted him to suffer for his treatment of Milly. Cruelty to any animal was unjustified. Then there was the emotive subject of her husband's damaged danglies …

She picked her spot carefully. In the corridor leading to the library. Doreen had shown her how to set the trap and it was now behind her, unlocked and primed. The other women were gathered safely in the kitchen, the door bolted. Celeste did not want any of them around to distract her while she dealt with this exceptionally unpleasant man. Besides, she had all the help she needed waiting nearby. A back-up. Reserves. The cavalry.

'Won't keep you a moment, Mr Johnstone,' she said evenly when he finally appeared. His angry calling for his comrades had been getting louder, signifying both his approach and increasing exasperation at their absence. She needed to show him she was not afraid and peered at her reflection in a mirror hanging on the wall, checking her make-up and tousling her hair unnecessarily in that way women have perfected specifically to annoy men who are in a hurry. 'I think you'll find you're on your own. Your associates are now all, shall we say, indisposed. Forgive me for sounding harsh, but I won't be losing any sleep over their predicament.'

Miller padded towards her, knife in hand, his face contorted with rage. 'What do you mean?'

Celeste dabbed on some lippy. 'Are you thick or something? Does the employment of words with more than one syllable cause you difficulty?'

Miller paused, frowning. Well that was unexpected. Of all things, he hadn't bargained for an English lesson from the stuck-up bitch.

After one final check in the mirror to ensure all was perfect, Celeste turned to give him her full attention. 'Let me explain more simply. The girls have brought your men down. All of them are now neutralised, two very painfully indeed. Looks like it's just you and me, Humph. I'd like to ask you some questions about the brains behind your brawn, but somehow, from the expression on your face, I don't think you'll be offering any information, and I'm certainly not going to tell you anything about our plans, so shall we crack on?' she said in a businesslike tone, uncoiling the whip casually, the chain wrapped around her other fist and dangling almost to the floor. Miller felt a wash of uncertainty. He recognised a creditable adversary when he saw one. Still, he had the knife, a generous physical advantage, full knowledge of martial arts, a complete absence of conscience and a ready predisposition to sadistic violence. A winning hand.

'Sod plucking the parrot,' he said coldly. This was now personal. 'I'm going to hurt you in an entirely different way.' Things had fallen apart badly. He needed to deal with this ginger cow, extract his men and execute a strategic withdrawal. Netheridge would have to come up with a different plan to deal with her perverted prick of a husband. 'I'm going to enjoy this.'

'So am I,' she replied with a sunny smile.

Miller advanced again, crouching low with arms spread wide, a carefully cultured murderous expression on his face. To his slight concern, she did not retreat. Usually, people retreated. Actually, they almost always retreated, often with commendable alacrity. More like fleeing in terror than retreating, but not this time. He knew he cut an intimidating figure, ex-special services guys always did, but the woman stood her ground.

'Time to be afraid,' he said very softly, pointing at her with the knife.

Celeste sighed wearily. 'Save your clichés. I've met – and bettered – far worse than you. You're a bully and a coward, Humph, and compared to Martin Shufflebottom, you're little more than a petulant, pusillanimous pussycat.'

'A what?' Miller had been called many things in his life, but never that. A blush of righteous indignation coloured his face. 'And who the hell is he?'

Celeste spotted the flush. Yes, you've still got it, girl. Tease him some more. Undermine his confidence, make him think defeat is a possibility, then force him into a mistake. It had worked at school, no reason to think it wouldn't work now.

'Martin is a rage-filled psycho. You know, a proper man. He'd never hide behind a knife. Fists, teeth and boots are his weapons. Balls of steel, that one. Entirely out of your league, Humph. I mean, come on, even I can see you've got hands of beer-softened veal.'

Miller went hot. Goaded by her mocking, he pounced. Cut first to incapacitate, then enjoy.

His lunge was anticipated. Celeste twisted to one side, spinning away before lashing at him with explosive strength, the whip hissing like an enraged cobra. Carried by his momentum, Miller fell into the stroking leather. Pain, indescribable in its intensity, erupted in his neck and shoulder. The knotted tip of the whip curled around his face and excoriated his left cheek and eye. Miller yelped, which in itself was unusual. He hadn't yelped since inflicting an unfortunate zippering injury on his Old Man during a hasty exit from a Benghazi brothel while moonlighting for Gaddafi in '98. Rawhide slid across his face, trailing wetness. He touched his cheek and looked at his fingers. Not tears – blood.

Celeste knew she could not underestimate this man and got in a return stroke with the chain while he stared at his blood-soaked fingertips in shock. Her target was the knife. Heavy steel links crunched around his hand, breaking all manner of delicate bones, but Miller, too, was full of surprises, and instantly switched the blade to his left hand. His arm swung, back and forth, slashing at her, a diabolical grin on his bloodied face, but she held him at bay with the whip and chain.

'You're good,' he rasped, 'but you're still mine. Never had me a ginger clacker before.'

243

'Don't get your hopes up, Humph.'

They circled each other warily, the library now directly behind Celeste, the Turkish carpet perilously close to the backs of her heels. Miller leapt in, feinted to the right and the blade drew a vivid scarlet line across Celeste's forearm. He expected her to cry out in pain, or at the very least flinch at the wound, but she merely chuckled, face flushed, eyes bright, her lips parted and wet as she casually licked up the trail of blood.

Miller was astonished. She displayed all the signs of a woman bordering on profound sexual excitement.

'Venha cá!' she called suddenly.

'What?'

'I'm so sorry, I tend to sneeze when I'm aroused.'

'You're a bloody nutter,' hissed Miller. He'd had enough. Time to end this farce. 'The world won't miss you one little bit.' He advanced, blood in one eye, murder in the other. 'First you, then your parrot.'

'Duck,' she said.

'I thought he was a macaw.'

'No, duck!' repeated Celeste.

Realization swept over Miller and he spun around – just in time to get a faceful of claws.

Bertie's impact was tremendous. He'd heard his mum's summons in their secret language – known to the rest of the world as Portuguese – and swept up in a blue blur to crash into Miller, his sheer inertia staggering the man. Claws sank deep into flesh, puncturing, tearing horribly at his cheeks and mouth. This man had hurt Milly, his mate. This man was attacking his mum. Cold, primal fury consumed him. The beast took over, replacing his normally unruffled amiability. He buffeted with his wings, body draped over Miller's crown, shrieking a fighting call.

Bertie knew from previous experience exactly how fragile human ears could be and homed in on his favourite target, stabbing Miller with lightning speed. His dagger bill parted skin like a scalpel, its tip grating along the mastoid bone and separating a large part of Miller's ear from his head. He screamed. Yelping no longer cut the mustard.

Celeste stepped to one side as Miller lurched past and, balancing on one heel, lashed out with a brutal stamp, dislocating his kneecap. The kick helped him on his way. He stumbled onto the Turkish carpet, one leg collapsed and useless, arms flailing for balance. Blood spurted from the side of his head, his catastrophically damaged ear hanging down and flopping against his neck. The trap tipped instantly and he began to slide down. Bertie released his grip and, in one fluid movement, swooped on into the library through its open door. Terror consumed Miller. His one remaining workable leg pumped frantically, but the carpet offered no purchase. Down he tumbled into the gaping darkness below, eyes bulging, his face a twisted mask, but at the last moment his arm went back and the knife arced through the air, embedding itself into Celeste's thigh.

'Norton Village Hall, Protect Yourself Combat Course for Women! Shove that up your frock, Humph!' she yelled into the black pit as the trap swung back up to close with a thump. Cheeks still blushing with excitement from the fight, she calmed herself with a few deep breaths before looking down, her attention now drawn by the lancing pain in her thigh. The knife protruded dramatically. Abstractly, she noted it was in an almost identical place to the stabbing James had received from the gold-nibbed Prime Ministerial pen. His and hers wounds – now there's true love for you!

Gripping the haft, she pulled the knife from her thigh, blood bubbling under her trousers. The wound was clean and sharp-edged. At least Miller had done her the courtesy of keeping his blade keen. It stung viciously, but was not deep – his last desperate throw had been wild and without any real force. 'Bloody amateur,' she snorted. 'Couldn't even throw a knife properly.'

She had a quick look around to make sure she was alone, then gave her thigh a good hard poke, just for fun. The prod could not in any way be described as a diagnostic method recommended by the medical profession, but it did produce a disturbingly dreamy look in her eyes.

She'd always had an ambivalent relationship with pain, always walked the fine line between it and pleasure.

Heat blossomed inside, ignited by the excitement of the fight and then stoked by the throbbing wound, but personal gratification would have to wait. Reluctantly, she turned her mind to more immediate matters. Her thigh required dressing and she badly needed a cup of tea. She hugged one wall to bypass the deadly carpet and hobbled into the library. Bertie was perched on the back of a sofa cleaning his bloodstained claws.

'I love you, Mummy,' he said happily.

Celeste threw the bolt to lock the trap. 'I love you, too, my brave little soldier. Come on, let's find you something nice to eat.' She limped away towards the kitchen and some sticking plaster, Bertie waddling along at her side.

CHAPTER SEVENTEEN

'We really should call an ambulance,' said Doreen. She stared in dismay at the red stain on Celeste's thigh.

'For this? Don't bother. I've hurt myself more plucking my eyebrows.' Celeste flexed her leg experimentally. 'I can't believe I'm saying this, but it's just a flesh wound. Jeez, I sound like Randolph Scott.'

'But –'

'Don't sweat it, Doreen. The skin's hardly broken. It looks a lot worse than it is. There was no force in the throw. There, I can walk already.' They stood in the kitchen. Cutie and Martha had divested themselves of their trendy apiarist protection, Jenny was filling the kettle, Celeste hobbled around the table as if to demonstrate her mobility and Sandra nervously turned her diamond-shaped piece of wood over and over in her hands.

'So they're all accounted for, all five? Good. Jen, where's yours?'

'Blinded by pepper-filled tomatoes, then rendered unconscious by frying pan and handcuffed to the conservatory.'

'A little over the top, but I like your style. Cutie?'

'Hopefully suffering major anaphylaxis locked in the potting shed.'

'And the remaining three in the oubliette. Excellent,' smiled Doreen. 'Well done, girls.'

'Any chance we can question Humph?' asked Celeste. 'He might be more talkative now I've softened him up a bit. I need to know who sent them. A day or so in the dark with his ear hanging off should make him more amenable.'

Cutie started giggling. The girl was irrepressible. Even Martha, wan and still embarrassingly damp, had to hide a smile behind her hand. Doreen looked at them and sighed wearily. 'All right, what have you two done?'

'We stored Norman in the oubliette last time we were down there.'

Doreen stared at them in disbelief, then burst out laughing. 'Oh dear. That should get them worried.'

'Who's Norman?' asked Celeste.

'Our skeleton. Dates back to the twelfth century, hence Norman. The bones of our resident ghost.'

'So those men are stuck in a hidden pit?'

'Yes.'

'In total darkness?'

'I didn't see any of them carrying a torch.'

'No hope of escape?'

'None.'

'With a skeleton for company?'

'Yup.'

'And the most unpleasant of them half bleeding to death.' Celeste pondered for a moment. 'Then we only need give them a couple of hours. Meanwhile, I could murder that cup of tea.'

The kitchen was a mess. Jenny tutted irritably and started gathering plates, clattering out her anger. Miller's mobile still lay on the table. Cutie examined it carefully. 'Mmm, password protected,' she murmured. 'Let's have a think about this. Psychos are surprisingly predictable. Adolf Hitler's birthplace? No. Pinochet's first name? Hmm, not that, either.'

'What about famous Humphreys?' suggested Celeste.

'Bogart? No, sorry.'

'Lyttleton?'

'Bingo! Give that girl an ice cream,' chuckled Cutie. She delved deep into the phone, nimble fingertips dancing over the touch screen.

'What have you got, Geraldine?' asked Celeste.

'Firstly, I'm uploading his entire content into a new password-protected account on the cloud. That'll ensure we have a copy, whatever happens to this phone. While that's chugging away, I'll just have a peep at his latest ...' Cutie's voice trailed off as she quickly discovered a preponderance of calls to two particular numbers.

'These texts indicate his boss is a man called Netheridge, but he also has a close association with someone called Matthew Black. Hmm, the sly bastard. You won't be surprised to know he's double-crossing Netheridge. Black knows everything. They both appear to be in some sort of high-power commercial cabal. There's some names here that sound awfully familiar.' Cutie continued to scroll. 'Interesting. These are extremely wealthy men. From London.'

'The men from the east, as Maggie foretold,' said Doreen.

'And that's not all. I'm afraid you're not going to get the luxury of a couple of hours, Celeste,' Cutie added urgently. 'We're not out of the woods yet. Humph sent a text not half an hour ago. Probably the last thing he did before Sandra made her show-stopping appearance. Netheridge is on his way here right now with Milly. Black, too, but he's after something else entirely, something valuable beyond measure.' She turned Miller's phone to show Doreen the screen. A red-haired beauty stared back. 'Humph's told Black about our art. He's coming to get Helen!'

Black took no notice of the Hall at all. Its ancient peace and beauty did not call out to him, its weathered grace unappealing in every way. He already had plenty of homes and all of them much larger and grander than this old country pile of dust and spiders. He was much more interested in what the Hall contained. He parked his Mercedes right by the front door, its boot lid already humming open. Time was of the essence. This was to be a speedy entry, quick snatch and flying exit. Miller had texted the all-clear. He had the women corralled and was now engaged with Netheridge in the kitchen, giving him a guaranteed window of about ten minutes to snatch the art and be long gone. Miller would then melt away with his men after disabling Netheridge's vehicle and calling the police, leaving young Adam to face the music. He grabbed a stepladder out of the boot and, easing the front door ajar, slipped inside.

The grand entrance hall lay silent and empty. Black scanned the walls. Holy crap on a cream cracker, Miller hadn't been joking! There were pieces here of national importance. The Reynolds alone was magnificent, the Gainsborough worth a fortune, but he'd not come for them. When it came to art, Black was motivated entirely by beauty. His gaze locked on to the painting above the fireplace.

Helen of Troy.

The portrait was glorious, its colours rich and vibrant. Helen of Troy as a redhead. Sandys had been inspired, his vision incomparable. In Black's view, Rossetti's effort paled into insipidity. Yes, this would be one of the crowning glories of his collection. What a find. In a rare moment of philanthropy, he resolved to give Miller an extra bonus for his efforts. He hustled forward, planted the stepladder and, climbing to the top step, carefully lifted the painting off the wall. Close up, the portrait was utterly beguiling and for a moment he lost himself in those wonderfully smouldering eyes, wallowing in a moment of indulgent introspection. Yes, he'd come a long way over the years.

For a while, Black had accumulated wealth merely as a precaution against poverty. This was at the very beginning of his career when a return to the impoverished mediocrity of Swaffham remained a distinct possibility, but once he'd developed a liking for destroying his commercial rivals, the Black juggernaut really moved into top gear, creating truly obscene amounts of profit. He didn't waste his hard-earned on any fancy accountant, but personally distributed his income amongst numerous offshore accounts, keeping only one hand-written record of his investments in his safe at home. Better that way. No electronic trails for the tax authorities to follow. Through a unique process of legitimization involving several Central American states, the money was washed cleaner than a Sunday morning football kit before oozing unctuously and discreetly into tax havens all over the globe. Black discovered, as only the very seriously rich do, that not only does money beget money, but that a lot of money begets a lot of money.

By this time, his pan-European paint cartel had really established itself, generating vast sums of profit on which he found himself increasingly disinclined to pay any tax. Which in turn boosted his income – and so the financial merry-go-round gained speed, dumping truly astonishing amounts into his several hundred accounts.

Which he then liked to spend on the finer things in life.

Such as adding to his personal and very private art collection. Private by necessity, of course. Black would pay for a painting if he absolutely had to, but certainly not if it could be obtained for nothing. The rest of the population would call this stealing, but Black, with his warped morality, merely saw it as an act of accumulation from unprotected sources. His art collection now filled a huge hidden basement below his London townhouse and included paintings by Vermeer, Cezanne, Monet, Matisse and Pablo Picasso, works that had been stolen to order over many years. Miller was good at this. The man was a talented procurer of valuable art, either by direct theft from galleries, or by tracking down lost masterpieces and pinching them from other illicit collectors. Vincent's Poppy Flowers had recently come into Black's possession by this route, snaffled from a drug baron's country retreat near Stoke Poges.

And now here was Helen of Troy. A pre-Raphaelite

treasure. God, she was so beautiful – and so easy to take. Black liked to get personally involved if the situation was safe enough. He'd driven the getaway car from Stoke Poges, chortling all the way home when Miller told him he'd left a magic marker penis scrawled on the wall where the van Gogh had been hung. And now he stood in this empty hall with the picture in his hands. This was going to be so easy.

'Good afternoon.'

Black spun around at the sound of the voice, still grasping the canvas. A man stood a few paces inside the open front door. Damn, should've locked it, cursed Black to himself. Too late now. He hadn't heard the other's approach, such had his attention been consumed by the masterpiece in his hands. The stepladder wobbled alarmingly.

'Now, you wouldn't be thinking of stealing that picture, would you? How about sticking it back on the wall and then we can have a little chat.'

But Black had already been seduced by Helen and was loath to let her go so easily. He had no intention of relinquishing his grip. 'I must get off this ladder. The painting needs to be rehung properly,' he said gruffly, already stepping down. 'It's also heavy. I'll put it on the table.'

Unknown to Black, the man he now faced was experienced in these little dramas and recognised the warning signs. There was no doubt Black was freeing himself up for action; the bigger man, he was obviously confident in his physical prowess. He was impressively broad-shouldered, bulky and grizzled, but he was also no spring chicken.

Black thought furiously. This stranger he now faced was tall and wiry. In a physical conflict, Black knew he could take him. He was good at making the right decisions in moments of crisis, an invaluable talent for a businessman of his calibre, and he trusted his judgement now. With the picture safely out of the way, he turned to face his opponent. 'Listen, Lanky, you have two choices. If you're clever, you already know what they are.'

'Indulge me,' came the polite reply. 'And it's Mr Lanky to you.'

'I'll give you the chance to leave,' he said evenly. 'I'll even throw in ten grand as an encouragement. All you have to do is walk away and keep your mouth shut.'

'That's a *very* generous offer. And the other option?'

'I beat you to a pulp and leave with the painting anyway.'

'Ah, the bully's bargain. Haven't heard that one for a while.' Lanky's hands remained in the pockets of his coat. He showed no inclination to prepare himself for action so Black made the mistake of assuming he'd got his way yet again.

'I'm so happy you've made the right decision.'

'Have I now.' Although concentrating entirely on his opponent, Lanky became peripherally aware of movement up in the gallery behind Black. Excellent. A witness. A woman. She had the sense to stand quietly, looking down at the two men. His day was getting better all the time. 'Tempting though your offer is, I still can't let you kidnap Ginger,' he said genially.

Above the two men, Sandra stood silently, peering down at the tableau from behind the heavy stone balustrade. She'd heard voices and come to investigate. The man with his back to her had obviously been in the process of stealing Helen of Troy – the portrait lay on the table with his hand resting on the frame in a blatantly possessive manner. He emanated a compressed aura of menace. His opponent was also middle-aged, but much slighter in build. He showed a lot of bottle confronting the larger man. She rather admired that and found his determination to protect Helen impressive. He was also quite handsome, in a sort of lean, intense way. Nice eyes, and baldness suited him. Mmm, actually, he was a bit gorgeous.

Black advanced. 'You going to be a problem?' he growled menacingly.

'Only where you're concerned.' Lanky's hands stayed firmly in his pockets.

'One last chance. A man like you could well use twenty grand. You could buy a coat that fits, for a start.'

'Twenty!' he chuckled, eyebrows raised in surprise. 'My, you are desperate.' The more dangerous the situation, the cooler he became. Up on the gallery, Sandra quietly began to drool.

'Out of my way, Baldy.'

'Now that's just plain rude.' Would it be a charge or a swing?

It was a swing.

Black knew he was strong enough to flatten his adversary. His fist arced – but completely failed to reach its target. Lanky ducked and twisted with lightning speed, no mean feat for a man with a comfortable number of years under his belt. With hands suddenly free, he grabbed Black's collar and, using the man's own forward momentum, tripped and shoved him face down onto the floor, following up his winning move with a none-too-gentle thumblock. Black grunted and tried to throw him off, but got a hard knee in the back of the neck for his efforts, his nose squashed painfully against the floor. Lanky pinned him to the ground, using his weight on Black's neck to subdue him effortlessly. He struggled, cursing prodigiously, but could not break free.

'Language! And in front of a lady as well.' Lanky rummaged through his mac pocket. 'Now, let's see, where are they?' he murmured, producing a tube of mints. 'No, not them, but I'll have one anyway.' Another search uncovered a tissue. 'Hardly,' he said urbanely, peering up and winking at Sandra. He was so damned cool. Parts of her were becoming very warm indeed. Ovaries, long dormant, began to tremble with anticipation. 'Ah, here we are.' To her surprise, he conjured up a pair of handcuffs, snapped them around Black's wrists, hauled him roughly to his feet and threw him into a chair. 'Sit!' he ordered forcefully, pointing a warning finger, then straightened his tie and turned to Sandra with a broad smile. 'Hello, gorgeous. I'm Detective Sergeant Wilfred Thompson. I'm a good friend of Celeste Timbrill. And Bertie. Now, I know they're around here somewhere ...'

Netheridge wrestled with the cage, dragging it along the floor, the macaw inside protesting indignantly at its mistreatment. Without the wheeled stand, it was bastard heavy and awkward to handle. 'Shut it!' he snapped. Unsurprisingly, the bird refused to comply and continued to squawk and shriek as it struggled to maintain balance on its perch. 'No witty remarks? I thought you were quite the conversationalist,' muttered Netheridge irritably. 'Seems I was mistaken.'

'Forties! Fisher! FitzRoy!' screeched Milly.

'That's better,' he said sarcastically. He lugged the cage and its unhappy occupant through the back door. He'd slipped the van in behind the stable block alongside Miller's. Several other cars were also there. His gang members. All were well out of sight from anyone arriving at the Hall. Careful chap, was Miller. Netheridge had absolute confidence his man was in complete charge of the situation.

Once inside, he looked around. No one was about. A pang of unease tempered his impatience. He was totally unaccustomed to field work, preferring to stay safe and warm in his office, directing operations from afar, but recently he'd found this prudence lacking in excitement. Miller was always full of such interesting and amusing anecdotes each time he returned from an operation, and Netheridge found himself wanting to share those experiences. This jaunt down to the Cotswolds was an ideal introduction. The target was soft, the women so easy to subdue, the results ridiculously easy to attain, yet the silence permeating the house was eerily disturbing.

Miller had texted the all-clear and should have been waiting at the gate, but the man was nowhere in sight. Netheridge cautiously made his way down a passage and into the large kitchen. Plates and mugs were strewn about. Man debris. No woman would leave such a mess. Well, at least that meant Miller and his crew were on the premises somewhere. He listened, but could hear no voices. Still, it was a big house. With a cellar. Netheridge dumped the large cage beside the table, thankful to give his arm a rest. Who would have believed a bird could be so damned heavy? Gazing around, he felt a half-drunk mug of tea. Still warm. So they were definitely here. Somewhere.

'Come on, Chuckles,' he said to Milly. 'Let's find Miller.' He wasn't a nervous man by nature, as his business rivals could confirm, but the tranquil house made him uneasy. Perhaps he wasn't up to fieldwork after all. For god's sake, show some backbone – it's just a sleepy old pile that smelt of cooking and lavender. Dragging the cage again, he headed towards the only other door in the kitchen.

'This way, Mr Netheridge, if you please.'

Netheridge froze. The distant call, echoing down the corridor ahead, made his heart hammer. It wasn't Miller. In fact, it wasn't even male. Damn, one of the bitches must still be free, but how did she know his name? He'd have Miller's eyes for this. Netheridge couldn't stand a sloppy job. Grabbing a carving knife from the table, he crept forward, scanning the passage for any dangers. Mercifully, his meteorologically obsessed companion stayed silent.

He came to a cross-corridor. One way seemed to lead to the back of the house, the other opened into grander rooms. He paused, uncertain, then heard a voice talking softly to his left and, taking a grip on the knife, stole in that direction, although the scrape of metal cage on wooden flooring rendered a silent approach impossible.

His original plan still held. Find Miller, secure this woman, whoever she was, and abuse the bird in front of its owner, pressuring her into submission. There might need to be some slapping and punching as well. Perhaps a bit of sexual aggression. It was a good plan, well thought out and, so far, faultlessly executed. He'd received a text. Timbrill was languishing in the Roman dungeon, handcuffed to her companions. The delicious irony warmed Netheridge's cold soul, fortifying his resolve. The tables were definitely turned. He crept forward again and emerged into the main hall. What he saw left him speechless.

A redheaded women stood over a seated man, talking to him quietly, her back to Netheridge. It had to be Celeste Timbrill. Her flame hair was nationally recognised. The seated man was obscured, but then she turned and moved to one side, revealing his identity.

'You!' he exclaimed. 'What the hell are you doing here?'

Matt Black sat on a chair, morose, angry and scared all at the same time. The paint magnate was dishevelled, as if he'd been in a fight, and was obviously handcuffed. He glared at Netheridge, but stayed silent.

'Good afternoon,' said Celeste evenly. 'Would you mind telling me what you're doing with that poor macaw?'

Netheridge recovered from the shock of seeing Black. He was a tough man. Not much bothered him. He'd get to the bottom of Black's involvement soon enough. 'Concerned for his welfare? How touching,' he sneered.

'I really don't like to see animals mistreated,' said Celeste grimly. 'It's unnecessary. Cruelty demonstrates a damaged person.'

'Oh, damaged, am I? That's bold talk from someone who's loved one is under my control.' Netheridge shook the cage and Milly protested with commendable volume. Celeste stepped forward, but stopped at the appearance of the knife. 'Close enough, Timbrill, or I'll cut the bird.'

'Threatening a captive animal – that must present quite a challenge to your courage,' she mocked.

'Let's cut the clever talk,' hissed Netheridge, keen to get the deal done and be on his way. Where the hell was Miller?

'I agree. You'll stand a chance of understanding the conversation then.'

Her sarcasm ruffled Netheridge. She showed no timidity or fear, even though he held a blade to the macaw through the bars. Her affection and love for the bird was well known, yet she seemed immune to threat. She even ignored the wide smear of blood streaked down one leg from a wound that obviously looked painful. An uncharacteristic nervousness roiled inside. Get a grip, man, he told himself savagely. With Miller nowhere in sight, he'd have to do the job himself, and what a pleasurable job it would be – the snotty cow was a real mouthy whore. Right, do what you're good at and scare the living crap out of her.

'Shut your mouth, Timbrill, and listen. I have no qualms about brutalizing this bloody bird. He's my hold over you, and you have control over that pathetic GIMP of a husband of yours. Do what you're told or the parrot gets plucked. I'll be sending you a feather a week if you don't toe the line. In a month he'll look like a Tesco turkey at Christmas. I imagine it's a painful experience. Shall we put it to the test?' He reached in and yanked out one of Milly's back feathers.

She was not impressed. Not at all. There was an almighty screech. 'Ahh, Sole!'

Celeste burned with anger, yet still smiled at Milly's pithy reference to the notoriously restless shipping area located off southern Ireland.

'My sentiments exactly,' she said grimly. 'Time to finish this farce.'

'One feather not enough for you?' snarled Netheridge. 'Let's try again.' He reached out again and got a fingertip removed for his trouble. Milly's bill was as sharp as a razor. Her powerful head darted forward, snakelike, and she struck with all the anger of an outraged harpy engaged in a bout of enthusiastic Friday night hair-pulling outside a Chesterfield nightclub.

Netheridge squeaked with pain, cradling his spurting finger, blood trickling down his wrist. What the blazes was going on? Things were not going his way – and that didn't happen very often. Anger and frustration boiled up, a dangerous combination in such an unstable character – and where the hell was Miller?

'Miller!' he roared. 'Miller!'

The Hall remained ominously silent. 'Ah, so his name's Miller. I didn't put him down as a Humphrey Johnstone. Thank you for the information, but I think you'll find he's unable to help.'

'What!'

'Your man and his inept little gang are safely imprisoned. They can't offer assistance. You're very much on your own.'

Netheridge paled, suddenly aware of his vulnerability, a reaction not unnoticed by Celeste. 'Now, while we've been waiting for your arrival, I've had a nice little chat with Mr Black here. He's been most co-operative. Seems he's very concerned about you, Adam. A small matter of wolfsbane.'

'What?'

'You would know it as monkshood. It appears you're an enthusiast for this particular poison. Mr Black was worried some might come his way. That's why he and Miller have cooked up a little plan to get rid of you.'

'Plan?' snarled Netheridge. 'What the hell are you talking about?'

'Oh, so you weren't aware Miller has been working for Mr Black. That must be a shock. It was Miller who suggested you came down to watch proceedings, wasn't it? Once you were here, he and his gang had planned to melt away with the macaw after calling the police, leaving you to face arrest and multiple charges.'

'You bastard!' Netheridge hissed, his face contorted. A cold rage consumed him.

Miller's treachery must have come as a mortal blow. The man was reeling. Time to play her trump card. 'However, although Mr Miller is unable to join us, I do have someone here who's very keen to see you.' She whistled shrilly. Nothing happened for a few seconds, then Netheridge became aware of an approaching clatter, an odd scratching.

Bertie scampered around a corner, his long tail swishing from side to side on the old oak boards, claws clicking. 'Hello, Mummy,' he called happily.

'Hello, Bertie. Look who's here.'

She pointed and Bertie trilled in joy, his head bobbing up and down. 'Milly. Here's Milly.' He started purring very enthusiastically. Milly squawked in response.

Netheridge's eyes bulged. He stared in turn at the two macaws. Celeste smiled grimly at his confusion. 'You're really not having a good day, are you?'

'What? Who?'

'Talk about the weather, did she?'

'She?'

'You got the wrong bird, moron. You never had Bertie. That's Milly, his mate. She was at the cottage on love leave when Miller came calling. The clueless knob took the wrong macaw. I guess he thought it would be easy, after all, how many hyacinths can there be in Prior's Norton? Well, you nasty, truly repellent, cretinous, festering, chlamydia-raddled pustule of a man, the answer is two. Your paid halfwit really excelled himself on this occasion.'

'Mummy?'

'Yes, my darling.'

'Milly.'

'Yes, it's Milly.'

'Feathers.' Bertie saw the blue curl at Netheridge's feet.

'Yes, Milly's feathers.'

Bertie waddled forward. Netheridge hurriedly stepped back. Milly squawked again. Bertie answered. Netheridge looked at Celeste, a ghastly expression on his face. Bertie looked at the feathers, then at Netheridge. He stopped purring.

'I would strongly recommend running at this point,' she suggested. 'My baby has previous in these matters.'

Bertie advanced in silence. Until that moment, Netheridge would have thought it ludicrous for a brightly coloured macaw to express any kind of menace, but no longer. In his eyes, Bertie's laughably waddling gait transformed itself into an implacable swagger. Claws clicked on the oak boards: sickled, needle-tipped claws. Netheridge retreated cautiously, maintaining as large a distance as possible from the blue bird, suddenly very frightened indeed. He continued to back away, then Bertie spread his wings, dropped his head and hissed in a clear display of aggression.

Time to leave.

Netheridge bolted. The macaw had a formidable reputation. Having already sustained one painful injury, he wasn't terribly keen to add another. What a total balls-up, but he was confident the situation could still be salvaged. However, above all, he now needed to get away. Even out of the country, where he could orchestrate a policy of targeted damage limitation based on generous disbursements to ensure no further action would be taken. Then he'd have Black and Miller. Goddammit, he'd have them if it was the last thing he ever did.

Consumed by fury, he found himself running blindly. The kitchen was down this corridor, wasn't it? In his growing panic and confusion, he neglected to notice a foot thrusting out from a doorway to send him sprawling.

'Going somewhere?' enquired Wilf casually. Tripping

was his favourite interception technique. Netheridge scrambled to his feet, waving the knife wildly, his other fist clenched to try and stem the flow of blood. Christ, it always looked so much easier in the movies. Wilf raised an eyebrow sardonically. 'You going to use that, sonny, or are you planning a whittling demonstration for the WI?'

His dry comment humiliated Netheridge. 'Back! Get back!' he screamed.

'Don't be a daft bugger,' sighed Wilf. This wasn't the first time he'd been faced by a blade. 'Just drop the knife and we can keep this civil. No? Oh well, have it your own way.'

Wilf slowly and oh-so-casually took off his mac and hung it neatly over one arm. He adjusted his tie and, at the exact moment Netheridge frowned in perplexity at the odd action, tossed the mac over his knife arm. Netheridge jumped back, but Wilf, displaying a fine turn of nimble speed, kicked the inside of one knee. Netheridge collapsed with a grunt and Wilf was on him in an instant, wrestling him to the floor. He stamped on Netheridge's hand, breaking two fingers, and wrenched the knife free. Netheridge screamed, struggling violently, but Wilf had him pinned down in the traditional way, knee grinding hard into the back of his neck. He looked back towards the hall where Celeste and Sandra watched. Bertie stood at their feet.

'No cuffs,' he said conversationally.

'Here,' called Celeste. 'Take these.' She tossed the handcuffs she'd salvaged from Miller's coffle. Wilf caught them in mid-air and snapped them around Netheridge's wrists. It was done with casual panache and, Celeste suspected, entirely for Sandra's benefit. The poor woman was more flushed than a King's Cross loo! She looked like she was about to pass out.

'Oh my God, Celeste,' she whispered. 'D'you think he'd do that to me? You know, with the handcuffs, I mean?'

'You can always ask. I'm sure he'd oblige. Then what?'

'I'm not going into details – but I've a strong suspicion I'm about to start wearing my ankles as earrings!'

CHAPTER EIGHTEEN

'You wore my helmet?'

'I'm afraid so. It was the only one I could find.' Wilf put the crash helmet down on a table.

'That's because I made James tidy his away the other week.'

'What! You knew there was only one helmet in the garage?' spluttered Wilf.

'Oh, yes. I wanted to see how well you carried pink. Would you put it on again so I can take a picture?'

'Certainly not,' he sniffed. 'I don't like being played with. Besides, I have my reputation to consider.'

'I think the girls would still like to see you with it on, especially Sandra. Only real men can wear pink.'

'Pink,' said Bertie distinctly. Now, that was an easy word. He snuggled next to Milly on the back of a chair, the two macaws rubbing shoulders. She trilled happily and preened him. Wilf suspected she was just glad to be out of her cage at long last. It had been cramped for such a big bird – and Netheridge's callous treatment hadn't helped. He didn't know too much about macaw body language, but he was pretty sure Bertie would be getting a lot of sex over the next few days.

Nice to know someone was.

They stood in a little group in the main entrance hall watching Cutie hang the portrait of Helen back on the wall above the fireplace. Doreen supervised with the obligatory, 'Up a bit. No, on the left. Down a fraction.' Jenny bustled in with a tray of steaming mugs followed by Sandra carrying a huge Victoria sponge and stack of plates.

Martha had at last managed to freshen up and came trotting down the stairs. 'Please tell me someone's finally called the police,' she said. 'I don't want any men littering up the place for a second longer than necessary. Present company excluded, of course,' she added with a twinkly smile at Wilf. 'You can stay as long as you like, young man.'

'Young man! Muscle! I like this place,' said Wilf, thrusting out his chin and straightening his tie.

'Yes, Wilf called them,' said Doreen. 'They're on their way, along with an ambulance. Jenny did a proper job on Lardy Arse. He's still unconscious.

'I have to say I'm impressed with you all,' said Wilf, accepting a very generous slice of cake and a mug of tea. 'On every level,' he added, giving Sandra a winning smile. 'These were no ordinary burglars.'

'We look after our own down here in the sticks,' said Doreen. 'Gloucestershire women know how to defend themselves.'

'Remind me not to cross any of you – especially the cook!'

'Do we know who they actually are?' asked Martha.

'That's for the police to find out.'

'I'm so sorry I brought this on you all,' said Celeste, 'especially you, Martha.'

'Forget it. I'm all clean and dry now. Still got a bit of a twitch in my hand, though. I'm sure it'll soon subside.'

'I didn't want to involve anyone else because of the potential danger,' said Wilf, 'but we would have been overrun without you ladies to help. I don't think Celeste and I could have handled them all. Thanks to you we now have all the grunts and two of the ringleaders in custody.'

'And we've recovered Milly safe and sound. Colin will be pleased.'

'So their motive was purely political,' said Sandra. Although everyone in the room knew exactly what was going on, they had to play act for Wilf's benefit. Celeste had warned them of his perspicacity. He would be a difficult man to deceive, but then all the women who had ever lived at the Hall had been deceiving men for centuries and were very, very good at maintaining the Sisterhood's secrecy.

'Yes,' said Celeste. 'Black and Netheridge are members of a group of high-powered city moguls who have been trying to corrupt James. When he refused their invitation, they turned their attention to me and Bertie.' She stroked his back affectionately and he began to purr in contentment. 'They planned to kidnap Bertie and hold him as a guarantee of our compliance, but their stooge, Humph, whose real name is Miller, nabbed the wrong macaw and took Milly instead. Wilf is an old friend and experienced detective in the Met who agreed to help. Doreen offered sanctuary and that's why we're all standing here.'

'But Black?' asked Martha. 'He was after something else?'

'As far as we can gather from Miller's phone, Black came solely for the art. He and Miller were planning to melt away with Milly after Netheridge arrived. They would then call the police anonymously, leaving Netheridge to face multiple charges. Apparently, Black was worried he would be poisoned by Netheridge and wanted him out of the way.'

'What an absolutely charming bunch.'

'That's what avarice does for you.'

'What about you, Wilf?' asked Sandra. 'How did you get here?'

'Celeste's idea. We knew her home was being watched. By decamping to Temple Hall, she forced Miller to follow, flushing him out.'

'It was actually Bertie's suggestion,' said Celeste.

'I then followed Miller here with Bertie. Normally, an experienced team like Miller's would have been hard to defeat, but you lot managed it without too much difficulty.'

'You came on a motorcycle?' Sandra seemed inordinately interested. She stood beside Wilf, fluttering eyelashes and twirling a lock of hair. Celeste suspected that had they been alone, she would already be riding him like a Rocky Mountain rodeo queen.

'Er, yes.'

'How brave,' she husked, breathily.

'Riding the bike or wearing a sparkly pink helmet?'

'Both. And then?'

'We holed up in a copse, keeping a distant eye on Miller's van, and settled in for the duration. Have you any idea just how noisy the countryside is at night? Bloody foxes and God knows what screeching and yowling all night long. Then Miller's gang arrived this morning and they all moved off to the Hall. We tried to follow, but I couldn't get the damned bike going again. I think it was sulking after such a long journey. With no alternative, I gave it a push and coasted down to the Hall. Well, I coasted, Bertie flew. We stashed the bike in some bushes to stay out of sight and it's just as well we did. Black's Mercedes drove past and pulled up at the front door. He got out a ladder and disappeared inside so I went to say hello. Once he was cuffed, I left him with Celeste. Netheridge arrived with Milly, I picked my spot and just waited to pounce. Bertie heard Celeste's call because he suddenly took off into the house. The rest you know.'

'And you saved Helen,' cooed Sandra adoringly.

'Well, I – um, I just stopped Black,' replied Wilf, a tinge of embarrassment colouring his cheeks.

'Netheridge, too, and he was armed with a knife.'

'I only tripped him up.'

'Modesty. I like that in a man.' She pecked him on the cheek. 'Thanks, Wilf. We'd have been heartbroken if the portrait had been stolen.' She picked up the helmet and stared at it thoughtfully.

Gravel crunched outside. Car doors slammed. Martha opened the front door to reveal two policemen. 'Ladies,' said the driver, touching his cap. Wilf liked the gesture. Not many Met officers would have been so polite. 'What's been going on here, then?' he asked in the traditional manner, accepting a tea and slice of cake. 'Thanks, Jen.'

'Everyone, this is my cousin, Greg. I wondered if they'd send you.'

'Pot luck. I just happened to be on duty. This is PC Paul Brush. Call him Basil. Everyone else does.' He nodded at his vulpine partner, who was already tucking into his Victoria sponge. 'Martha, Cutie, you two OK?'

'We're fine, Greg.'

'You, I know,' he said, pointing with his cake. 'You're Mrs Timbrill, the Leather Lady. Can't mistake the hair. Nor the bird, whichever one it is.'

'Hello, my name is Bertie and I'm very pleased to meet you,' said Bertie, addressing the policeman politely.

'Occasional rain,' added Milly.

Greg gave Bertie a suspicious look, as if searching for a hidden ventriloquist, then turned to Doreen. 'Are you her sister, by any chance?' he asked. 'Same hair. Nothing gets past me, you see.'

'Not quite, but we are very distantly related,' she said. 'I'm Doreen and this is Sandra.'

'And who might you be?' Being a gentleman, Greg turned to Wilf last.

'Detective Sergeant Wilfred Thompson, Metropolitan Police, Greenwich Borough.' Wilf flashed his warrant card.

'That expires tomorrow,' said Greg, munching sponge.

'Yes, it does, but it's still valid until then.'

'Righty-ho. Welcome to Gloucestershire, sir.'

'Thanks, Greg. It's Wilf, by the way. Forget the formality. I've had thirty-five years to get thoroughly sick of it.'

'You made the call?'

'I did.'

'Something about burglars, attempted murder, assault

269

with a deadly weapon, cruelty to animals, conspiracy, corruption and kidnapping. Get that a lot in Greenwich, do you?'

'Not this month,' smiled Wilf.

'Dangerous place, Temple Guiting. Jen, this is a great sponge, by the way. All right, who's going to fill me in?'

'Best call for a Black Maria first. You're going to need it.'

'Showing your age, there, Wilf,' said Greg, making the request into his lapel mic. 'They haven't been black for decades. We call 'em COWs down here. Cages On Wheels.'

'Of course you do. Why would you call them anything else?'

'You all seem remarkably relaxed considering the nature of the emergency call. Mind telling me who I'll be putting in the COW?'

'Probably better if we show you,' said Jenny, 'but finish your tea first. There's no rush.'

Greg was no fool. 'Right,' he said slowly and carefully. 'Where are they?'

'Oh, you know, scattered around the place,' she replied airily.

'I think you'd better show me.'

The little group moved on into the house.

'These two Wilf dealt with,' said Jenny. 'First, the poisoner.' Netheridge was in a broom cupboard, handcuffed and pale-faced.

'I advise you to let me go immediately,' he said evenly. 'If you don't I'll ensure you never work again. Anywhere. I can make your life a waking misery. All of you! I'll find out where your families live and hound them mercilessly. There'll be no hiding.'

'Yeah, sure thing,' said Greg, slamming the door in his face. 'What a nasty little runt. Let's leave him in there until the van arrives.'

'Next, the art thief,' said Wilf. Black was locked in a

270

nearby toilet and sat on the pan. Wilf opened the door to a torrent of foul-mouthed abuse and threats. 'Oddly enough, I find this one better company,' he said mildly, locking the door again. 'Just a thought, Greg, and I'm not teaching you to suck eggs, but I've a feeling he's been stealing paintings for a long time. Might be wise to warrant up and search all his homes. Check for secret rooms. You never know what you might find.'

Martha scampered ahead into the library. Jenny stopped Greg just as they reached the Turkish carpet. 'I wouldn't go any further,' she said. Martha unlocked the trap and pushed on the carpet edge with her hand. It swung down on its finely balanced hinge, revealing a deep, dark pit.

'Jesus!' muttered Greg.

'It's a tippy-trappy thing,' said Cutie. 'An oubliette. Our ancestors knew a thing or two about dealing with burglars.'

'How many are down there?'

'Only three.'

'Only!'

'I lured two in using my perfectly formed middle-aged arse as bait,' said Sandra proudly.

'That's my girl,' murmured Wilf. He'd taken a discreet look at her rump earlier and decided it was notably delicious.

'The other one is badly injured.'

'How?'

'Well,' said Celeste, 'that's my fault. We were having a knife fight when –'

'A what?' spluttered Greg, incredulously.

'Technically, I didn't have the knife, Miller did. All I had was a whip and length of chain,' she explained. Greg stared at her in frank astonishment. 'He cut me on the arm, I went for his eyes with the whip, then broke his hand with the chain. Bertie waded in to sever an ear, I think I dislocated his kneecap with a kick and he threw the knife into my leg as he went down into the pit.' She displayed

271

her bloodstained trousers as evidence.

'Holy crap!'

Wilf nudged the stunned policeman. 'Feisty, isn't she?'

'You're not bastard kidding.'

'And there's more to come.'

Martha locked the trap shut again and the party moved on into the garden. 'This one was after Cutie and me. We're not sorry for what we did,' she added with a sniff. 'He deserved it. He had a knife as well.' She unlocked the potting shed door. Skinner sat cross-legged on the floor like a puffy Buddha. He looked up as the door opened. Even Wilf, a hardened officer of many years' experience – even he winced at the sight. Skinner's face, neck and arms were obscenely bloated. Multiple stings blotched his discoloured skin. His injured eye was completely closed and wept sticky tears down his cheek. Distorted lips, tumescent and a horribly unnatural shade of scarlet, hung slackly to reveal a blackened, swollen tongue.

The man was a real mess.

'How?' asked Greg.

'Bees,' replied Cutie. 'Lots and lots of bees.'

'Baz, better take this one back to the hall.'

'Sure.' Brush hauled Skinner to his feet and handcuffed him. 'Come on, Elephant Man, ambulance won't be long.' Greg saw the knife on the floor. 'No one touch that,' he ordered. 'Forensics will want to see it.' He looked around the potting shed. Bee carcasses littered the shelves. 'Jesus!' he swore again. 'Any more?'

'Just one,' said Jenny, 'but I'm afraid he's in a bit of a state.'

'You mean he's even worse than that guy!' Now in considerable shock, Greg just looked at her.

'He was going to rape me,' she protested. 'He made it pretty obvious when he got his dick out. Small cock, but big mistake. I would have warned him what was coming, but he'd used this stun gun on Martha.' She handed it to Greg. 'Made her pee her pants. As far as I'm concerned, he got what he deserved.'

'And what did he get?'

'Oh, only my Dorset Naga peppers.' She led them into the greenhouse.

'Jesus!' muttered Greg yet again. He seemed to be stuck on the one word, his mind incapable of expressing itself in any other way. Leach lay moaning softly, one wrist still handcuffed to the iron stanchion. He'd rolled over on to his back. Dried blood encrusted his mouth where he'd cut his lips falling face down, several teeth jagged and broken. His nose was squashed flat by the impact of the frying pan, but all that was actually inconsequential compared to the damage inflicted by the chilli missiles. Both eyes had completely disappeared. Flesh swollen beyond endurance bulged from each eye socket, grotesquely distorting his face, the skin febrile and leprous.

And then there was his knob! Wilf and Greg involuntarily cupped genitals in a shared instinctive gesture of protection.

Their own – not each other's.

The damage was catastrophic, the colour a spectacular purply-reddish-burgundy-orange. Leach's willy no longer looked like a willy. To be honest, it didn't even look like anything that should be near a human body, let alone attached to it. Greg couldn't bear the sight and turned away, suddenly nauseous.

'Promise me you'll not tell Mum,' pleaded Jenny in a small voice. 'Please!'

An approaching siren gave the two men a timely and valid excuse to exit from the greenhouse. The ambulance arrived first, followed in short order by the COW. The number of constables in attendance swelled to four. Vehicles congregated in front of the Hall. It began to look like the car park of a stately home on a sunny Bank Holiday Monday. Netheridge and Black were frog-marched into the back of the van while Skinner and Leach

273

received treatment in the ambulance under close supervision by several officers. 'Bloody Norah,' muttered the paramedic, administering a generous injection of morphine into Leach, 'I thought my missus had a temper!'

Returning to the library, Martha unlocked the trap and Wilf slid an extending ladder down into the oubliette. The two Toilet Thugs emerged first out of the darkness, blinking myopically, and found themselves promptly arrested. Finally, Miller crawled up the ladder, his numerous injuries apparent, bloodstained head swathed in a makeshift bandage ripped from his shirt. Despite these wounds, Greg wasn't taking any chances and got him handcuffed in a jiffy. Miller's eyes widened momentarily when he saw Wilf, then the shutters came down and his face went blank.

'Just a minute, Greg. I've a feeling we've met before.' Wilf's preliminary search revealed the heavy sap. He hefted the nasty weapon. 'You can add assaulting a police officer to all the other charges,' he said grimly. 'I've got the lump to prove it.'

Miller did not react at all, but he glared at Celeste as he was led away. Engines fired up and the emergency services vehicles departed to either police station or hospital, depending on the physical condition of their occupants.

'I want that thing made safe,' ordered Greg, nodding at the trap. 'There's going to be lots of our people here and I don't want to have to fish them out every five minutes.' He excused himself and walked off to consult with his colleagues.

'Where on earth did you get all those handcuffs?' asked Wilf.

'They were originally intended for us, but I know a useful little party trick involving a bent hair grip,' said Celeste.

'Of course you do.'

'That's where the chain came from as well.'

'And the whip? No, don't answer that. I know you never travel without one.'

'Not this time. It was a present from Martha, and very useful, I have to say.'

Cutie and Martha pulled up the ladder. The trap door swung shut and was locked.

'What will happen to Miller?' asked Celeste.

'Well, for a start, I would imagine he'll find spectacles difficult to wear,' mused Wilf. 'But that'll be the least of his problems. In my opinion, judging on what you've told me, he will almost certainly be charged with your attempted murder. By throwing the knife he showed deliberate intent. If found guilty – and I don't think there's the slightest chance of any other verdict – sentencing usually starts at around twelve years.'

'Good. I won't be losing any sleep over that.'

'Now it's safe, would you show me the library again,' said Wilf suddenly.

'Why?' asked Cutie.

'I'm curious as to why there's an oubliette positioned here, at its entrance.' He walked in with the women and looked around, professionally examining the long, low room. He scrutinised the windows, the doors and even peered up the chimney.

'These books must be valuable,' he finally said.

'Some of them are,' agreed Doreen.

'But I guess most have been added over the years. There couldn't have been that many in here when the house was built. Hardly worth such sophisticated protection, it seems to me, so I'm intrigued as to why so complex a defence was placed here.' He saw the polished brass oval set into the wooden floor beside the massive fireplace, its surface engraved with "IN".

'What's this? An "In" button to what? If I push on it does a secret panel open or something?'

'A secret panel leading where?' asked Doreen evenly.

'A hidden room, maybe.'

'Sorry, nothing so exciting. These are the initials of Isaac Newton. He came to stay once and this plaque marks the spot where he was sitting when he invented the cat flap. We're very proud of it.'

'The cat flap?'

'That's right.'

'So if I step on it, no concealed door will open?'

'Try – see what happens.'

Celeste glanced nervously at Doreen. Cutie bit her lip. The atmosphere suddenly tightened. A wash of nervousness swept through the group of women. Wilf glanced up through shaggy brows, the only part of his head that still sported enough hair to even vaguely warrant such a description. Celeste knew he'd sensed their uneasiness. He raised one foot and cautiously pressed on the plate. Nothing happened.

'What did you expect – a nuclear missile launch?' said Martha sarcastically.

He relaxed, but the look he gave Celeste was thoughtful. She knew him well enough to realise he was not entirely satisfied. No doubt he would be bringing up the subject at a later date.

'No, I guess not,' he admitted.

They left the library. Wilf peered over his shoulder and noted with surprise that Martha was very careful to lock the doors behind them. Interesting. None of the other rooms in the Hall were locked, so why did she do that?

Greg met them in the entrance hall. 'Now we've dealt with the bad guys, would anyone care to tell me why they were here?'

Wilf's explanation was a masterclass of descriptive prose. Years of appearing as a witness in court had honed his technique. Greg listened, notebook in hand, pen scribbling furiously. 'In short, you're dealing with a high-level conspiracy to corrupt an MP. Miller's phone provides enough evidence to arrest the other three men in their cosy little club. I'm sure further revelations will duly come to light. These men have been doing this for a long time.'

'This is way above me,' said Greg. 'I've no doubt it's going to turn into a major investigation.'

'You look like a man who could do with another cup of tea,' said Doreen.

'Thanks, that would be lovely.' Jenny went to make a new pot. More cake arrived.

Sandra sidled up to Wilf. 'Got a minute? There's one last thing I think you should see.'

'What's that?'

'Best I show you.'

'It's not another poor soul in handcuffs, is it?'

'Not quite, but play your cards right...'

Wilf pursed his lips. The other women were busy plying Greg and Baz with double chocolate layer cake, so they slipped away unnoticed. She led him into the pantry and closed the door.

'Well, what have you got to show – good grief, woman!'

Sandra unbuttoned her blouse to reveal a black satin bra and tipped her breasts out of their cups. With his attention suitably engaged, she pounced, ripping at his clothes. His trousers were forcibly dragged down to his knees, leaving crumpled shirt-tails flapping in front of his middle regions.

Such a thing had never happened to Wilf.

Sandra hoiked herself up onto a marble shelf, naked arse squashing a punnet of Jenny's strawberries in her haste. Juice squirted across the cold stone. She stretched her legs wide and up, drawers hanging off one ankle. She grabbed Wilf's lapels, pulled him in close and kissed him hard. Wilf's eyes bulged, as did other parts. An industriously inquisitive tongue wormed into his mouth. Even Wilf, as unseasoned in the art of love as a man could possibly be, began to realise the likely outcome of the encounter. Her kisses took on an urgent intimacy.

'This is totally unprofessional,' he gasped, surfacing for air. He couldn't tell if the giddiness he felt was through lack of oxygen or awakening passion. 'Good job I'm leaving the force tomorrow.'

'Stop talking and start shagging!' she panted. Her hand disappeared between his shirt tails. She rummaged and emerged with her prize. Wilf gasped while Sandra grasped. She kneaded urgently. 'Come on, Wilf, you know you want it.'

'Do I?'

'Got any handcuffs?'

'Er … sorry.'

'Next time, then.'

'There's going to be a next time?'

'There will be if you wear this!'

She plonked the pink crash helmet on his head. Wilf giggled. He hadn't giggled for decades. Frankly, he'd never had much to giggle at, but the sight of Sandra lying back on the slab in a pool of mashed strawberries, brown eyes smouldering, tits wobbling, legs wrapped around his waist and ankles crossed in the small of his back, put him in an excellent frame of mind. She guided him into port with a sigh and shudder. Wilf liked the sound very much, the dreamy sensation even more, and began to hump vigorously, decorum long gone and antlers flapping in time with his thrusts. Sandra moaned, pinching her own nipples, and tumbled into an intense, grunting climax. Wilf followed swiftly, eyes rolling back, his face blushing deep red under the sparkling coral-coloured helmet, knees wobbling and tongue hanging out.

At least he'd lasted longer than Bertie – but only just!

'Anyone seen Sandra?' asked Doreen.

'Not for a while. Come to think of it, Wilf's gone as well.'

'Are you thinking what I'm thinking?'

'God help us,' muttered Celeste. 'What have I done!'

'We're here,' said Wilf a little too breathlessly, scampering in a little too hastily and certainly a little too guiltily.

'I was just showing Wilf around the house,' added Sandra, trying to straighten her mussed auburn hair. Colour stained her cheeks and throat. Her blouse was buttoned awry.

'I'm sure you were,' observed Doreen dryly.

'There's something different about you,' said Cutie, eyes narrowed suspiciously.

'Can anyone else smell strawberries?' asked Martha.

Greg drained his cup. 'Ladies, we need to take statements from you all,' he said. Probably best to do this at the station.'

'How do we get there?' asked Doreen.

'We'll have to go in the van.'

There was a squeal of excitement. 'In a police van? Girls, I'm not going out looking like this.' Doreen led the stampede upstairs.

'Oi! Come back! Where are they off to?' complained PC Brush.

'You're a bachelor, aren't you, Baz?' said Celeste. 'Hope you're not in a hurry.'

'I'm afraid you'll have to come as well, Mrs Timbrill,' said Greg.

'That might be a problem. My priority is Bertie and Milly. I want to get them settled as soon as possible. This has been traumatic for them both.' She thought for a moment. 'Listen, let me take them home and I promise I'll come to the station tomorrow morning and make a statement then.'

'Sounds reasonable.'

'Can you go with the others?' she asked Wilf. 'Keep them from wrecking the place.'

Wilf slapped Greg on the shoulder. 'Sure. You'll need all the help you can get, my boy.' The police station was bound to have a convenient cupboard somewhere private that he and Sandra could employ usefully while waiting for the others to make their statements.

'I'll phone Colin when I get home, let him know we have Milly back safe and sound.'

Another police vehicle arrived. 'Here come forensics,' said Greg. 'The SOCOs will want everyone out while they do their thing. Ladies!' he called up the stairs. 'Your bus is departing now.'

A clatter of heels announced the return of the women. All four had coiffed their hair, applied make-up and changed into smart clothes and appropriate interview shoes. Even Martha. Celeste gave Greg an encouraging pat on the arm. 'Good luck,' she murmured. 'I've a feeling you'll need it.'

Doreen took Celeste to one side as the others piled into the police van. 'Thank you,' she said earnestly.

'For what? Saving democracy or introducing Wilf to Sandra?'

'Either one or the other will make my life much more bearable, although it's too early to say which.'

'My pleasure.' They hugged briefly and Doreen climbed into the van. Greg and Baz were already struggling to cope.

'Can we have sirens and lights?'

'What's that button for?'

'Why won't this window open?'

'I like your helmet!'

'Where do you keep the CS gas?'

'How does this breathalyser work?'

'My, that's a big truncheon!'

'It's like herding blancmange,' muttered Wilf, getting in last. The police van hummed with happy chatter like a charabanc on a trip to the seaside.

There was only one empty seat – and it was next to Sandra. She patted it and smiled.

AND FINALLY...

'In we go!' said Celeste, opening the front door of the cottage. Bertie scampered over the threshold, his tail sweeping from side to side like a long blue brush. Milly followed closely, trilling happily. Celeste had no fear she'd make a bolt for freedom. A crowbar wouldn't be strong enough to separate her from Bertie's side. The two chattering macaws hopped and fluttered up onto the perch and dipped heads to the nut bowl.

Celeste made sure they had plenty of food and water before going upstairs. The cottage was, as always, a haven of peace and tranquillity. No sound could be heard, but for birdsong outside and the occasional distant crack of shattered Brazil nut. She closed the bedroom door, stripped off her filthy and bloodstained clothes and took a long, relaxing bath, treating herself to extra bubbles. Her wounded leg still smarted, but the cut was clean. The paramedics at Temple Hall had not seemed unduly concerned. Sitting at her dressing table, she replaced the dressing before applying a little make-up and lipstick, then dried her hair. She'd always appreciated how lucky she'd been with her unique colour, despite having endured many examples of ginger bigotry over the years, but to learn that it would never go grey struck her as deliciously ironic. She gathered the wavy tresses back into a flowing ponytail and pulled on a pair of thigh-length red leather boots to conceal her injury, tugging hard on the silk lacing to snug the long boots pleasantly tight.

Turning to her wardrobe, she unlocked and swung open the double doors. There were no clothes inside – it was not that kind of wardrobe – but that certainly didn't mean it was empty. A large, black leather papoose hung there, swathed in straps and buckles, zips and poppers. A hooded head emerged from the top, anonymous and blank. Celeste stroked a hide-clad cheek fondly, unbuckled the gag covering its mouth and very tenderly kissed the exposed lips.

'Time to return to the real world, my gorgeous Kneeling Man,' she murmured.

A tongue licked the lips. 'Hello, darling,' whispered James unsteadily. He squirmed against his bondage, leather creaking softly. He'd been cocooned for well over a day, having arrived unannounced by taxi the previous afternoon just as Celeste was about to leave for Temple Hall. She'd needed to get him out of the way quick, to keep him safe and concealed from Miller's view, and using the wardrobe had been the obvious answer. The thing was, she hadn't even needed to persuade him inside!

Celeste unbuckled the blindfold. James blinked, squinting in the light, and caught sight of his wife, naked but for the stiletto boots. 'You look perfect!' he murmured.

'As do you, my helpless leather slave.' She kissed him again very tenderly and started loosening straps.

'Now then,' he said as the leather slackened, 'has anything important happened while I've been meditating?'

THE END

Well, maybe not. It seems Bertie has time for one final adventure…

PUBLISHER'S NOTE

The author, by his own admission, has led an entirely uneventful life. He has assured us that for long periods of time, not a great deal of note happened. This is the natural consequence of being a resident of Gloucester. He has frequently expressed an earnest desire for this situation to continue and this was the case up until the point *Bertie and the Hairdresser Who Ruled the World* was completed.

Inexplicable occurrences began to plague the author shortly after the first draft of the manuscript was electronically transmitted to our office. He noticed an unusual hesitancy in his email, the telephone developed a curious echo and a mysterious vehicle always seemed to be parked in the street close to his house. He became convinced he was under constant surveillance and conveyed his concerns to us on a number of occasions. We, in turn, tried to allay his fears, but to no avail. The author became increasingly agitated and felt that, although the Sisterhood of Helen is an entirely fictitious organization of his own making, this story had somehow touched a nerve.

On the morning of September 5th that year, Mike set off by bicycle intending to visit friends. Neighbours later recalled him talking to a red-haired woman near his house. He has not been seen since. The police have conducted extensive enquiries, but are at a complete loss as to his whereabouts. The case remains open to this day.

A few months later, residents of the Cotswold village of Kineton noticed a cyclist riding through the countryside near their village who, when approached, claimed to be a

Polish plumber with no knowledge of English. Unfortunately, the questioner happened to be a former resident of Cracow, who established very quickly the cyclist was as deficient in Polish as he claimed to be in English! The bearded man was reported to be of similar age and build as the author, but despite persistent enquiries by the authorities, his actual identity remains a mystery to this day.

Kineton lies just over a mile from Temple Guiting…

For more adventures featuring

Bertie...

If you're a fan of *Yes, Minister*, *House of Cards*, and farcical British humour, then – meet Bertie!

Bertie is a big blue parrot – a Hyacinth Macaw from Brazil. He's also very intelligent, and he loves his owner Celeste.

Celeste, meanwhile, is doing some *loving* of her own – with James Timbrill, MP – newly appointed to the Cabinet, James is a devoted public servant. He's also a devoted masochist, and in Celeste he thinks he's met his match on the kink front.

But some people aren't so keen on James. Political machinations behind the scenes mean that events are in place that could bring the Government to its knees. With some surprisingly inept criminal masterminds on James's trail, it's up to Bertie to save the day – but will he risk it all for a bowl of nuts?

For more information about **Mike A. Vickers**
and other **Accent Press** titles
please visit

www.accentpress.co.uk